To union members,
Keep the faith and
continue the fight.

WILDCAT

A Novel by Micheal Micallef

This is a work of fiction. Names, characters, places and incidents either are the product of the author's imagination or are used fictitiously, and any resemblance to actual persons, living or dead, business establishments, events or locales is entirely coincidental.

ISBN: 9798316995233

Cover design by LDMedia

ldmedia.ca

To all the men and women who have

lost their jobs due to a plant closure…

what if?

"We paid the price to get here.
We'll pay the price to stay."
Eddie Fitzpatrick (Local Union Rep)

Prologue

Labour Day

evening

A convoy of headlights approached the factory from the south on Patillo Road with one purpose in mind. The silence of the clear night was broken by the combined roar of the vehicles' engines as they crossed over the railway tracks and turned into the shipping driveway of Border City Stamping. The lead vehicle was a large pickup truck, its front grill fitted with Bull bars, and it smashed through the chain-linked gates easily, snapping the sliding aluminum bar holding the two sides together. The other vehicles followed through the swinging gates and past the guardhouse toward the shipping area. The last vehicle, another large pickup, stopped just inside the gates. Two men got out of the truck, one with a sledgehammer in hand while the other held a heavy chain and closed the gates. They straightened the gates as best they could, then wrapped the chain through them and padlocked it. The truck backed up close to the broken gate and the two men jumped onto the bed of the truck. After opening the tailgate, the men struggled to push out a couple of concrete blocks against the mangled gates. They tapped on the truck's side to let the driver know they were done and the driver proceeded to the shipping bays. The men in the bed of the truck looked out at the road to ensure no one had heard them. With all the other companies along the industrial corridor of Patillo road closed for the holiday no one was aware of the illegal entry into their place of work. It was 10:36 p.m.

Inside the factory was organised chaos. At the shipping bays, pickups were backed into the three bays offloading barbecues, propane tanks and picnic tables. A man with his long hair tied up in a ponytail was directing where each cooking unit was to be placed. Just inside the back of the factory, cars and SUVs were unloading boxes of food, sleeping bags, blankets, pillows and suitcases. A petite brunette stood on top of one of the picnic tables shouting out instructions for the placement of the rest areas. Men and women were scurrying past the stock area with whatever they could carry to different parts of the factory. Someone had put on the lights, the place illuminated as if starting the midnight shift. But this wasn't that.

Outside, there was activity to secure the factory. An equipment moving crane sitting idle at the end of the shipping driveway was hot-wired and driven to the front of the factory. Cutting across the space between the chain-link fence and the building, the crane was positioned at the other gates protecting the office parking lot. These were also chained and padlocked. Following the crane was a lift truck that backed up to the back door of the guardhouse. Another lift truck travelled back down the shipping driveway to the mangled gate where the female driver nudged the concrete blocks against the gate and then positioned the lift truck across the back door of that guardhouse. She walked back to the shipping bays, joining the two men who had positioned the crane and the other lift truck.

The employee turnstiles were disabled from the inside, electronically, causing them to become locked into place. The genius of the group, a man wearing thick-lens glasses, was able to gain control of the factory by overriding the security system.

The process of securing the factory took fifteen minutes, and was completed well before the time employees were expected to show up for work on the midnight shift, 11:30 pm start time.

The shipping guard reported to work five minutes before eleven. Able to get into the guardhouse by the front door, he saw the lift truck blocking the door to the inside of the fence. He used the guardhouse phone to alert management of the employee takeover of the factory. They had achieved their purpose.

Reece Kincaid answered his cell phone just after one in the morning…

"If I went to work in a factory, the first thing I'd do
would be to join a union."

Franklin D. Roosevelt
(32nd President of the U. S.)

PART 1

JUNE

(Three months earlier)

1

Reece Kincaid wasn't through half his daily tour of the shop floor when he realized the mood was very negative. Men and women stopped him, and their work, to talk. They stood with their arms crossed, or shifting from one foot to the other, talking about past contracts. The employees were projecting their fear and anger concerning the company at him. It was times like this that Reece almost regretted having taken the union position. Almost.

He was surprised when the membership had first voted him in as a steward; when he was just a baby-faced, second-year full-timer, working as a press operator. The membership had wholeheartedly accepted the young man with the light brown curly hair, slender but muscular build, and genial demeanor as their representative in the union. His conviction to represent these people became very strong during his short time working on the line, he'd been very aware of the working conditions and safety issues that the workers faced every day. As a steward he made it a habit to connect with the employees, touring the plant each day.

That was nine years ago. Reece was thirty-three now, his continued boyish looks often belied his responsibilities as Committee Person and Benefits Rep. He maintained the practice of a daily tour of the shop floor when he became Committee Person four years after first being elected as steward and continued to do so today, even with the extra duties pressed upon him. The mood on the floor was due to the lack of contract talks with the company and Reece was the only source for the employees to vent their anger to. He was feeling more and more alone in the battle.

Border City Stamping, BCS as it was informally known, was an auto parts manufacturer making parts ranging from small dampers to the complete assembly of rear axles for vehicles. In all, 602 components were built and shipped to Chrysler, Ford, and General Motors, the top three North American automotive companies. Originally situated on Drouillard Road in Windsor, BCS was created in response to the need for automotive parts to feed the huge automobile market only minutes away from the Windsor-Detroit Ambassador Bridge.

BCS was extremely successful and expanded its operation to become one of the first manufacturers to relocate to a larger facility on Patillo Road in Lakeshore over forty years prior.

In its heyday, BCS had close to a thousand employees. When Reece was hired, there were 750 working on three shifts. On this warm morning in June, the number of employees hovered around 400, on two full shifts and a midnight shift of about fifty people.

A management staff of thirty-two consisted of a plant manager, salaried personnel in accounting and payroll, foremen over three shifts and security people. The plant was functioning at only seventy-five percent capacity, but not because of employee output. The struggle to gain more work, or in the least, maintain the work it had been doing for decades, was an issue that puzzled almost everyone who worked there. Including Reece.

Reece was only able to make it through the Press Line, the oldest part of the plant, where two- and three-ton presses still churned out small products like gas tank straps, sliding door channels, and sub-assembly parts, before being inundated with employee concerns, specifically about the new contract

In the past, contracts were negotiated and settled six months before expiry of the existing one, usually by summer shutdown in July. However, new owners, Industrial Metal Products, had acquired BCS ten months prior, and hadn't approached the union to begin talks about the impending contract. Reece believed they wouldn't be talking to the union for a while. The BCS management team had changed drastically, and most decisions were being made from the IMP head office in Toronto.

Above the din of the large presses, Reece tried to explain all of that to the people, but they weren't listening. Doom and gloom seemed to be the general consensus.

Reece moved along to the far side of the plant entering the Welding Cell. The *whomp-whomp-whomp* of the presses faded away, replaced with the *zap-zap-zap* of the spot welders and arc welders creating melded metal parts. Newer automation, FANUC robotics, included a transfer line of arc and spot welders, along with manual welding stations, where completed assemblies of axles, front and rear bumpers, and cross beams were made.

The smoke from the welders gave off a metallic smell as Reece rounded the end of one transfer line. An employee that Reece would rather have avoided signalled to him.

"Reece, can I see you for a moment?" Nick Campo removed his welding helmet, placing it on his ergonomic chair. He laid his welding gloves on top of the helmet and smoothed out his matted black hair, tied up in a ponytail, and then wiped his hands on his leather apron. His two-day growth of a beard looked scruffy, grey-flecked and uneven.

"Something needs to be done about those fucking vents." Nick gave a slight tilt of his head toward the workstation where he repaired any incomplete welds to the axle.

"I know, Nick," Reece opened his notepad and read something. "I have the requisition form for the filters to be changed out. The supervisor was given a copy, and he says they'll be fixed during lunch break." Reece now handled all safety issues as part of his union duties.

Nick rubbed the back of his neck. “It’s about time. I’ve been complaining about it for over a week.”

“It’ll get done.” Reece closed the notepad. The clanking sound of a welded axle being placed into Nick’s workstation by the automated robot had both men turn to face it.

Nick tapped the toggle lever beside his workstation, twirling the rotating station the axle rested in, and then tapped the toggle switch again setting the station upright. Another handling robot came in to grab the axle and lift it out, carrying the part to a final rack. Nick had purposely sent the axle to inspection without having checked for incomplete welds.

Reece tried to move on. Nick stepped in his way, legs spread and hands on hips. “What’s going on with the contract talks?”

“Nothing,” Reece answered.

Nick blinked. “Nothing? What the fuck! You guys holding back on us?”

Reece sighed. Nick was the first to support the union and the first to bash it. And he was good at riling up the people. Too good. Reece wasn’t going to play that game.

“There haven’t been any talks, yet,” Reece said.

Nick picked up his helmet and gloves and sat on his chair. "What does the union plan on doing?"

"What would *you* have us do?" Reece responded, a slight dare in his voice, though he wasn't going to reveal the union's stance about the contract on the shop floor, especially not to Nick. There was a time and place for informing the membership about union news and the floor wasn't one of them. "You seem to have the answer, so tell me what to do."

"For one, I'd let the membership know about the delay." Nick jabbed his helmet towards Reece. "And then I'd approach the company to start talks…"

"Hold on, Nick," Reece interrupted. "You know that's not how it's done." Nick stood quickly but Reece put up his hand. "The membership is smarter than you give them credit for. They know we'd tell them if anything was happening. Be a little patient like they are."

"Patient!" Nick spat out. "That's the union's answer. Be fucking patient?"

"We'll inform the membership about any updates at the meeting." Reece's cell phone rang. He took it off its holder on his hip, looked at it. "I've got to take this." Reece sidestepped Nick while he put the phone to his ear.

Nick grabbed his welding helmet and gloves, all the while sneering at Reece, as another welded axle was placed in his workstation.

2

David Bainbridge sat on one of the two black leather couches in the private room of the office of the President and Chief Executive Officer of Industrial Metal Products. The decor was modern, black and silver being the colours of choice. A few times a year he had the opportunity to be here, mostly during celebratory occasions, when deals had been successfully completed.

Today, the large flat screen TV on the wall was off, the big speakers in the corners were silent, and the only noise was the ticking of the pendulum clock on the sideboard table. It had been over fifteen minutes since the end of the team meeting. As he waited patiently, enjoying the view of the bright afternoon sky through the large windows to his right, Bainbridge wondered why he'd been asked to wait here, alone. During the meeting with the team assigned to negotiate the upcoming contract for an automotive parts company, Border City Stamping, Bainbridge noticed Silva's anxiety about the strategy to be used in the talks. Silva constantly interrupted the discussions amongst the members of the team to give direction or suggestions. Bainbridge was perplexed by Silva's manner. The strategy was used successfully over the years with other companies under their control and the team was virtually the same.

Industrial Metal Products was created by a European company spreading its talons to the expanding auto parts markets in North America in January 2012. Bainbridge had been hired shortly after, in May of that year, as Chief Operating Officer. They'd liked his management practices, and their working agreement had flourished making it one of the most successful enterprises in the industry. The recent acquisitions of automotive manufacturing firms alone had doubled the scope of the operations they'd had in North America. Bainbridge felt that this success would continue, even with Silva's doubts about the upcoming negotiations.

The door opened and Massimo 'Max' Silva entered, stopped just inside and closed the door gently. Silva, fifty-two years of age and of Italian descent, had a tanned complexion, a dark, thick moustache and straight black hair, slicked back, receding at the front. He wore a black suit, tailored perfectly to his lean frame, with a crisp white Armani shirt opened at the collar, a small gold chain around his neck. His Italian leather shoes looked like they'd just come out of the box. He quickly stepped towards Bainbridge, hand outstretched. Bainbridge slowly rose from his seat.

"I'm sorry to be so late, David. I got caught up in some other affairs." Silva pumped Bainbridge's hand and gestured with his other hand towards the bar. "Would you like a drink? I sure could use one. Scotch or Amaretto?"

"Scotch is fine," said Bainbridge. He wasn't a big drinker, but he didn't want to refuse his boss. Bainbridge stood about six inches taller than Silva, with broad shoulders, a full head of silver hair, and a salt-and-pepper beard, neatly groomed. He was dressed more casually than his boss. Designer jeans topped with a short-sleeved, blue denim shirt gave the impression of a man who enjoyed the outdoors instead of one tasked with running a major corporation. His grey loafers were worn but they were comfortable. Bainbridge liked being comfortable. His reputation had preceded him, making his appearance a concession the employer accepted.

Silva decanted Scotch into two tumblers, adding cubes of ice into each. He handed one over. "Here's to making the world dance to our beat," he said hopefully.

They both took a healthy gulp of their drinks after a quick salute. Silva moved away from the bar to the big windows displaying the heart of downtown Toronto. The office was high enough to view most buildings all the way to the harbour. The lake was spotted with a variety of sailing vessels from tankers to leisure craft. Bainbridge joined Silva, both men looking out at the picturesque site. Bainbridge enjoyed this quiet moment, aware of Silva's mood, and waited for the breaking of the ice.

"David, I asked to see you alone to talk about your trip." Silva emptied the rest of his drink leaving only the cubes of ice rattling in the glass.

Bainbridge cradled his drink in both hands. He eyed Silva in the reflection of the window. Silva glanced nervously at Bainbridge.

"There are a few things you need to know that can't be discussed in our group meetings. Information that will help you in your negotiations," Silva continued, his gaze seeking a reaction from Bainbridge.

Bainbridge didn't reply. He took a sip of his drink.

Silva turned, put his glass down on the table between the couches, and sat on one, leaning comfortably, one arm across the lush leather back. Bainbridge waited a couple of seconds before moving back to his previous spot, facing his boss. Even though Silva was his boss, Bainbridge, at age 62, acted like an equal. After all, it was Silva who was worked up about something, not him.

"David, you know the history of Border City Stamping. Tell me your impressions, and I'm not asking about performance or profitability. I want your gut feeling about the place," Silva said.

Bainbridge was correct in his assumption that Silva was anxious about the details of the negotiating tactics the team was going to use. Bainbridge had sensed that his boss was looking for something other than financial benefits concerning this purchase.

Bainbridge decided to ask a question that had been bothering him from the onset of the purchase. "Why did we purchase this company in the first place?"

Silva raised his hand to lightly brush his moustache. "Why do you ask?"

Bainbridge smiled. Okay, his boss was treading lightly. He placed his drink down on the table, leaned forward with hands out front, palms up. "Border City Stamping is not really a huge enterprise. It's a stand-alone operation. Granted, it does have a number of solid contracts." Bainbridge shrugged his shoulders, putting emphasis on his next words. "*But it is only one facility.*" He settled back into the sofa. "I'm sure our other companies could eventually outbid it for future contracts. The price we paid for it; we could surely have put that money to better use."

"What would you say if I told you we were asked to make the purchase?" Silva asked, leaning forward.

“What do you mean?” Bainbridge remained relaxed, putting one arm on the back of the sofa.

“I mean, what if I told you that it wasn’t my idea to make the purchase,” Silva said.

Bainbridge considered this new information. “Who would want to buy it and why?”

Silva paused, leaned back and crossed his legs.” Interested parties that made it known that we could benefit from the purchase.”

Bainbridge knew all the details of the operation and the future viability of the factory. Though he hadn’t been involved in the acquisition, having been busy with another negotiation, nothing had indicated that it was a prime business acquisition. “But *how* could we benefit from purchasing Border City Stamping?”

“David, you’ve been there a few times, correct?” Silva asked.

“Sure,” said Bainbridge, aware that Silva was switching tactics.

“What did you think of the people there?” Silva continued.

“The management team we put in place is capable. I…” Bainbridge stopped mid-sentence because Silva was waving his finger at him.

“I don’t mean the management. I want to know what you think about the workers.” Silva straightened. “We know about their work ethic. They’ve won loads of quality awards. But what do you think about their attitude towards our purchase of them?”

Bainbridge nodded. He understood where this conversation was going. Most of the issues when dealing with a new acquisition were regarding the new contract. The first contract under new ownership was challenging, and in the case of Border City Stamping, dealing with the wage disparity in relation to the other holdings of Industrial Meta Products, was a challenge Bainbridge was prepared to deal with. The negotiating team’s most pressing matter was to lower the cost of operating, and this meant going after wages and benefits.

“If you’re asking if I believe we’ll have a problem getting concessions from them, I’m sure we will.” Bainbridge’s confidence showed in his disregard toward Silva’s question, picking up his drink and taking a sip.

Silva ground his teeth, his jaw line pulsing with tension.

Bainbridge continued, “But I’m also not worried at all. We’ve already taken some work from them showing our power. This has set the tone for negotiations. They’ll fall in line just like the others have.”

"What makes you so sure?" Silva asked, leaning in again. "I mean, how far will you go to get what you want? More importantly, how far do you think they'll go to resist?"

Bainbridge felt a fast chill run up his spine. Did Silva doubt him? Never had Silva questioned his ability to handle contracts and reign in the cost of any operations they had purchased. His past record, before being hired as COO, was the reason he was sought after. He'd never been questioned before. His ego kept him silent.

"David, what you may be running up against is nothing like you've experienced before. This plant " — Silva ran his hand through his thinning black hair — "its members are very active in the union. In their city, BCS has been influential in union leadership and union power. Other workers in different factories emulate what they achieve with their contracts."

Bainbridge wasn't sure where Silva was going with this because it wasn't like they hadn't dealt with union shops before. But there had been one instance where Bainbridge had failed to get concessions from a union shop. Bainbridge spoke up before Silva could continue. "So, we bring them down and it will show the others that we aren't to be messed with," Bainbridge said confidently.

Silva shook his head. "Maybe I'm not making myself clear, I'm sorry. David, this group has been active in work disruptions in that city for decades. Their members have been leaders in the local unions, many even on national committees. They picket not only their own lines but competitor companies who are seeking concessions as well. They've even been influential when supporting their customers who are members of unions when they've been on strike. They are extremely militant when it comes to workers' rights."

"Max, do you doubt my ability to deal with this group?"

Silva again sat back, his hand reflexively moving to his moustache. The moments seem to stretch on interminably. Finally, he sat up and continued the conversation. "David, the people who asked that we purchase Border City did so with a specific reason. They implied that if we fulfilled their request, we could benefit hugely from them. They have had enough with this group hindering their agenda."

Bainbridge could tell Silva was uneasy about something. Being addressed by his name each time was annoying and a sure sign of Silva's anxiety. He had done the same thing during the team meeting. Remaining in his relaxed posture, he put out his hands as if he were giving up. Not knowing what to ask, he waited.

"David, these interested parties would like nothing else but to rid themselves of this group." Silva brought his hands together, elbows on knees. “They would be grateful if Border City Stamping no longer existed.”

3

Home was a refuge for Reece. The raised ranch in the middle of a cul-de-sac was one of the first built in this development in Tecumseh over thirty years ago and the house Reece grew up in. He had purchased it last year when it had come onto the market. The changes made from when his family lived in it were evident and practical for the older couple who had inhabited it the last seventeen years. What once were two smaller bedrooms that he and his sister occupied had been made into one large master bedroom. His parents’ bedroom was now a den. The kitchen space remained the same, only updated, with new cupboards. The living room carpeting he remembered from his youth was replaced with hard-wood flooring. The basement had been made into an entertainment room from its original workshop his father had created. Today the workout equipment and small office occupied the space that the previous owners had filled with a pool table, wet bar and TV room. Barbequing home-made burgers on the three-tiered wooden deck that replaced the old cement patio, Reece felt comfortable in the updated old digs. It also held many good memories, especially of his father. With Father's Day just past, he felt his father's presence in this house he now called home. There hadn't been a celebration of the day since his teenage years, after the passing of his father. With no children of his own, the day passed like any other. Hurley, their four-year-old beagle, lazed under the lone elm tree, escaping the hot sun. The sound of a car door closing prompted Hurley to scurry to the gate where, a minute later, Shannon Stewart entered the yard.

Reece and Shannon had met at the University of Windsor during a student rally against rising tuition rates. He had been in his third year of business administration while she was in her freshman year of law. They married five years later and were now into their eighth year. She had kept her maiden name because she liked her individuality in her professional career as a corporate lawyer. They had never really talked about having children, the pursuit of their careers taking precedence. They were even teased by their friends, who had children, with the moniker 'Ken and Barbie'. He didn't mind.

Shannon crouched to pet Hurley, her slender legs showing as her skirt rode up her thigh. Her black hair hung down her right side partially covering her taut white blouse. She looked up at Reece. "It smells great. Nothing too fancy, I'm sure." The aroma of hamburger grilling on the barbecue prompted her teasing.

"You know me. Simple is good." Reece, in shorts and a muscle shirt that showed off his toned arms and calves, held out a glass of wine for her. She stepped up on the deck, accepting the Pinot Grigio, and planted a kiss on his lips. The table was all set, complete with all the condiments and dinnerware. "Hamburgers and coleslaw, what more could you ask for?" He tapped her glass with the bottle of beer, the third one he'd had since coming home from work two hours ago.

Shannon placed her waistcoat and briefcase on a lounger. "This drink is more than enough." She sipped from the glass as she sat at the table.

Reece retreated to the barbeque with spatula and serving plate in hand. "Tough day at work?"

"Not really." She made space for the food on the table. "Just the usual procedural documents that had to be filed in court. But some people make everything harder than it needs to be. You'd think I was filing papers to bring down a major corporation." She frowned as he placed the tray down.

"I'm sure your charm helped to hurry the process." The comment was made out of jest due to her reputation. The nickname 'Beauty Bitch Barrister' had been tagged on her because of her tenacity and the lack of patience she had exemplified in the courthouse. Many colleagues and officers of the court had whispered their

‘BBB’ within earshot of her, making no apologies for their comments.

Shannon shot him a glare and blew him a pursed kiss for his sarcasm. “And how was your day? Boring, as usual, or mind-numbing would be more appropriate.”

“Touché!” Reece raised his Coors Light to her and smiled. “I guess I deserved that. But, actually, today was crazy in the plant. People are getting nervous about the contract talks.”

Shannon stopped midway from the serving tray to her plate with a hamburger patty on her fork and looked over at him. “You’ve started talks?” Slowly she placed the patty down.

“No, we haven’t and that’s what everyone’s getting worked up about. They’ve been so accustomed to having a settlement by now that they think the worst is going to happen.”

Shannon went about preparing her meal, head down but eyes shifting up and down. “What is it they expect?”

Reece waved his hands about. “There are some crazy ideas going around on the shop floor. Rumours fly freer than the birds.” He spread relish over his burger before continuing. “I had one guy suggest that the union make a proposal to the company to jump start talks. It doesn’t happen that way.”

They both ate their meals in silence for a while. Usually, they tried to avoid talking about their respective jobs because of differing opinions and they wanted their time together to be stress free. Her career at Ellis and Unger and Associates had risen rapidly as she dealt with corporate takeovers which contributed to her attitude toward the ordinary worker. She saw them as a hindrance toward management and was not hesitant to say so.

"Any mail today?" Shannon asked.

Reece had been waiting for this query. "The usual bills and junk mail."

"Nothing from any university?" Shannon stared at him. "You would tell me, right?"

Reece reached for the bowl of coleslaw. The query was about his application for a position in the Faculty of Education at three different universities in Ontario. Shannon had urged him to apply with the hope that he would get in as a mature student. He had applied to please her, especially after the recent acquisition of BCS by IMP had put some doubt into her mind about the factory's future. His heart wasn't really into it and the lack of a response was a good omen for him. Not so for Shannon.

"Reece, I don't understand why you oppose the idea of bettering yourself." She took up her glass of wine.

"Let's not start with this again, okay," he pleaded.

She reached over to take the bowl of coleslaw from him. "I'm just concerned that one day you'll realize that you've wasted your life in a factory. Here you have a chance to have a more meaningful vocation."

"I'm fine with the work I do." He waited for her to look at him. "Making sure those people get what they deserve, helping them to understand their benefits, and seeing that they are treated with respect for the work they do is meaningful to me."

"More like baby-sitting a bunch of adults who are too lazy," the condescending tone of her voice revealed her attitude, "or too stupid to care for themselves." She shook her head and continued with her meal.

"That's harsh, Shannon. You've met many of the people I work with, and I think you came away with a better view of them than that," Reece pleaded.

She put down her burger and sighed. "Okay, maybe I'm generalizing too much but you have to admit that most of your effort is spent on those who don't deserve to be represented, let alone working for that kind of money." She forked a patty from the plate and leaned over to offer it to Hurley, who snatched it and retreated to the elm tree.

"Who is to say one person deserves representation over another?" He knew of the public sentiment that auto workers earned too much and that they were seen as spoiled by belonging to a union. Shannon was never shy about voicing her opinion along those same lines.

"You know you could pursue the same type of work as a teacher?" She was trying another angle to get him to consider the career choice. "After a few years of teaching you probably could run for a union position. Those people would appreciate your efforts more."

"There's no guarantee I would even get a teaching job." Reece brought up a point against her argument. "Two years of schooling, with no guarantee, is a pretty expensive alternative. I think I'm better off staying where I'm at."

"With the uncertainty of that industry," she hesitated, glancing away from his stare. She sighed, returning her eyes to him, his head cocked to one side and squinting. "I mean, you know, with the recent closures of other factories and the market just rebounding from the pandemic, are you sure Border City can survive?" Shannon took up her burger and bit into it, all the while watching Reece for any reaction to her question.

"It's doing fine." Reece answered with slight anger in his voice. "We've survived before and we'll get through this difficulty, no problem."

Shannon shook her head slightly, forked some of the coleslaw, and ate without replying to his rebuff.

"That's enough now. We could debate this issue all night, but it would only ruin our time together." He smiled at her, hoping to avoid further conversation that would lead to confrontation. "Let's change the subject. What do you want to do tonight? Cheap movie night?"

Shannon returned her attention to eating, ignoring his question. With time he hoped she would accept that he was content with what he was doing. If being content was enough for her.

4

"It's not as easy as that." Scott Wilson, Plant Chair at BCS, sat back in his swivel chair as he tried to sum up the situation for the other three people present in the meeting at the union office. Elected to the position only last year, Scott seemed to have gained a few pounds on his short frame, his flabby jowls attesting to that fact.

In the small room afforded the union were Reece, listening from his small desk across the room from Wilson's desk, Brock O'Rourke, the union steward, representing the workers from the midnight shift, and Phil Gagnon, an employee who was the subject of this meeting.

"Why not?" Brock leaned over Wilson's desk, all 6'5" and 240 lbs, trying to control his temper. With both fisted hands supporting him he implored Wilson to give a better answer. "Before his recent problems, Phil was a perfect employee of more than twenty years. Can't they see that?"

"No, they can't!" Wilson raised his voice to counteract Brock's confrontational stance. "They only look at what he's doing for them now and his missing time" — he paused while he sat forward, reaching for the sheets on the table — "fourteen days in the last three months is not acceptable to them." He dropped the attendance sheets, spinning them so that they slid between Brock's arms. "There's nothing I can do."

Phil sat up in the chair that was positioned against the wall. His eyes were bloodshot and his face haggard and unshaven. Besides working the midnight shift, he had recently run into personal problems that made him sink into despair. "I can't afford to be suspended for that long," he finally spoke up.

Wilson clasped his beefy hands as he replied. "But Phil, missing one or two days a week like you have the past two weeks indicates a problem to the company that they see no other recourse but to suspend you. They've tried to warn you with verbal and written warnings."

Phil slouched in the chair. "I can't be without the pay."

"Maybe two weeks off will make you see the value of your job." Wilson slid over an envelope, the official notice of suspension.

"C'mon Scott, that's bullshit!" Brock grabbed up the envelope and whipped it against the wall behind Wilson. "You know they're just using Phil as an example for the others."

Wilson shot up from his seat. "Brock, the discipline is warranted just on the absenteeism alone. If they really wanted to nail him, they could have brought up the incidents where Phil came into work drunk."

"No way are you using that as an excuse to not defend him." Brock stood erect, towering over the shorter Wilson. "The company had already dismissed those charges." The two men were at a standstill.

Reece had risen from his desk and approached Brock, putting his hand on Brock's shoulder, gently steering him away from Scott's desk. "How about we calm down, guys, and figure out what we can do for Phil."

"There's nothing we can do." Wilson shot Reece a glare. "They have followed progressive discipline to a tee. This is the next step." The term 'progressive discipline' was a practice by the company whereby a worker is disciplined for work disruptions in stages, the mildest, or first step, being a verbal warning to the ultimate, or final step, being termination.

Brock stepped back, running his hand over his bald head. Phil's eyes darted from man to man to man, like the ball in a pinball machine. Wilson remained standing, defiant.

Reece glanced around and then stepped to the door, resting his hand on the doorknob. "Maybe we should suggest that Phil go on S&A and get treatment for depression. His recent family situation warrants an excuse for his unusual work habits and the uncharacteristic missing of time. We can make a case that the recent circumstance of his wife leaving him, with the children, has brought on this unfortunate change. His past work record shows he's a good worker." All three men listened intently to Reece spin his idea. "There is precedence with this company allowing an employee to seek help and receive S&A while doing so." He turned to Phil. "You could attend rehabilitation for a month at a facility recommended by the company whereby your attendance would be mandatory for you to receive payment." Sickness and Accidents benefits (S&A) were provisions in the collective agreement that allowed a worker time off work, with pay, to recover from an illness or an injury.

Phil cocked his head to the left and upwards at Reece. Brock had moved over to lean on the file cabinet. Wilson had retaken his seat.

Reece continued while moving back to his seat. "We would be right in proposing this solution." He looked over at Wilson.

"I suppose we could." Wilson had picked up the envelope and placed it with the sheets on the table. He addressed Phil. "In the meantime, you cannot miss any time while we arrange this. Your suspension was to take effect Monday, so you have the rest of this week to show up." He paused. "You think you can do that for two days?"

Again, Phil just nodded. Brock bounced away from the cabinets. "He'll be fine. Just make this happen." He flicked his hand at Phil, pointing to the door. The two men exited.

Reece watched Wilson. The chairperson's cheeks were flushed, his double chin quivered as he seemed to be mumbling to himself. Finally, he squinted at Reece with intensity. "You think that will solve his problem?"

"I think the man needs help," Reece replied.

"And what about Brock? He can't keep coming in here undermining my authority." Wilson swayed back and forth.

Reece knew that Brock really pushed Wilson on many matters. Trying to favour one over the other was like choosing between a father and a brother. Scott had shown Reece the workings of the union while Brock was like the brother Reece never had. “He’s just doing what he thinks is right for his people.”

“And I don’t?” Wilson stopped rocking. “I have everyone to think of and the company breathing down my back. It’s not easy.” Wilson opened a drawer of his desk and took out a pill bottle.

Reece stood up and approached Wilson. “I know the times are hard right now, but we need to take a step back from the overall picture and see things from their eyes. The employees are looking for direction and leadership.” Reece took the seat Phil had been in.

Wilson shook out a capsule and reached for his coffee cup. “Are you implying that they aren’t getting that from me?” He put the blood pressure pill in his mouth, washing it down with his coffee.

Reece didn’t need a confrontation with Wilson. “Scott, you’re juggling too many things right now with all these disciplinary actions, the upcoming negotiations, and your duties at the local. Maybe you’ve got to slow down and rely on others to help you. Let me handle Phil’s case and let the stewards know that they’re going to get increased attention on the floor from the foremen.”

Wilson acknowledged Reece's comments with a slight nod. The two men were very aware of the company's renewed conviction to follow policy and regulations as set out in the collective agreement. It was contract time and they both knew the company enforced the rules more stringently in the hopes of suspending people so as to use them as negotiating chips. This resulted in more cases like Phil's that pushed the union to the limit. Representing the employees was a top priority for the elected union officers. Reece wasn't sure Wilson cared.

5

Both garage doors were opened, front and back, to allow the slight breeze to pass through to cool the two men. Brock O'Rourke was bent over the engine of the Ford F-150. "That'll do it. Your truck is all tuned up for another year." Brock slammed down the hood and turned to face his father who looked on from the comfort of a lawn chair at the rear of the garage. Rufus, the family chocolate Labrador retriever, lay at his feet. "Why don't you get a new truck so we don't have to do this every year?"

"Because I don't need one." Gilbert 'Gil' O'Rourke rose, tapped the box of his red pickup, and walked to the fridge just inside the doorway. "I said when I retired that it was going to be the last truck I got." He tugged on the fridge handle.

"But that was fifteen years ago, Pop. You can afford to get another one." Brock was wiping his hands with a rag.

Gil closed the fridge, taking two beers from it. "It still runs good." Brock joined him at the doorway, accepting one of the beers.

They stood together looking out to the yard. Father and son were about the same height with Brock having about a hundred pounds more on his frame. Brock's home was situated on four acres of land just outside of Belle River. The ranch-style house spread across the yard, facing the county road, was to the right of the driveway. Its appearance was enhanced by the Bonsai trees, rose-bushes, many flowers, and lawn ornaments Brock's wife Margaret had planted in front of the house. The back yard stretched out with an above-ground pool, complete with enclosed deck, and a garden that grew tomatoes, peppers, carrots, corn and squash, bordering the right side of the property. Just behind the garage to the end of the property line was a pole barn that held Brock's toys; an ATV, boat, motorcycle and Ski-doo. Way back, beyond the fields of soybean, was a small forest that seemed out of place in the vast openness.

"How's it going at work?" Gil, at 80 years old, kept his grey hair slicked back making his gaunt face seem long. The jeans and collared shirt were baggy on him.

Brock pointed his bottle down, allowing Rufus to lap up the last little bit of beer. "Wilson has no clue what he's doing. The guy's useless." His muscle shirt was drenched with sweat, and he wiped his forehead with the rag.

Gil took a quick swig of his beer before replying. "I thought he was the logical successor to Dunbar? He seemed the right man for the job."

"He was the only successor, no-one challenged him." Brock faced his father. "But that doesn't mean he's cut out for the job. The guy doesn't have a feel for the people he represents." Brock walked back into the garage to fetch another beer.

Gil watched his son and waited for his return before probing more about the situation. "I remember Scott as a union steward when I was there, and he seemed genuinely concerned for the people. Even at the local, Scott jumped into a bunch of committees and seemed driven to do good for the membership." Gil had been President of the local union, advancing from Plant Chairperson of BCS, representing the membership in one form or another for over twenty-five years.

"He's driven all right. For his own good." Brock frowned. "He wants your old job at the local. He spends more time down there than he does at the plant. It's the stewards and Reece who take care of the people, not Scott."

Gil dangled his bottle at his side, still almost full. "Reece is doing a good job there?"

"Sure, if it wasn't for him, we'd have no representation with the company." Brock noticed a slight smile from his father. "He's the one everyone goes to when they have a problem and lately that's happening more often than I like to say. He should've run against Wilson last year." Brock harrumphed. "He would've won easily but instead he agreed to not oppose Wilson and keep his position as committeeman. Now they've added the Benefits position to him." Brock shook his head while taking a big gulp of his beer.

"His time will come." Gil sipped at his beer and his face twitched. "What's going on there?"

"People are being put up for suspensions or getting written up for piddly-ass stuff. The company is coming down hard on everyone." Brock paused. "Scott keeps telling the people that the company has the right to discipline them, and he gives excuses for not wanting to defend them. He's such an arrogant ass."

"What are you doing about it?"

Brock stared open-mouthed at his father. "I do my job. I try to reason with the foreman, but they have instructions to discipline. When I meet with Scott, I remind him what he's there for." Brock had started at BCS right out of high school. Now, twenty-two years later, he held the position of union steward. "Pop, he's not the right guy we need to deal with this company."

Gil looked Brock straight in the eyes, his grey pupils like bullets. "So, what are you going to do about it?" He crossed his arms, the beer tucked in the crook of his arm.

Brock frowned and shook his head. "What do you want me to do?"

"For one, stop talking trash about Scott to everyone," Gil almost whispered. "You don't think I hear things down at the local?" Gil stepped onto the grass and turned to face his son. "It doesn't help you and it poisons the membership's faith in the union. We can't have that."

Brock took a pull from his beer, accepting the criticism. Whenever father and son got together it seemed their conversations were always about work. Brock had followed in his father's footsteps, working at BCS and filling a position in the union. Gil had earned respect from the membership during his years of service and Brock tried to live up to the expectations. He just wished that his father would acknowledge his efforts, once in a while. He bent down to scratch Rufus's ear.

“Son, you need to reel in your personal feelings about Scott and understand what the people need to hear during this time. They need positive feedback.”

“But Pop, there’s nothing positive to speak of.” Brock straightened up, spitting to the ground. “No contract, no talks, nothing. What do you want me to spin...lies?”

“No, that’s not what I’m saying. Be like Reece and take care of your people. Tell them that the process will work itself out and that the union is looking after their interest, that’s all.” Gil extended his beer bottle as a gesture of conciliation.

Brock tapped his bottle with his father’s bottle. The present union executives didn’t have the respect of the membership and Brock had a hard time supporting them.

“Daddy, supper is ready!” A small voice broke the tension. The two men turned to see Gillian, Brock’s youngest daughter, running from the house to them. She had a genetic condition, Down-Syndrome, but her wide smile and flowing shoulder length blond hair made her the darling of the family. Rufus bounded to her. “Grandpa, you’re staying for supper too, right?” She hugged him.

Gil patted her head. “Of course, pumpkin.” She looked up at him, a huge toothy grin on her face. He wiggled his fingers at her, a sign they shared. “I’m going to sit beside you.”

She giggled as she tore away from him. The affectionate signal meant he would be tickling her while they ate. "I'll tell Jackie and Evie that you're sitting by me." She yelled back as she ran back to the house, Rufus in tow.

Gil peered at his son who was watching his girl, a smile escaping his grizzled face. "That's only one reason why you need to take care of things at work. They all depend on you." Brock was the sole income earner in the family, Margaret being a stay-at-home mother and wife. It was a rare feat in today's world. Gil clamped his hand on Brock's arm as they made their way to the house.

6

"Okay, so he's coming later this afternoon," Reece replied after having been filled in about the upcoming visit of an executive from the main office by the plant manager Lena Kersey. He was standing in for Scott, who was at the local. "What's the purpose of this visit?"

"Mr. Bainbridge expressed a desire to meet with Scott, and yourself, about the future of Border City Stamping." Lena sat in one of the chairs along the wall of the union office.

Reece had come to appreciate her candour when dealing with any issues from productivity to health and safety, and employee conduct. Even coming to the union office instead of just calling to inform him of the visit showed her genuine concern for BCS. It had only been a little over six months since she secured the position of plant manager, vacated by the unexpected death of the previous plant manager last September. But today she seemed to be holding back, somewhat nervous in relaying the message from the parent company. During their conversation she was constantly picking up and placing down a pen, avoiding eye contact, and hesitating to answer any queries Reece had about the visit.

Lena Kersey had raised a lot of eyebrows with her appearance as its new plant manager, at the young age of thirty. Her slim figure, dark complexion and eye-catching look had prompted many lewd remarks by the male employees. She deflected them with a graciousness that impressed Reece, yet she was firm in denouncing the act as harassment that would not be tolerated in the workplace. The female employees welcomed her stance and eventually all employees saw earnestness in her role to make BCS a successful enterprise. She had introduced a number of cost-saving measures to the production process and had implemented many changes to the daily operation that improved efficiency and productivity.

"He's a little late for that." Reece sat at his desk. "He should have thought about it two months ago."

She slowly stood and turned to look out the door window into the main office. Reece couldn't help but appreciate her appearance; dark blue pants with a white blouse that accentuated her features. She turned back, slowly walked toward Scott's desk, and leant up against it facing Reece. With a forced smile, she continued the conversation. "I understand your concern with the shutdown so close. Mr. Bainbridge didn't elaborate but he did ask me to arrange accommodations for him to the end of the week."

Reece now took a moment to answer, getting up from the chair and walking to the personnel file cabinets on the left. He turned back to her, leaning on the cabinets. "I've never really had to deal with him, you know, with Scott usually accompanying him on his tours. I've maybe spoken to him offhand once or twice, but Scott has said that he's a serious type of guy...all business." Reece put his hands in his jean pockets. "What do you make of him?" Reece wasn't sure whether her loyalty was to BCS or to the parent company, IMP. By asking her about some insight into Bainbridge, he hoped to clarify that point. "Being in your position, I believe you would have an idea of what he wants?"

Lena raised her hands in supplication. "I don't, really? There hasn't been any discussion from head-office about the talks." She crossed her arms. "He did request that I have all personnel files available for him," she paused, "including retirees."

"Why?" Reece bounced off the file cabinet, glancing at it as if these files were being exposed. He went to his desk and turned to face her, copying her pose, leaning back against the desk with arms folded.

"I don't know." She answered honestly. "I'm not privy to his thoughts, but," she shrugged, purposely ending her sentence in doubt, not sure whether she should share her concerns over the upcoming contract.

"What?" Reece implored. "You must have some idea what he wants, right?"

"No, I don't." She decided to trust Reece. "But I'm concerned about the direction they are going with BCS." Lena unfolded her arms, her palms up. "When I first got here, BCS had a reputation of being a quality company with lots of work, but then parts were moved out and layoffs occurred." Reece nodded and she continued. "I didn't understand why that was happening when I hadn't had a chance to make any improvements." She forged on with a determined mind. "I went to work, and we saw improvement across the board. Yet, more work was taken away." She shook her head.

"What's bothering you?" Reece could tell she wanted to say more.

"Only my opinion, you understand?" She re-crossed her arms. "Why would the parent company take away a profitable product from BCS unless it was to send a message?" Her eyebrows rose, prompting Reece to answer.

Reece just shrugged, waiting for her to finish her thoughts.

"To show who's boss," she flatly responded. "I believe Bainbridge, on behalf of International Metal Products, plans to exercise their authority as the parent company to get you, the union, to accept their demands. Is that a tactic you guys are accustomed to?"

"Yes, they try to flex their muscles, so to speak." Reece appreciated her honest opinion.

Lena continued before Reece could elaborate. "I've never been involved in a negotiation, with a company or a union." She stood. "This is all new to me and I can't really offer more insight into Bainbridge's strategy." She pushed off the desk and went to the door. She pretended as if she were going to leave but then abruptly about-faced. "I hope it doesn't ruin our relationship" — her eyes bulged, and she stammered — "I mean, our working relationship, that is."

Reece recognized her discomfort and offered her an out. “I guess we’ll have to see.” He smiled. “Are we done?”

She grabbed the door handle, opened the door slowly, tilting her head a bit toward Reece with a pert smile, and exited.

Reece felt they had an ally on the company’s side, but time would tell whether his intuition was correct.

7

Bainbridge watched as the rider got off his Harley Davidson and entered the Tim Horton’s with his helmet still on. This location just off Highway 401 at Comber was chosen seven months ago, a rendezvous the informant felt safe to show his face. This was the fourth motorcyclist in the last fifteen minutes to show up at the coffee shop, with most of the vehicles using the drive-through, and the small coffee shop was virtually empty. Bainbridge was amused by the informant’s efforts to conceal his identity, going so far as to make it even difficult to make contact. Bainbridge couldn’t phone, text or email but instead was instructed to use a code of numbers indicating date and time of rendezvous on the informant's weekly pay stub whenever he wanted to meet. Sitting at the far end of the cafe, with a view of the parking lot, Bainbridge watched the rider go to the counter. The man wore a leather jacket, ordered his coffee by putting up his shield, keeping the helmet on, and then gazed around the shop, nodding in Bainbridge's direction. He paid for his drink, grabbed the hot cup and strolled over to the corner table. Before Bainbridge could address him, possibly by name, the rider spoke. "What do you have for me?"

Bainbridge passed over an envelope. "I will have something for you after I hear about the union meeting." He couldn't help but smile at the scared eyes peering from the helmet. This was taking precaution to another level, hiding behind a helmet and jacket.

The rider put the envelope inside his jacket. He hesitated a second too long.

"What are the chances of you getting on the negotiating committee?" Bainbridge asked while putting his hand out inviting the rider to sit. Getting the informant on the union's negotiating team would be a great advantage for Bainbridge to undermine their strategy.

The rider shook his head. "It all depends on who runs against me. The membership can be very fickle when it comes to choosing that third man."

Bainbridge smiled. “Aren’t you liked by your fellow workers?” Bainbridge had sought out a ‘stool pigeon’ shortly after the acquisition of BCS, just like he’d done many times before with other companies, finding this one eager to rat out his fellow workers.

The rider’s eyes narrowed. “I’ve got to go.” The rider turned to head out of the coffee shop.

“What’s the mood like on the floor?” Bainbridge asked, forcing the rider to turn back.

“Mixed.” The rider pronounced, his nervousness apparent by the shuffling of his feet, wanting to get away as quickly as possible. Bainbridge wasn’t going to make it that easy for him. “They don’t like that negotiations haven’t begun and some are getting nervous.”

“What have you told them?”

The rider placed the coffee on the table and took his gloves from his pocket. “I give them the union line that we’re waiting for the company.” He paused while slipping the gloves on. “Is that why you’re down?”

“Maybe,” Bainbridge answered tersely. “Are you afraid that the union won’t be ready?”

“There’s nothing to be afraid of. You haven’t given them anything.”

Bainbridge tapped his valise on the chair next to him. “I’ll have something for you to distribute on the floor. The earlier we get it out, the better."

"When?" The rider asked, staring at the valise.

Bainbridge answered. "I'm at the plant this week."

"No way." The rider blurted out and then looked around before continuing. "You know the agreement. Never at the plant."

"Okay, back here." Bainbridge paused, looking out the window at his car, a black BMW 328i, as he stirred his coffee. After a few seconds that seemed like an eternity to the rider, who was tugging at his gloves, Bainbridge continued. "Monday afternoon, one o'clock."

"Too early," the rider replied, "same time, here." He clapped his hands, once, shooting a glance at Bainbridge's Rolex.

Bainbridge looked down at his watch and then back up at the rider, a smirk on his face. "Okay, four o'clock."

The rider turned and walked out of the coffee shop. His coffee remained at the table.

8

Local 123 was an old bar converted into a union hall almost twenty years ago. The large dance floor, now used to hold membership meetings, was reduced in half by a sliding folding partition. The rooms above, that used to be apartments for rent, consisted of offices for the President, Vice President, Benefits Officer, and the Financial Officer. The motto of the local, not official, but spoken by the membership; '*Local 123, what can you do for me?*'

There were only about forty members in attendance, half being retirees and laid off workers, due to the meeting only dealing with general business and the election of one person to the negotiating team. For Reece, sitting at the front with Scott Wilson and Brad Dunbar, President of the Local, the low attendance shed a poor light on the attitude of the workers about the union. That this meeting would attract less than ten percent of the membership was not a good sign for the union. The murmur resonated throughout the hall, small groups formed, huddled willy-nilly, amongst the rows of chairs. The three men sat at the front table up on the low stage. Dunbar, a tall, heavy-set man with crew-cut grey hair, sat to the left of the podium. He had ascended to the President's position after having served as plant chairman of BCS for many years. He aspired of moving up higher in the National Union's office. Wilson, seated next to the podium, poured himself water from the pitcher, took a sip, and then stepped up to the microphone centred on the podium. Reece sat in the farthest chair, on the right of the podium, intentionally, having been instructed that he would not be presenting anything in this meeting. He was fine with that.

"We'd like to start the meeting, so could everyone take their seats and quiet down." Wilson opened the meeting. The shuffling of chairs subsided as the crowd settled in. Wilson took another drink and then continued. "I would like to call this meeting to order. If you would like to take some time to read the minutes of the last meeting before we open it up for discussion." He took his seat while the membership pored over the sheets handed out at the door. Wilson whispered to Dunbar before he stepped up to the microphone.

"Are there any questions or comments concerning the information before you?" There were no gestures from the crowd indicating anything was to be asked. Wilson waited a few more seconds before he pronounced. "Then I move to accept the minutes of the meeting. Do I have a second?"

A few people raised their hands and Wilson pointed out one person. "Jerry Olsen seconds the motion. We shall now proceed with today's business. The agenda for today is general business and the election of one person to the negotiating committee. Do I have any other issue that needs to be added to the agenda?" A man stood up, his hand raised, from the middle of the assembly. Wilson acknowledged him. "Nick, what else would you like to add?"

Nick Campo wore his black hair slicked back, shoulder length, while his face was more stubble than beard. "I would like to add that upcoming negotiations be discussed and why hasn't it yet happened?" A buzz rose from the crowd.

Wilson waved his hands up and down." Okay people, quiet down. Nick, we were going to discuss that today, anyways."

Nick threw up his hands. "Then why wasn't that put on the notice? More people may have shown up if they had known you were going to talk about it."

Wilson bent down from the podium to whisper to Dunbar. Returning to the microphone, his hands waving to quiet the crowd, he hesitated to say something against the rising noise. A shrill whistle pierced the air, followed by a shout. "Everyone, shut up!"

"Thank you for that." Wilson nodded to his right at the man who had quieted the crowd. "People should have realized we were going to talk about the negotiations when they read we were electing a person to the committee. That's not to say this meeting is for suggestions, which will come later. There really isn't anything to discuss because the company hasn't approached us to open talks."

Another person stood up. "Didn't you meet with someone the other day?" The murmur started up again.

Wilson waved everyone down. "Yes, we met for a few minutes, but nothing was presented or suggested for opening talks." He paused, waiting for the murmur, but it didn't appear. "Let us proceed with this meeting and we'll discuss the negotiations, or lack of, when we clear everything else."

Nick, who remained standing, pointed to the stage. "Then why is Brad here? He doesn't normally attend our meetings unless it involves negotiations."

The crowd burst with chatter, questions being asked from all over the room. Wilson stepped away from the podium as Dunbar rose. They conversed for a few seconds while the crowd was silenced again by a loud whistle.

Dunbar moved to the microphone. "Okay, Nick, I'll answer your question. I'm here to support Scott and Reece in their relating the events up to now in the negotiations. Unfortunately, there is nothing going on and I expected they would meet some resistance by the membership for the lack of talks. It's not their doing, it's the company's. So, if you would just sit down and let them get through the meeting, you'll be updated with what's happening." He left the podium and re-took his seat.

The crowd was stunned by the abruptness of the President's words, becoming silent. Nick shook his head but sat down anyways.

Reece watched with a detached mindset. The short meeting with Bainbridge on Friday hadn't gone well. His bombastic rhetoric about securing a contract had enraged Scott, Bainbridge spouting off about corporate structure. Scott had stormed out of the meeting, leaving Reece to warn Bainbridge that his attitude would hinder any further talks unless he curbed it and came to the table with an understanding that the union and the company were partners. Reece came away with the feeling that Bainbridge didn't see it that way.

The meeting proceeded with the general business and then eventually led to discussion about the negotiation process. The crowd heard that the company preferred to wait until after the shutdown to commence with negotiations and they were content to take as much time as possible. The membership was reminded that the current collective agreement ran to the end of the year. Wilson then spoke about the electing of a member to the negotiating committee.

"This is the first time this is being done to fill the void that was created when the Benefits Representative was eliminated when the new ownership demanded that the committee be reduced." Wilson paused for effect. "And I would like to remind the membership that it was whole-heartedly agreed to reduce the committee by a vote of the membership in a previous meeting." The crowd burst with chatter, some yelling profanities at Wilson who stepped aside for a few seconds. After a shrill whistle once again quieted the crowd, Wilson returned to the microphone. "Reece now takes on those duties as well as his own as plant committee person. This elected position of a member from the ranks was also brought forward by the membership as a checks and balances for the committee." Catcalls rose from the crowd. "I now call for nominees to be elected for the position to stand."

Three men stood for the vote: Brock O'Rourke, Nick Campo and Jonathan Prentice. Reece reasoned that each nominee had their good points and their bad points with the membership. Brock's father Gil, in attendance, was the past president of the local which gave Brock an edge, but he was a hot head at times. Nick opposed everything management stood for, which could be a hindrance when negotiating a contract, but was a believer in the rights of the worker to earn a good living and he supported the union. He was also known to criticize the union, openly, to the membership. Jonathan, called John in the plant, was the union steward on shift one. He seemed smart, involved in a few committees of the union, and very knowledgeable about the collective agreement and union policy. His downfall, according to the workers on his shift, was that he was too friendly with the supervisors, an easy prey to do their bidding. That Reece had a preference over any one of them didn't matter as the membership in attendance would decide who the third person on the union's negotiating committee would be. Their names were listed on a large paper on an easel and smaller tickets were handed out to the crowd. They were to vote for the person they wanted by selecting the number beside that person's name. The slips were collected by the election committee who then went out of the room to conduct the count. During this wait, minor issues were dealt with concerning the recreation committee and donations to charities. The election committee returned with the result. Brock was elected.

9

"Nice putt," Reece said as the golf ball dropped into the hole after travelling thirty-five feet.

Shawn Bennett strolled up to retrieve the ball. “Just reading the line. You should have no problem with that five-footer.” He stepped aside as Reece set up.

Reece tapped the ball, sending it slowly towards the hole. It stopped two rotations before the cup. He nudged it in and then bent to pick it up.

Shawn replaced the flag. “All flash with those drives but no finish.” Slightly shorter than Reece, lean yet muscular, he playfully punched Reece on the arm and chuckled.

The two men grabbed their bags on their way to the next hole. They’ve been best friends since grade school. They had each other’s back and earned the respect of the other guys in the school. Through high school and university, they had competed together in several sports such as hockey, baseball, martial arts, and track. This helped them maintain a competitive friendship. When Shawn was teased because of his Asian look, his mother being Vietnamese, Reece was there to defend him. Shawn had his back when he struggled with the loss of his father, being a friend to confide in. Shawn had gone on to become a police constable while Reece pursued his union officer duties. Shawn noticed Reece being rather quiet during their Sunday morning round of golf.

“It’s been over an hour now and you haven’t said five words.” Shawn placed his bag down on the fourth hole at Rochester Place Golf and Resort. “What’s eating you?”

Reece glanced over and shyly answered. “Shannon.” He rummaged in his bag for the scorecard.

“Now what did you do?” Shawn teased as he lifted his driver out of the bag. “You want to talk about it. I’m no expert, being single, but women can sure be a mystery.”

Reece returned the marked-up scorecard to his bag and took up his driver. Shawn went through his set up and then drove the ball down the middle of the fairway. Reece followed suit, driving his ball forty-five yards further and sliced to the right. They shouldered their bags and started their walk.

“I’m just confused why she didn’t take vacation time with me.” Reece adjusted his ball cap. “She said she’s swamped at the firm, but I find that hard to believe. She knew about the shutdown. She could’ve gotten ahead on her work or put it off ’til she got back.” He frowned while he faced his friend.

Shawn placed his sunglasses from his cap to his face. “Didn’t you two go away in January? Maybe she doesn’t have more time.”

“She has three weeks, just like me.” Reece recalled the week in Mexico at a resort. That was such a good time, which now seemed so long ago. What had changed, he thought?

They stopped just before Shawn's ball. While he put his bag down, he replied. "Have you talked to her about it? I mean, you know how hard it is to figure out what they want. She might not know that you're upset about it."

Reece backed away to let Shawn prepare to hit. Shannon knew he was upset about the matter, having talked about it extensively the last few days. She even mentioned that she may have to go to the firm's head office in Toronto during Reece's time off. That really set him off.

Shawn hit away, the ball landing to the right of the green. He groaned, aware that Reece was closer to the green and was already one stroke ahead of him.

"She knows," Reece answered Shawn. "She just said she couldn't afford to leave the cases she has on the go. She promised she would take the time later but that doesn't do me any good." Reece had his arms resting on the shouldered golf bag. "I think there's something else going on."

Shawn tilted his cap down, hiding his face even more, along with the sunglasses. He placed his 9 iron in the bag and then shouldered it. They walked towards Reece's ball.

"I think she's mad at me for not wanting to go to teacher's college," Reece spoke up.

"Why don't you want to go?" Shawn grinned. This was an opportunity to change the subject.

"I'm happy where I'm at." Reece's red face showed the effect of the sun. "Plus, there's no guarantee I would get a job teaching."

"Being at Border City suits you after all those years in university?"

"Definitely, it does," Reece replied. "Everything I learned I put to use." He looked over at his playing partner who was shaking his head. "What? You don't agree?"

Shawn crossed in front of Reece to go to his ball, walking backwards, to reply. "I think you wasted all that money, for where you're at." He tipped his hat and then turned to go to his ball lying in the rough just off the green.

Now it was Reece's turn to shake his head. Why did those close to him not see his work as worthy? Reece believed in what he was doing and even felt that his education had set him up to follow this path. Taking business administration and psychology prepared him for the toughness in dealing with people on both sides, the company and the membership. It was his task to show them. Shawn surely could see he was doing okay.

He placed his bag down, grabbed his pitching iron, and went through his routine. He waited as a train raced by, this hole running parallel to the tracks. His high arc shot landed on the green and rolled to within ten feet of the cup. Taking up his bag, he watched Shawn chip onto the green for his third. Walking up to the green he saw Shawn's ball inside of his own. They met on the green, putters in hand, and continued the conversation.

"Maybe Shannon wants you to get a profession that fits your education." Shawn spotted his ball and took up the flag out of the cup, placing it down away from their line. "She has done that with her education and maybe wants the same for you."

Reece knelt behind his ball to read the line. "I do have a profession."

"Working in a factory is what you went to university for?" Shawn took up a golfer's stance, leaning on his putter with his legs crossed.

Reece didn't answer but instead rose and pretended to concentrate on his putt. Recalling why he went to university and then ended up at Border City Stamping muddled his concentration. He was good with numbers but didn't want to go into accounting. Business administration seemed like a good idea, remembering that he thought he could parlay that into a career with a big sports company, maybe even a professional team. But then he began working summers at BCS and thought maybe a management position could be had. Working everyday on the shop floor with the people changed that for him and when he landed a full-time job at BCS, right after graduation, he knew what he wanted to do.

"And is that profession going to last?" Shawn asked.

Reece froze for a second during his practice putts. "There's a future there. This new company's just playing hard ball. They see we're still making a profit for them." He straightened up and addressed the ball.

Shawn added. "Still, you're not sure what their plans are for the plant. Maybe looking at some other options wouldn't be a bad idea."

Reece shook his head as he lined up the putter, never glancing at the hole. His stroke was firm causing the ball to lip out and scoot a foot to the left of the cup. Shawn scooped up the ball with the back of his putter and tossed the ball to Reece. "Just like your putting, it's not a sure thing."

10

The room was ideal for their meeting. It was long and narrow, without windows, and supplied with two oblong tables butted together, and enough chairs for everyone. In the past the room had been used for training purposes and agenda meetings with company and union personnel. Both of those scenarios were no longer practiced.

Bainbridge requested a meeting with the union to set the tone for negotiations. Scott Wilson, Reece Kincaid, and Brock O'Rourke were accompanied by Brad Dunbar. The preliminary talks, as Bainbridge called them, was to set out the schedule of talks for the contract. He had informed the union of his team's arrival later that day. Their job was to go through the language of the present contract and make suggestions of change. The debate was whether they would be suggestions or ultimatums. Bainbridge tried to downplay the importance of this part of the process. His main concern was the eventual issue of wages and benefits.

Bainbridge sat in the middle of one of the tables with Lena Kersey to his right at the other table. Opposite them sat Wilson with Kincaid and O'Rourke on either side while Dunbar sat at one end of the table, furthest from Lena. Pads and paper were provided for each person. Nothing had been written, yet. Discussion had been relatively friendly with Bainbridge apologizing for his outburst at the previous meeting. He was setting them up.

"These negotiations will determine your ability to secure future work." Bainbridge had rolled up the sleeves of his denim shirt and had files spread across his side of the table. The remark was meant to spark some reaction.

Wilson huffed and then replied, “We had secured future work, but you took it away.”

Bainbridge smirked, “That work was never guaranteed for here. It was decided that one of our other facilities was better suited for the work.”

“More like it was cheaper labour,” Wilson shot back.

“That was not a factor.” Bainbridge shuffled some papers, never looking down at them. “The customer was satisfied with the choice due to the savings on transportation and border issues.” Bainbridge paused, noticing the doubtful expressions across the table. “Regardless, you should not base the talks on what you may have had but rather on what you aim to secure.”

“It’s hard to do that when we don’t know what we’re up against.” Wilson was taking the lead. “What’s the company using as a parameter to meet their goals?”

“Now that BCS is part of our corporate structure it’s imperative that it fall into line with our operating costs in relation to all the other plants.” Bainbridge despised using the acronyms for both companies but had been shot down using the full titles by the union as being too formal. He refused to say the acronym for Industrial Metal Products. They knew the names of the companies. “You’re all bidding for work.”

“That’s bullshit,” O’Rourke spat out only to be silenced by Wilson putting up a hand in his face.

Bainbridge smiled thinly. “Before we delve into contract talks, let me make it quite clear that this meeting’s intent is to lay the groundwork for further negotiations. You, as a committee, need to get up to speed, so to say, about our policies and guidelines. As well, the future of BCS will depend on its viability in respect to the other holdings we have. Again, you’re all bidding for work. These points will help you decide how you view our offer.”

Dunbar spoke up, “In the past negotiations were handled by the plant manager.” He eyed Lena across the room. “Are we to assume that’s no longer the case with your presence?”

Bainbridge answered, putting out his hand towards Lena on his right, staring at Dunbar, ignoring her. “Miss Kersey will be fully involved with these contract talks.” He slowly turned his head to take in the other union members, ending to finally look at Lena. He had hired her with the intent of putting someone inexperienced at the helm of BCS. Hoping that it would result in a downward trend for the auto parts manufacturer, she had surprised him with her improvements to the operations and the subsequent high efficiency rating. Even taking away some work didn’t deter her from creating a productive work environment.

"But let me make it abundantly clear. I have full authorization to oversee these contract talks and abide by the policy set out by the new owners. BCS is no longer its own entity. It now comes under the umbrella of a whole network of automotive suppliers we own or have a share of." Bainbridge laid his hands flat on the table and directed his attention to Wilson. "The competition has just gotten tougher because you are now dealing with a corporate structure that's used throughout all the plants. Your ability to adapt to that structure will determine your future."

"You mean increasing your profits at the expense of the workers." O'Rourke spoke up, this time leaning forward and continuing. "Don't think we aren't aware of *IMP* buying up companies and slashing their wages and benefits. That's not going to happen here." The emphasis on the acronym for the parent company was meant to rattle Bainbridge.

Bainbridge sat composed. "There are many factors to take into consideration when evaluating a plant's operating efficiency."

"And BCS's quality and productivity should stand for some consideration," Kincaid interrupted, drawing Bainbridge's attention.

"It's expected that BCS will maintain its level of work" — Bainbridge paused, a smug look on his face — "but need I remind you that the purchase of BCS was to save it from bankruptcy."

"Wait, that has nothing to do with the workers." Wilson's face was red, his jowls quivering. "The problem occurred because of negligent owners, or should I say, sons. You can't take it out on the people who've made this company a success because of two spoiled boys who frittered away their father's legacy."

Wilson was referring to the two sons of Jacob Ermler, one of the founders of Border City Stamping. Ermler and Benjamin Rollins created BCS just after the Second World War, supplying auto parts to the Big Three; Chrysler, Ford and General Motors. When Ermler passed away in 1999, his share of the ownership transferred to his two boys, Eli and Isaac, who had never stepped foot in BCS. They instead drained the coffers of the company to the point of bankruptcy. The previous manager, Theo Epstein, had been able to keep the struggling enterprise afloat until last year when he was informed that the two negligent owners had accepted an offer from IMP. His untimely death coincided with the takeover which occurred in September.

"Regardless of the circumstances that brought us to this point, BCS now falls under the guidance of the corporate structure. It's the desire of my employer, and yours, to reduce the operating costs of this facility to be able to compete in the global market that has come out of this recent recession. We must be very competitive if we want to survive." Bainbridge challenged.

Dunbar spoke up, "We're aware of what's happened over the last few years and are receptive to ideas that allow us to share in the success of this company. But it's hard to be efficient when the facility is operating at only about three-quarters capacity because work has been taken out of here. Bring that work back, or secure similar work, and this facility will show you productivity, quality and efficiency as it has in the past."

Bainbridge flopped open a folder. "Filling this place with work may not solve the problem of costs that this firm has on its books. Do you know that there are more people receiving retirement benefits than there are people who work here? The legacy costs alone make this facility expensive to operate."

Wilson spoke, "Bring back the work and the hundred people on layoff and the ensuing profit from throughput would surely offset some of the benefits' cost."

Bainbridge pulled out one sheet from the folder. "You don't understand what I'm getting at. Even if we were to do that, the premiums that are paid out for benefits have sky-rocketed over the last few years. Bringing back people will only increase those premiums. We need to get a handle on them."

"By coming to some reasonable ground, our membership can pick up some of the cost of their benefits through a co-pay," Kincaid countered, quite aware of the cost of health care benefits. He directed his next comment to Lena, hoping to get a favourable response. "Miss Kersey, are you aware of this practice?"

Kersey finally spoke up, "There have been many companies who have introduced co-pays as a way to reduce the obligation of the company. Most employees don't mind, considering the alternative of reduced benefits, or paying for benefits totally on their own." She glanced at Bainbridge who seemed to be ignoring her statement.

Bainbridge seemed mesmerized by the sheet in his hand. "But what about those already receiving retirement benefits? And those eligible soon? Their costs are too high. Do we go after them for premiums?" He gestured toward the men on the other side, slightly waving the paper in hand.

No one answered. The lull in the room seemed interminable. Bainbridge forged on.

"I'll give you an example." He raised the sheet in his hand. "We have a retiree here going on fifteen years. Over the last four years his medication costs have risen dramatically, to the point where last year alone it was $85,000.00. That's one employee! Imagine the premium on him. What's his condition?" Bainbridge scanned the sheet, with a photo of the person attached to the summary of health care costs and then placed the sheet on the table for all to see. "It seems he has multiple myeloma and has been receiving treatment for it for the last three years.

If he continues, for say, three more years, the cost is close to $300,000." He paused to look around the table. "The man should be dead; he's costing us so much."

O'Rourke shot up out of his chair and leaned across the table. "That's my father you're talking about" — he pointed to the paper — "and if he were here, he wouldn't put up with this bullshit you're handing us." Kincaid had stood up and gone over to restrain O'Rourke, somewhat, by placing a hand on his shoulder. O'Rourke glanced a second at Kincaid and then turned back to Bainbridge. "That man gave a lot of years to this company and represented them fairly and with dignity. Unlike you, scum-bag, who come in here with only one thing in mind, your bottom-line."

"Take a seat, Brock." Kincaid gently pulled O'Rourke to his chair. He then turned his attention to Bainbridge. "This committee doesn't need you to incite us with your callous disregard for the people who've worked here and helped to build the good reputation Border City Stamping enjoys. When we negotiate, we do so in good faith and with no malicious intent." He tapped O'Rourke on the shoulders and returned to his seat.

Bainbridge placed the sheet back in the folder and closed it up. "I'm sorry I upset you. But I want it understood that negotiations are not something that can be done with emotions attached. The *bottom line…*" he held

O'Rourke's attention for a second, "...is that this is a business, and we all have to bear in mind the cost of running a business.'

"Fuck you," O'Rourke replied.

Wilson leaned into the centre of the table. "Well, Mr. Bainbridge, we don't see it that way. Emotions will play a part because *we are* talking about people here. Not machinery, not parts, and certainly not your *bottom line.* This is their livelihood we're negotiating and as far as we're concerned" — Wilson swept his hand to include all of the committee — "our *bottom line* is their ability to earn a decent living, provide for their families and plan for their retirement. You, sir, better take that into consideration when we next meet." He pushed away from the table, gathered his material and walked out of the room. He was followed by Dunbar.

O'Rourke slowly rose from his chair, glaring at Bainbridge. "We don't take kindly to bashing our members, retirees included." He stormed out of the room without his materials.

Kincaid hesitated a second at the door. Bainbridge smirked while gathering up his material. Lena made eye contact with Reece and tried to smile. Reece commented. "Not a good opener, and definitely at your expense." He turned and walked out.

11

In the union office, the four men fumed over the meeting with the company. Wilson swiveled back and forth in his chair as the conversation bounced from one to the other. Dunbar sat in one of the chairs along the wall with his legs stretched out and crossed. Reece was at his desk with papers spread across the top, adding very little to the conversation. Brock was the only one standing, or pacing rather, smouldering over the meeting. Attempts to calm him down only seemed to fuel his fury even more. The others had been through this type of tactics, but for Brock, it was the first time. After a few minutes of rehashing the gist of the meeting, a consensus had been made that further talks wouldn't occur until after the shutdown. This would allow a cooling down period and time to research the company, Industrial Metal Products.

"Who is this guy Bainbridge?" Dunbar's tone was sharp.

Wilson replied, "Besides being an asshole, he's the company's trigger man. He's been around from the onset. I think he was the person who directed the takeover?"

Reece spoke up, “He’s a very determined man. I’ve looked up his past and this guy doesn’t give up no matter what happens.” The three others gave Reece their undivided attention. His desk was littered with paper, a result of his research. “Before going to work for IMP, Bainbridge had his own consulting firm. He helped companies downsize, eliminating jobs, whether it be a factory, a chain of stores, an oil company, whatever. He had a philosophy that was born from his previous failure in business. I have a printout of an article in a paper,” Reece took up a sheet of paper. “From the Chicago Chronicle in April 1996 that reviewed the man. Bainbridge had married into a textile company and almost immediately created a new line of clothing called Jay-Lo.” He glanced at the men. “Not the J-lo you guys are thinking.” Brock chuckled. “It was named after his wife, obviously pleasing the family. This company’s success came in making suits, dress shirts and the like and Bainbridge convinced them to go into the sporting clothes like jogging suits, track pants, shorts and t-shirts, et cetera, et cetera. This was in the 80’s, just when the health craze was building. Everything was made in the United States. There were a few production plants scattered around Chicago and the products were distributed throughout the Midwest and the Northern states. But get this” — Reece shook the paper — “then Nike and Adidas and the like from overseas began making their appearance in

Walmarts and Targets and all those cheaper brand companies flooded the market. Bainbridge couldn't compete with their lower costs and pricing. By 1994 the company was losing money. They claimed bankruptcy that year, closing all the operations including the suit clothing line. By this time Bainbridge controlled everything and he sold the buildings, the land, and the machinery, all of it. He even lost his family, getting divorced and estranged from his children. And get this" — Reece looked up from the paper in his hand, not needing to quote — "he doesn't apologize for this happening, instead states that his wife and kids were spoiled, never appreciating what he provided for them."

"What a jerk," Brock blurted out, shaking his head.

"This article goes on to quote him," Reece read it out loud to the others. "My costs were too high. Labour was prohibitive with the union not favourable in scaling back their wages to help keep the work going. I had no choice but to quit." Reece put down that sheet and took up another one. "A few years later, Bainbridge pens an article in the Business Quarterly, *The Stakes*, in which he states his consulting firm's principle. It goes on to say that North American companies needed to rein in higher labour costs if they wanted to survive. More foreign companies were now selling in the United States and unless the American companies didn't seize the opportunity to either lower their existing labour cost or go overseas to make their products they were going to lose in the long run. His firm helped companies to reverse their trend by downsizing their operations. He slashed companies' costs by getting concessions from their employees, eliminating jobs that were deemed redundant, and overhauling their industry standards regarding wages and benefits."

Wilson interrupted, "He's a consultant working for IMP?"

"No, Scott." Reece shuffled some papers around before picking up another one. "I have here an article from June 2012, from the Canadian Business Magazine, *The Capitalist*, that announces Bainbridge's appointment to IMP. By 2005 businesses weren't using Bainbridge because of September 11, 2001." Reece looked up to ensure the others got the significance of that date. "He states in this article that he was pushing for companies to do more after the terrorist attacks because of the crippling effect it had on industry. They could use it as an excuse. But companies felt it would look unpatriotic for them to burden the American people with more layoffs, more closures, and they decided that Bainbridge was not the answer. Except, IMP did! They lured Bainbridge from his firm. In fact, he closed it, lock, stock and barrel, and moved into the position of Chief Operating Officer of IMP." Reece put down the sheet.

"We really have a maverick here," Dunbar said. "He thrives on this stuff. It seems his sole purpose in life is to bring everyone else down to make up for his past failures."

"Ain't that the truth?" Brock snidely commented, standing against the door. Reece gave him a queer look, confused why Brock would pass judgement on someone he just met.

Wilson thumped the desk with his fist. "Bring it on."

12

The lunchroom was virtually empty with many of the workers enjoying their time outside in the warmth of the early summer. Picnic tables were scattered about the front lawn, separating the building from the parking lot, filled with workers who brought their own lunch. Many employees used the half hour paid lunch time to go to nearby restaurants. The cafeteria had once been a 'hot canteen' during the previous ownership but that had changed since the takeover. The caterer was ended at the onset leaving only vending machines and microwaves where once a huge grill, a countertop, a cooler, and a large fridge and freezer had been. Tables and chairs were scattered throughout the room trying to fill the emptiness. Only two of these settings were in use. The first, just inside the doorway, had four men engaged in a game of euchre while they ate. The second group of four men were situated across the room reading the proposal that had made its way onto the shop floor only the day before. There was competition between the conversation these men were trying to have and the burst of excitement from the euchre players.

"This is crazy! How can the company expect us to accept this offer?" Nick Campo pushed a copy of the proposal into the centre of the table.

Paul Fields, a wiry guy with thick lens glasses sat directly across from Nick. To Nick's left was John Prentice, two seats over, the steward on this shift. Beside Paul was Renny Percinni, the janitor on the shift, who was absorbed with his meal of tortellini and Ciabatta bread.

It was rather odd that these four men shared a table, their background so diverse from one another. Nick had the least amount of seniority, fifteen years at BCS, after having lost a job at the General Motors transmission plant. His hatred towards management stemmed from that experience, ten years wasted, having to start over. Nearing age forty-five, he didn't want to have to go through that again. John, 38, had just made eighteen years, the last four as the steward. The other employees, who had elected him, came to regret their decision when they saw how easily he bent to the supervisor's discipline against them. John reasoned that the employer required the employee to put in a solid eight hours of work, anything other than that, he was unable to defend them. Paul was an enigma to everyone. Well-educated with a calm persona, he was in his twentieth year at BCS, holding the position of leader in one of the areas of the plant. He had declined an offer to be a supervisor a few years back, stating that he didn't need the headaches of managing the people. Yet, he helped many employees adapt to the influx of automation over time, teaching them how to use the computer consoles at their workstations, especially the older workers. He also was near 45 years of age. Renny was the most senior of the four, thirty-two years and counting. He was content with coming in every day, doing his job and collecting his paycheck. Over the age of sixty — no-one really knew how old — Renny enjoyed coming into work.

Paul glanced up from his reading. "Nick, you're getting all worked up for nothing. This is a tactic they use to get us scared. The union has already come around to tell us to ignore it."

John wiped his mouth before speaking. "The company is really low-balling this time. And I think they may be serious about it."

“Get real, John. Don’t add to the fear.” Paul gave a look of disgust and a slight shake of the head.

“Nobody can live on these wages,” Renny piped up. “I would be better off to retire.” He winced at the thought.

“Maybe you should?” John looked at Renny. “The pension isn’t going to grow under this proposal. In fact, they want to discontinue company funded pensions. You’re one of the lucky ones that would have a full pension.” He winked at Renny.

“But what would I do every day?” Renny was scared that he wouldn’t have BCS to come to each day.

“Make wine or something like that.” Nick’s sarcasm didn’t hide his feelings about high seniority people hanging on when they should be gone. The full company pension was earned with thirty years seniority making Renny eligible. “Those laid off wouldn’t be sorry for you, Renny.”

Renny ignored the rebuff by forking tortellini and shoving it in his mouth.

John spoke, “Nick, maybe you’ll end up wishing you had a pension like Renny. How many more years do you have to make up what will be lost?”

Nick stopped munching on his sandwich. “That’s bullshit. I’ve put in too many years now to start my own retirement plans." He snatched back his copy from the middle of the table. "Hell, with what they want us to go down to, I wouldn't be able to afford putting money aside for retirement." His face seemed flushed. "I'll have to work here until I'm dead."

Paul took off his glasses and pinched the bridge of his nose. "Guys, you're doing exactly what the company wants, getting panicky. Ignore this paper and wait until we meet with the committee. They'll explain everything and how to deal with the company."

The paper they were discussing was a two-sided sheet that was a proposal for negotiations on a new contract. The wages were cut by forty percent across the board; the pension would be ended by the end of the year, replaced with a contributory registered pension plan; health benefits would be slashed; vacation pay would be reduced by two percent; paid holidays would go from fourteen days to eleven days. Along with all these monetary cuts, a new work environment would be introduced that would limit seniority rights. The paper had made its rounds on all three shifts the last few days, alarming the membership.

"I'm not so sure the committee knows what they're dealing with." John uttered as he glanced down at his paper. The others stared at him as he slowly raised his head. "This company has already closed other plants they've purchased because they failed to accept a contract. They mean business."

"Okay, John, what do you know that the union doesn't?" Paul replaced his glasses.

"No, wait." Nick held up his hand. "He may be right. I have a brother-in-law in Toronto that lost his job years ago because his plant closed. They were bought out by this company during the recession and right away they were asked to change their contract." He was interrupted by the roar of the men at the other table. Nick was referring to the recession of 2008 when many companies closed shop. Even Chrysler and General Motors had succumbed to the recession, claiming bankruptcy in early 2009, only to be rescued by government bailouts and new ownership. He continued when quiet restored. "They refused and within a year the company moved all of their work out."

Renny turned up his palms. "They can't do that here, can they?"

Cheers erupted from the euchre table and Nick shouted back at them. "Keep it down. This is not a god-damn game we're dealing with here." Two of the men shot him the finger before resuming their game.

"You never know." John had the proposal in his hands, lightly tapping it upright on the table. "They can do whatever they want. They've already taken some contracts away from us."

Paul pointed to John's head. "John, did you fall off your bike on the way in?" John was known to brag about his Harley-Davidson Street bike. "Being a union steward, I would think you would be trying to calm everyone, not scare them."

John stood up. "I'm just trying to be a realist. As you've already seen, this company is different from what we've dealt with in the past. We used to have a contract before summer vacation. Not this time." He pointed the rolled-up proposal at Nick. "You should listen to Nick about his brother-in-law. Maybe lower pay is better than no pay."

John walked away towards the exit. Paul put his head down and whispered loud enough for the others at the table to hear. "What a fucking idiot."

"Management doesn't seem to understand the importance of the human factor."

Charles, Prince of Wales

PART 2

JULY

13

The drive to Toronto on Highway 401 was long and boring. Two two-lane roads split the landscape of farmland for four hundred kilometers. Flat land of corn, soybeans, or hay competed with pastures dotted with cattle or horses for the only scenery along this major thoroughfare of south-western Ontario. Traffic was light for this day and that suited Reece just fine. It allowed him to reflect on the last eighteen days while driving his Jeep Grand Cherokee to the big city.

Negotiations on a new contract hadn't started off well. In fact, it hadn't started at all after the ridiculous proposal the company presented to the union was immediately rejected. To top it off, the paper had found its way onto the shop floor upsetting most of the membership. The committee spent the last week before summer shutdown quelling their fears and anger. The vacation Reece was supposed to have had been taken up with more research on IMP and conferring with the committee members on strategy. He was confident that they were prepared to return to the negotiations with the company. He only wished he was as confident about his relationship with his wife, Shannon.

During the first week of the shutdown Reece had received three letters from the universities he had applied to for their respective Faculty of Education positions for the fall. All three politely informed him that his application was denied. Reece was okay with it but not Shannon. She went ballistic. Unbelieving their response, vowing to reverse at least one of them, she was adamant that he attempt to contact each one of them pleading his case. He stated that he really didn't care to pursue the matter, but that only fueled her anger even more. Some of that anger was directed at him. The arguments made the evenings hotter than the summer weather. Then, almost as if to punish him, she informed him that she would be working for her firm in Toronto during his second week of vacation. When he tried to reconcile with her by promising to send letters to the schools with the hope that she could change her plans she said that she couldn't pass up this opportunity for a possible promotion if things went well. She didn't elaborate on the 'things'. The debate came to a boiling point on the night before she left when he tried to reason with her that they were letting work interfere with their personal life. She replied that she wouldn't hold back her promising future while he allowed his to stagnate. She left for Toronto, and he spent the first three days doing meaningless yard work and playing golf. He woke Thursday morning feeling regret over their bickering and by noon decided to go to Toronto to surprise her.

His thoughts shifted when he listened to a song on the radio. 'Hollywood Nights' reminded him of his father. Sean Kincaid loved listening to Bob Seger. Reece missed his father, who had died in a car accident when Reece was twelve years old. Even though he was young, he still recalled the lessons his father bestowed upon him during their short time together. Reece found himself using many of the sayings from his father, one in particular. 'Far from the heart' was a phrase often said when his father consoled him over a minor injury or, more importantly, after a disappointment with a result either in sports or in school. It reminded him that whatever struggles one faced it was important to get strength from within, that anything that didn't destroy your heart made you stronger if you believe in yourself. Reece wondered if his dedication stemmed from his father's past. He recalled his father being heavily involved with the union. Reece gripped the steering wheel a little harder as he tried to remember snippets of his father's life. There were times his father came home from work at BCS only to head out immediately for some union meeting or rally. Mother would beg him to stay home, but to no avail. It was after a rally at another factory that was on strike that his father had the car accident. Four years after his father's death, Reece moved in with the O'Rourke's when his mother decided to leave Windsor. Reece was a year away from entering university and wanted to go to Windsor. She reluctantly agreed, leaving with his sister Roxanne, to her hometown of Haliburton. As the song ended Reece realized that the influence of his father, and the O'Rourke's, had paved the way for his career choice. He also wondered what his father would do with this present situation, at work and at home.

Reece convinced the receptionist at the Four Seasons Hotel to give him a passkey to Shannon's room after showing her pictures of them and showing her the flowers and small box that he was going to surprise his wife with. It was just after four-thirty when he entered the room. An L-shaped white leather sofa with a glass coffee table in front of it was on the right with a similar white leather chair at the end where Reece plunked down his small carry all. He placed the flowers on the dresser against the other wall that held a large flat screen TV and put the jewelry box on the coffee table. The bedroom, with an en-suite bathroom, was on the other side of the TV wall accessed by a French door at the end by the window. The room was rather extravagant for a junior executive. It seemed Ellis and Unger didn't spare expenses.

He figured she worked until five, with the offices being only a few blocks away. He had time to wash up and relax waiting for her to show. He pondered about calling her but decided he wanted to totally surprise her. While returning from the bathroom, he came upon her briefcase on the table near the window. He found it odd that it would be left here, and it was open. Unable to avoid looking at the papers inside, his interest was instantly piqued. Reece took up the top folder, sat in the chair, and began to read.

Three hours later Reece heard voices outside the door. Shannon entered, followed by a silver haired man with a scowl on his face. They both stopped inside the doorway when they saw Reece sitting on the chair facing the entry, the coffee table littered with papers.

"Who are you?" Silver-hair challenged, prevented from approaching Reece by Shannon putting her arm out to stop him.

Reece was already fuming and stood up to leave. "Ask her?"

"Reece?" Shannon blushed, embarrassed at first, and then angered when she noticed the file on the table.

"Are you the heavy in this transaction?" The older man spouted off.

"Shut up, Henry." Shannon warned, stealing a glance at him. She returned her attention to Reece. "Did you go through everything in my briefcase?"

"No," Reece pointed to the table. "I've seen enough." He moved toward the door. Shannon and Henry backed up against the wall. Reece snatched up his carryall from the dresser, leaving the flowers and the box. He hesitated a moment before Shannon. "More than enough." He stormed past them and exited the room.

14

Lena Kersey stared at the Surface Pro laptop for the umpteenth time, unsure of how to access it and curious as to what information it held. She was alone in her office and now had something else left over from the previous manager, besides the furniture. This one though had her undivided attention.

The week before the shutdown was chaotic. After the confrontation with the union committee, Bainbridge requested all personnel files for the team to view. Lena was not included in the process of preparing for the talks, except to fetch the files for them. When the company proposal found its way onto the shop floor, Lena was busy dealing with the employees and the union over the matter while still trying to maintain production. Bainbridge brushed away any questions she posed about the paper finding its way to the employees, stating only that they should take it seriously. She couldn't understand the purpose behind the tactic. On the last day of the week, Bainbridge informed her that she was required to work at BCS during the shutdown because a construction crew needed access to the factory and the grounds. Fortunately, she hadn't planned any trip, deciding to explore the county of Essex with its many summer fairs and historical landmarks. That idea was squashed with her spending almost twelve hours each day at BCS while the construction of a fence around the building was erected.

Border City Stamping was now protected by an eight-foot-high chain link fence on three sides. This fence separated the plant from the employee parking lot, employees now having to enter through one of six turnstiles activated by an electronically coded swipe card. There were two guarded gates: one to the shipping area on the south side and another to the visitor/office parking spaces on the north side. The guard houses at each entry were situated along the driveways, the fence splitting the building, half on the outside and half on the inside of the fence. The gates operated mechanically from within the guardhouse. The only section not fenced in was the rear of the plant that opened to a field of corn and a copse of trees.

Inside the plant, a crew installed a security system consisting of cameras around the property and inside the plant, the swipe-card turnstiles, and new employee logins at the workstations. All this security was monitored from a small office just down the hall from her and to be manned by more security personnel. Lena asked Bainbridge why all this was necessary. His reply was that it was necessary to protect the customers' products from theft and to prevent any unauthorized entry of personnel onto the property. Lena hadn't experienced either instance during the seven months she had been working at BCS.

Since she was not really needed for the actual construction, she had spent the time in her office trying to catch up on everything. Lena had been hired shortly after the acquisition of BCS. Having put in a few years in management positions with other firms, smaller and not all automotive, she had applied to a job opportunity online through *Monster.ca.* last September. The interviews were conducted over the phone and via *ZOOM*, at first, but then she was visited by Bainbridge at her last place of employment. *Mold-Perfect Ltd.,* a maker of die molds for plastic injection, just on the outskirts of Chicago, offered her more money to stay but not as much as Industrial Metal Products. She was also intrigued by the opportunity at BCS. Bainbridge seemed sincere in his assessment of her citing her education, her experience and youthful exuberance as factors in his deciding she was what they were looking for to manage BCS. The whole process happened rather quickly, and she bought his sales pitch and signed on in October.

It took a month to get the paperwork to work in Canada. She crossed the border at Detroit into Windsor in late November in search of a place to stay. She started work the first week of December and hit the floor running. With little direction from Toronto, she struggled at first but got her stride in short time. Having only been on the job a short time, she hadn't had time to thoroughly go through the personnel files. The only exceptions were for adding reports on discipline or health and safety issues such as injuries at work, Workers Safety Insurance Board (WSIB) claims or Sickness and Accident (S&A) claims. Sprucing up the office was also on her to-do list as she had been too busy to cover up the holes in the walls left from taking down the certificates, pictures and plaques of the previous manager, Theo Epstein. She didn't yet have any similar objects, except her diploma, and instead adorned the walls with some cheap landscape paintings. Two Dracaena plants on either side of the doorway helped brighten up the office and the decorating of her office allowed her to break up the tedious work of reviewing each employee. She was also contemplating adding a comfortable sofa or set of armchairs to replace the old wooden chairs in front of her desk.

It was while sifting through the files that she came across the laptop. Under the letter 'N', the Surface Pro was inside a file folder marked 'Negotiations'. After having charged it up with the corresponding charger found nestled amongst the files, she booted it up only to find it was password protected. Repeated attempts using 'BCS' or variations of it as well as combinations of numbers and words failed to open the programs, she closed the laptop and placed it at the right corner of the desk. Trying to continue with the reading of the personnel files, she kept glancing at the laptop until eventually she gave up her work and just sat there staring at the computer. Her imagination ran wild with what it held.

Did 'Negotiations' mean Epstein was preparing for these contract talks? Would he have done so way back then? He died last year during the Labour Day weekend, just before IMP purchased the plant. If so, would there be some set of guidelines or proposals that could help to make these contract talks go more smoothly? The meetings held before the shutdown seemed confrontational, each side vehemently opposing each other before details were even presented. Being her first time involved in negotiations of any kind, she felt overwhelmed. The union had approached her in the spring asking if there was a timetable set for contract talks and she referred them to head office in Toronto. She was too busy to bother thinking about contract talks. Now she was in the middle of it all, torn between BCS and IMP.

Lena liked it here. When she started the employees gave her a hard time, but the challenge of running such a big operation was exciting to her, and she refused to quit. She eventually won them over with her enthusiasm, encouraging their input on the initiatives she proposed to make BCS more productive. They seemed to have accepted that she was part of their team. Even the union warmed up to her, allowing her to implement some of the cost-saving initiatives without a hassle. Dealing with employee issues, whether it was health and safety related or, more recently, disciplinary actions, she had come to respect the union committee, especially Reece Kincaid. He came across as genuinely interested in the daily operation of the plant and they were able to agree on many issues, avoiding conflict with management over workers' actions. She was unable to offer some insight on Bainbridge but felt comfortable sharing her thoughts on the taking away of work from BCS by IMP to show who's boss. That first meeting confirmed her opinion. Not that she knew very much about Bainbridge or even IMP, having never been to the main office in Toronto. All contact with him, and the parent company, occurred here, in the office or on the shop floor. She had no idea why they purchased BCS but was glad they had hired her for the management position. Each day she became more comfortable with the people of BCS. She only wished she could feel the same about IMP.

She shook her head slightly, cleared her mind of these thoughts, and returned to the laptop. How could she access it? There was a friend from her university days, who dabbled in computers, which she probably could get to look at it. But should she take it home? Surely there could be no harm in her trying to access it. Bainbridge would be too busy with the contract talks to be interested and, if there was something in there that concerned these negotiations, he would appreciate that she found out about it. She reached over for the laptop, running her hands over the surface. She placed it in her large handbag hanging over her chair.

15

On the Monday morning after the shutdown, Bainbridge managed to convince the union committee, without the executive members of the national union, to meet with his team dealing with the contract language. In the boardroom they sat opposite one another but had yet to speak. Wilson, O'Rourke and Kincaid, the three men he would try to control their decision making, were vastly different in the union. Wilson, a beady-eyed, overweight factory worker who managed to advance into the union, sought a higher union position in the local. The position of President of Local 123 had a condition that the candidate comes from an existing unit in the local. The threat of BCS's demise would catch Wilson's attention and Bainbridge felt he could reel him in later. O'Rourke was new to the process and hot-tempered, exemplified by his outburst at their first meeting three weeks prior. He could easily be manipulated, too. Bainbridge had nothing to worry about with O'Rourke. But Kincaid was another matter. His background exhibited a man with conviction. Well-educated and well-liked by the employees here, Kincaid had risen quickly in the union during his short time at Border City Stamping. His dedication to the union and his responsibility to the membership were evident by his apparent disregard to further his own personal fortunes with a better career. The research done on the man also revealed the connection to a union champion of the past. Sean Kincaid, Reece's father, had forged a career in the union that was celebrated even today. The elder Kincaid worked for BCS and had risen in the union, becoming a vital member in the union's strike action committee. His legacy was cemented after his death in a car accident after participating in a union strike of another factory. The man was honoured at the local hall with a plaque that memorialized him.

Was the son following in the father's footsteps? Bainbridge had noticed the cool persona Kincaid exuded in their previous meeting and considered the young man an adversary. This man believed in his principles. Bainbridge was about to put up an obstacle that would test this man's ideology.

"My team has already taken the initiative to look over your present collective agreement and have come up with some suggestions." Bainbridge stood at the end of the table, his team on the right, made up of two young men, one from the 'Human Resources' department and the other from 'Accounting', who sat with binders filled with changes for BCS's collective agreement.

"Our language is pretty straight forward," Wilson replied. "Any suggestions for change will be opposed, for sure. We tightened it up to help this company during the recession. There's no need to tinker with it."

"I believe there is always room for improvement." Bainbridge nodded to his team. "Allow them to show you where they can be made, and it may help lessen the burden of financial adjustments."

"Nothing will be discussed until after the meeting with the membership." Wilson leaned forward placing his hands flat on the table. "Your present stance with respect to the proposal you submitted leaves very little doubt as to your intentions."

"Our intentions are the same as yours." Bainbridge bent down supporting himself on the table while glaring at Wilson. "And that is to keep Border City Stamping a viable operation."

"Bullshit," O'Rourke spat out.

"I don't think discussions should continue until after this weekend." Wilson palmed the edge of the table as if ready to push away and leave. "There is a lot of explaining to be done to the membership." Wilson was referring to the explanation he was given about the new security system and the fence surrounding BCS.

"Wait." Bainbridge glanced down at the table where his materials lay. "We've only just met one another. I believe you should hear from each one of my team."

Wilson interrupted, "I don't think we'll be going out for lunch together, so there's no need to pretend we're in this together."

Bainbridge needed them to stay a while longer. Also, Kincaid was too calm. The man sat still, not engaging in any of the conversation, or making eye contact with him. "But we are in this together, whether you like it or not. Coming up with a workable contract is in the interest of all of us here."

"We'll see if you believe that when we get down to the real issues." Wilson stood. "This meeting is over. There's nothing to gain from continuing today."

Bainbridge's cell phone buzzed. He put up his hand to Wilson. "Just a minute, please." He took up the phone, eyed the screen, and then placed it back down. "If you would take your seat for a couple of more minutes, I have someone else for you to meet." He motioned for Wilson to sit. O'Rourke shrugged his shoulders and Kincaid remained seated with his head down. Wilson sat back down. Bainbridge moved to the door. "Thank you. I'll be back in a minute."

A few minutes later the door opened, and Bainbridge returned with Shannon Stewart. Wilson and O'Rourke both looked dumbfounded. She stood to one side, clutching her briefcase with both hands while keeping her eyes on Bainbridge who addressed the group.

"Everyone, I would like to introduce our legal counsel for these negotiations, Shannon Stewart."

"No way!" Wilson shot up from his chair. "This isn't happening." He looked over at Kincaid, who had his head down but was ruefully smiling. "Reece, we won't allow this to happen, don't worry."

"Scott, if I may speak," Bainbridge said.

"Fuck this, let's get outta here!" O'Rourke now stood up, slamming his chair against the table. The two men on the other side jumped a little at the abruptness of the act.

Bainbridge concentrated on Kincaid. "Miss Stewart has been hired by the company to represent us during our negotiations and has made it quite clear that there is no conflict."

Kincaid slowly raised his head, a faint smile disappearing as he acknowledged Bainbridge. "I don't have a problem, either."

"Reece, what're you saying?" O'Rourke put his hand on Kincaid's shoulder. "Having Shannon work for them doesn't bother you? I can't believe you."

Kincaid rose from his chair. "I'm sure she'll do a fine job just like we'll do. Like Mr. Bainbridge said, we're all in this for the same reason. To get a fair deal." He walked past O'Rourke, faced Wilson, and said, "Let's go, Scott. I think the introductions are all done." He turned to O'Rourke and tilted his head. "You too, Brock." Kincaid then stared down Bainbridge. "Mr. Bainbridge has done what he set out to do. There's nothing more here." He led the other two out of the room.

16

The sun was slowly setting when Reece drove into the parking lot of the Tecumseh dog park. Hurley stood up on the dash, howling as he saw Shannon waiting at her car. At least he was excited to see her. Reece was anxious, but in a different way. When he returned home late Sunday, Shannon was not there. Instead, a note was left asking to meet. He had texted after her introduction as a member of the company's negotiating team setting up this place and time. She moved to the fence and turned facing him, fingering the necklace he had left at the hotel on the weekend, two doves signifying peace with one another. Reece was concerned that their peace was threatened. He had to hold onto Hurley to prevent the dog from jumping out of the window. Hurley scampered from Reece's arms when they got out of the Jeep.

"Hurley, my baby, how are you?" Shannon bent down to greet their pet. "I missed you so much."

Reece walked up to them, hands in his pockets. "He knew we were coming to the park but really got excited when he saw you." He moved over to the gate to the park, opening it. "C'mon Hurley, let's go for a walk."

The three entered the fenced in park. Hurley scurried away towards the other dogs while Reece and Shannon started their stroll. Both felt unsure how to start the conversation.

"I didn't know where Hurley was when I got home," Shannon opened. "It was pretty quiet this weekend." She furtively looked over at Reece.

Reece stared ahead at the dogs running in a pack. There were four of them. "I took him over to Brock's. Hurley loves playing with Rufus and the girls didn't mind having another dog around."

They walked along the path near the arena, the heat of the day cooling as the night fell, the cicadas beginning their nightly song. The awkwardness was apparent in their small talk and by their curt greeting to another couple they passed by who were holding hands. They stopped by the corner of the park near the homes separated by the wooden fence. They watched Hurley scamper around with one other dog. The park was emptying. They started to walk along the back fence.

After a few feet, Shannon got the courage to continue. "By the surprised looks on Scott and Brock's faces, I took it you didn't tell them what you knew. Thanks."

"I still don't know what to make of it?" Reece was surprised to hear his voice crack a bit. Reading the papers from Shannon's briefcase, a history of BCS and the union, along with a detailed description of IMP's corporate structure, revealed their strategy to get BCS to fall in line with it. Why didn't he disclose what he knew still puzzled him?

"I assume you received my texts?" She tried to grab his attention by walking slightly ahead of him, walking backwards. "There was no reply to my calls all weekend."

Reece didn't know if she was being genuinely concerned or confrontational. There was a hint of exasperation in her tone. "I got the text. My phone was off all weekend while I visited my mother and sister." He had spent the time in Haliburton where his mother lived with his sister and brother-in-law.

She moved beside him, a foot apart. "Do they know?"

"No, I told them you were working and that I took the opportunity to visit." Reece's family never approved of him marrying Shannon. Roxanne, his sister, figured something was wrong when he didn't answer his phone one time when they were alone. He confided in her.

"Well, I'm sure that scored me some brownie points." She sarcastically replied. She shook her head but continued. "I'm glad you didn't let on that you knew but David was pretty upset about your reaction."

"What are you doing?" Reece finally blurted out what he really felt. That she thought it was okay to take on this job confused him. That he allowed it to happen, even more.

She looked at him, a set jaw and steely eyes penetrating his shield. "I'm trying to further my career."

"By taking on this job? How do you figure that will advance your career?" Reece asked.

"If I didn't take this job, I probably would've been let go." She said matter-of-factly. He didn't believe her. "When Ellis-Unger was contacted by Industrial Metal Products, they specifically asked for me. The firm knew about your position and raised the concern about conflict of interest, but David insisted that I be the legal representative, and that there wasn't any conflict."

"How could he say that?" Reece was determined to be just as blunt as her.

"There is no personal gain for me to represent them in your negotiations." Before Reece could reply, she held up her hand and continued. "You represent your members; I'm only the legal advisor. No personal gain for either of us, monetarily or otherwise."

"How can you say that and believe it?" Reece said. "Everything I'll be fighting for will be your gain as well, being married to me. Wouldn't Bainbridge be concerned that you could give me inside information about their tactics or aim?"

Shannon winced. "David already brought that up after the meeting. He was so taken back by your reaction that he asked me if I had told you beforehand that I was representing them." She pursed her lips then continued. "I said no I hadn't."

"What, you lied to Bainbridge?"

"No, I answered his question." She stopped walking. "He asked if I *told* you, which I hadn't. Part of the condition of my contract was that I do not inform you of it. In my first meeting with David, he made that quite apparent."

"Stop calling him by his first name!" Reece hissed as he walked past her. He stopped after a few paces, turned to face her, stunned by her demeanor. "How long ago was that?"

She walked past him. "I was hired in June."

Reece stood still for a moment trying to comprehend everything. That she kept it from him for over a month set him on his heels. How many other secrets did she have? He turned and jogged to catch up to her.

"Can't you see that he's just using you?" Reece slowed to match her pace. "His sole purpose today was to throw us off."

"It didn't work with you." She smiled. "I thought of that but, I know how you are, and figured you'd see through that and carry on. As for Scott and Brock." She shrugged her shoulders.

"Bainbridge must be concerned that I may get information from you?"

"Not a concern." Her eyes sparkled. "Another part of the agreement was that I stay at the hotel during negotiations."

Reece nodded, not surprised. He suspected something like this when he had read the note and discovered a suitcase gone from their closet and some of her clothing. "What other conditions are there?"

She shook her head and then bent down to pet Hurley who had come running up to them. The sun was setting; they were now the only ones left in the park. They had managed to walk the full circuit of the park and were at the gates. She looked up at Reece with a weak smile. "I'm sorry to put you in this position but I have my career to think of."

Reece hadn't even mentioned what was really bothering him, yet. Seeing that they were alone, he figured now was as good a time as any. A few seconds of silence hung in the air, the cicada's song being the only sound. "What was that in Toronto?"

"Reece, there was nothing there."

"Not what I saw!" Reece raised his voice.

"It's not what you think," she answered just as brusquely.

Reece grabbed her by the arm. "Don't lie to me, too. What are you doing in the firm?"

She pulled away from him. "You men!" she almost yelled. "All you think about is sex." She sat down on the bench, Hurley at her feet. "That's what you think happened?" She bent down to pet Hurley to curb her anger. She glanced up at him. "You're so naive," she whispered.

"Explain it to me."

"Do you believe I've made it this far because of my education?" She hesitated. She had been at Ellis and Unger for three years, at their satellite office in Windsor. Shannon got up from the bench and walked to the gate. Hurley followed her as did Reece. Darkness was setting.

They moved through the gates to their vehicles. Shannon turned and waited for Reece to catch up. "Okay, all right, you want to know?" She nodded to him. "Most of these men already have enough money, power, and prestige to last them a lifetime but they all miss one thing." She eyed him expectantly. "Domination over a female, specifically their wives."

Reece started to say something, but Shannon put her finger to his lips.

"Let me finish before you say anything." She moved away to sit on the hood of her

Mustang. Reece leaned against the fence while Hurley lay down between them.

"These men fooled around for years on their wives who accepted it because of their faithfulness or desire to keep the family together, you know, raising kids, paying for college, whatever," she paused. "But now the kids are grown up and gone, the wife is more in the public eye attending banquets and fundraising events, and they don't want to be seen in that way anymore. They don't want to be publicly humiliated. So, they warn their husbands to straighten up, no more cavorting with the young girls. They threaten that they'll take them for every cent they have. They'll ruin their reputations and side-track their careers. Many of these men are worth a lot of money, like I've said, but more importantly, they seek political positions. So, they adhere to their wives' demands. But not all of them."

Reece bopped off the fence he was leaning on and tried to say something, but she waved a finger at him. He waited with fear and anger for her continued monologue.

"Over the last couple of years, I've come to know some of these women." Shannon crossed her arms. "They confided in me their situation and somewhat asked if I could help them." She took in a deep breath and exhaled slowly before continuing. "They wanted more leverage against their wayward husbands because they were threatened with losing everything. Those husbands who wouldn't adhere to their wives' demands to stop cavorting with the young girls, instead proposed to leave their wives, taking away all that they have, you know, the house, the luxurious vacations, the money. These husbands could care less if it was revealed about their infidelity. So, the women needed something else to get their husbands to straighten out." Shannon shrugged. "That's where I come in."

"What do you mean?" Reece was really confused.

"These men, like I've said, are high up in the firm and over the years have brokered many contracts with major corporations and government agencies." She paused. "Not all of them legally." She stood, taking a step forward. "Now what I'm about to tell you can't be shared with anyone." Her stern face got the point across to Reece. He waited.

"I uncovered some contracts that were favourable to one party over another, especially concerning the government, that could be considered unethical and illegal. Some involved kickbacks given to these men," Shannon said. "Now, I don't hand them over to the wives but instead" — she backed up and crossed her arms — "I've used them to get these men to stop fooling around and promote me within the firm."

"You're blackmailing them?" Reece blurted out.

"No, it's not that," she replied too quickly. "I'm getting them to see the errors of their way and by handing over the files to them, they find a way to promote me in the firm." She put out her hands, palms up. "It's a win-win. Their secret is kept, and the women get their men back."

"And you get promoted holding those secrets over them?" Reece was trying to understand the severity of her actions. "I'm sure you've kept files on them?"

"Did you not see some in my briefcase?" she asked.

"No, I was too absorbed with the file on BCS."

"Reece, these men can't afford a scandal over their work with the firm," she continued to defend her actions. "They would lose everything. By me keeping the files, they are assured that it would never go public if they stick to the agreement and keep me in the firm."

"Do you hear yourself?" Reece replied. "These men, you can't control. They'll find a way to discredit you..."

"Not while I hold these files," she cut him off.

Reece bent to pick up Hurley and headed towards his Jeep.

"Reece, this is nothing more than playing the game." She put her hand on his shoulder to spin him around. "I'm doing a service by cleaning up the perception people have about lawyers and making these men stay faithful to their wives."

"Now who's naive?" He held Hurley tight, too tight that the dog whimpered.

"I'm not naive!" she firmly stated. "I know what I'm doing is right, and," she purposely paused to get Reece to look her in the eyes, "that man was there to get his files in exchange for a favour."

"Another promotion?" His sarcasm made her wince. He stepped over to the Jeep and opened the driver side door. He shoved Hurley in and turned to face Shannon. "He thought I was there as your enforcer?" Reece recalled his comment.

"In fact, it was for you." She stepped forward to hold on to the door.

"For me? What do you mean, for me?" Reece had his hand on the steering wheel but remained standing outside of the cab facing her through the open-door window.

"That man's alma mater is the University of Toronto, and he works for Ellis and Unger." She begged with moist eyes. "He was going to put in a word for you at the faculty of education."

Reece shook his head and frowned. “Well, he works pretty fast then.” He got inside the Jeep and reached for the door.

Shannon blinked. “What do you mean?”

“They called today to offer me a position this fall,” he paused, noticing her smile. “I turned them down.” He slammed the door and started up the Jeep.

Shannon stepped back. A shocked expression showed on her face; a tear escaped one eye.

Reece backed up and pulled away.

17

The room was packed. In its heyday as a dance floor and bar the capacity was five hundred, comfortably. Almost six hundred employees, past and present, crammed into the hall at Local 123 occupying every folded seat, row-on-row, with more people lined up against three of the walls. The front had tables stretched across it where the committee sat facing the crowd. The only space was the middle aisle created to allow people to go to the microphone stand to ask questions and the outer edges of the assembled chairs, the gap lessened by those standing. The large attendance was because the meeting would be about the upcoming contract talks and that there would be a vote at the end of the meeting concerning strike action. The air conditioning didn't alleviate the heat in the room. The buzz throughout the room was concerning the actions by the company during the first week back from shutdown and the committee waited till the appointed time to start the meeting. Scott Wilson rose and stepped up to the lectern, asking that the membership take their seats so that the meeting could start. He didn't get a chance to begin.

"Scott, how could the union allow the company to put a fence around the plant?" A question was shouted from the crowd. "We feel like prisoners there now." A rumble rose to a crescendo with shouts coming from all corners of the room.

Wilson tried to quiet the room. "Everyone calm down and let us get into the details of what's happening and what we plan on doing about it." His pleas could hardly be heard over the clamour.

Nick Campo stood at the microphone in the middle aisle. "Scott, this meeting is an open forum for us to voice our concerns. You guys obviously need our suggestions on how to handle this company." Laughter and catcalls mixed to raise the ruckus to a higher level. Wilson looked bewildered, putting up his hands, looking for help amongst his fellow committee members. Even a few loud whistles didn't quiet the room. Gordon Noonan, the National Representative assigned to these negotiations, stood and conferred with Scott. He was the same height as Scott but skinny and younger, having advanced to his present position relatively quickly. He went to the lectern, raising the microphone to his level.

"Order in the room, order in the room!" Noonan's voice boomed over the noise. The crowd hushed. "This meeting isn't going to be a shouting session where nothing gets accomplished, and words are exchanged that may be regretted later. The only way it will continue is if you all will quiet down so that this committee can fill you in on the details. Anything else and we walk out of here." He scanned the room until only a few murmurs could be heard. Nodding to Wilson, he gave up the lectern.

Wilson adjusted the microphone, tilting it down. "Thank you, Gord. Now, we'll start this meeting by answering your concerns about what has happened at the plant while we were away on shutdown." Relating the events to the changes made, he made it apparent that the union had not been informed prior to the action and that they were just as surprised as the membership on their return to work. "They believe that the fence was necessary to protect the interests of their customers and to provide security to the premises. As to the turnstiles, the company wanted a more controlled process of tracking time and, again, of preventing unnecessary access to those not employed by BCS." A buzz emanated from the crowd, but Wilson's waving of his hands silenced them. "These are the reasons they've given to their actions. I'm just relating them to you." He paused. "Now, to the rules that they seem to have created with respect to the fence and gate, they want you inside the plant for the eight hours you're being paid." Again, a buzz began to rise but was quickly stopped by a shrill whistle. "We, as a committee, have already brought up the fact that your breaks are yours to do what you want but they insist that because they are paid breaks that you're required to be in the plant. This will be an issue that we'll have to deal with in negotiations." Wilson stepped away from the lectern to talk with Reece. The crowd didn't say a word. He returned to the microphone. "I'm going to let Reece get up here and fill you in on a little background about our employer. This will help you to understand what we have to deal with." Scott stepped away, allowing Reece to take up the lectern.

"I understand how frustrated many of you are after seeing all that has changed since coming back from vacation. We feel the same and believe there is more change to come." Reece paused to let that sink in. The room was quiet. "In my research of Industrial Metal Products, the company that purchased BCS, I've come to the conclusion that this company has one mission and one mission only, and that's to bring all workers down." A few whispers followed and Reece allowed a few seconds before continuing, shuffling some papers on the lectern. "To give you that sense I'll tell you how they came about. IMP was created from an automotive supply company out of Italy. Bruggi Motors is a manufacturer of engines and engine components for the auto industry in Europe, specifically for sub-compact and compact cars. They build small cylinder motors and components like carburetors, fuel pumps, power steering pumps and such, to give you an idea of their products. They are relatively successful considering Europeans buy smaller vehicles and have built a string of plants throughout Europe." This was where Reece wasn't sure about their wealth. Throughout his research, the one nagging thought was how they could afford to expand overseas? Bruggi was valued no more than BCS, about three-quarters of a billion dollars, whereas IMP's holdings of 23 auto-related operations made it a multi-billion-dollar enterprise. "They decided to invest in North America by creating a new company, sort of like a sister company, IMP, to buy up financially troubled auto parts suppliers. We all know about that scenario." He gazed amongst the crowd, nodding heads agreeing with his statement. "They set up an office in Toronto in January 2012 and shortly after made their first purchase of a string of auto parts suppliers just north of that city. These few shops made brake parts and wheel assemblies and were greatly affected by the events of September 11 as well as the recession of 2008." People acknowledged the events mentioned with grimaces and nodded heads. Reece forged on. "I won't bore you with the details of each purchase but most of you know how it's been over the last ten to twelve years with companies going under or being bought out. IMP continued to buy up troubled companies and built themselves a network of shops. Now, here's where their practice comes into play. The places they purchased were asked, or demanded, to make concessions to stay alive. Those that didn't agree were closed up, their work brought to those that did give concessions. I use the word concessions but in a lot of cases, especially the non-union shops, there were no options. They were told what the new wages would be, what their benefits would be reduced to and how they were to produce; hourly rates, yearly objectives and operating procedures in relation to each job." Reece looked out upon the assembly and noticed some confused faces. "Jobs were eliminated, and those duties were added to existing jobs. More work was put onto the worker for less pay. IMP increased their holdings threefold over the last few years. There were a lot of companies in trouble and IMP scooped them up. With respect to the union shops they acquired, many of them were closed because they fought against concessionary demands. Many of these were purchases in the U.S. but a few were here in

Canada. There were a lot of job losses in union shops whereas non-union shops grew, benefitting from the work obtained from the closed shops. IMP was basically union-busting and reducing the working man's ability to earn a good wage." Reece leaned over to get a drink of water, and the crowd grew antsy, the noise not too loud but noticeable. He returned to address the audience. "This company has grown from the misfortune of others, mostly the workers. They don't care. Their profits have soared and yet the people they employ barely make a living." The murmur began to build, and Reece held up his hands to quiet them. "Okay, everyone, I know I have painted a grim picture but there are some positives here. A few years back, 2018 in fact, IMP purchased a Canadian-owned firm in Ontario that produces instrument panels for General Motors. They were near the end of their contract and being a union shop they were prepared for negotiations to uphold what they had. They managed to get a fair contract, gaining in some areas, because they put IMP in a delicate situation. They ran their contract out without a settlement, and went on strike forcing the shutdown of those GM assembly plants for a week. General Motors, as you know, came out of bankruptcy and couldn't afford to be down because of a supplier problem. GM forced IMP to get back to the table and settle quickly, thus the union was able to secure a good contract." Reece paused a few seconds, noticing some grins in the crowd and sensing a glimmer of hope in the memberships' undertone. "The management team of IMP have already made it clear they seek concessions and that they want to control the daily operations of BCS with an iron hand. What we need to do as a membership is to understand what we're up against; to face this challenge as a united group and to stand strong." Reece abruptly stopped and returned to his seat.

The crowd seemed stunned for a few seconds but then the chatter started building up to a crescendo. Wilson got up to the microphone to regain the attention of the audience. The remainder of the meeting was spent going over the proposal that everyone had seen and discussing the committee's strategy in negotiations. That strategy involved using the National Union office resources to show the profitable operations at BCS and comparing it to other holdings of IMP. The membership was very vocal in their suggestions and in their condemnation of concessions. There was even a suggestion that the union not agree to begin talks until a more reasonable offer was put forward by the company. Noonan assured the membership that the talks opening on Monday would proceed only on the assumption that the proposal be off the table. When the mention of strike action was brought up to the membership, they whole-heartedly voted by a show of hands to approve it, if a contract could not be reached by the end of the year. The three-hour meeting provided the committee with a blueprint to conduct negotiations on behalf of the membership.

18

"What do you think, Lena?"

The mention of her name brought Lena Kersey out of her trance, and she focused on the other two at the table. Shannon had suggested this restaurant, a dark below-the-street-level Italian eatery, which allowed for some privacy. They were virtually the only people in the restaurant, a young couple in a booth across the room the only other patrons. Framed pictures of the Italian countryside adorned the walls and soft Italian music added to the dark atmosphere. Since leaving the hotel where they were staying the conversation had been a two-way interaction between Shannon and Bainbridge, in the car and at the restaurant. Now, after twenty minutes of being seated, her name came up.

"Umm...I'm sorry... what was the question?"

"How will the employees react to the changes in the language of the contract?" Shannon repeated. She and Bainbridge occupied the curved bench of the booth while Lena sat in the lone chair extending into the aisle.

Really, thought Lena as she quizzically stared at them. After all this time, from the moment Shannon was introduced, Lena had been virtually left out of the preparations for the negotiations. They had holed up at the hotel, along with the junior team, going over the strategy and reviewing the language changes they were to propose to the union. Lena, meanwhile, had to work. She spent every day at BCS doing her job and was briefed each night during their 'dinner meetings' with the whole group. She had taken the time during her busy day schedule to review their proposal and only now was she being asked her opinion.

"If last week was any indication, I believe not too friendly," Lena deadpanned. She was referring to the animosity that was shown by the employees over the physical changes that had occurred at BCS. They opposed the new system of swiping in to work, having to pass through a set of turnstiles. The surrounding of the plant by an eight-foot fence had also brought on a feeling of imprisonment and the enforcement of lost time due to leaving the plant during their lunch break had eventually caused the membership to rebel. On Friday the midnight shift had staged a 'sit-down' whereby production was halted, and it continued through the day shift. Lena was unable to get a compromise and by noon the plant was idled for the rest of the day as ordered by Bainbridge.

"Their action will be costly to their negotiations." Bainbridge raised his drink, a Manhattan, taking a sip before continuing. "I hope you have a list of those who started the problem?"

Lena kept her composure by lifting her own drink, a Bloody Mary, but didn't reply. She had no such list.

"They shouldn't believe things are going to stay the same forever," Shannon offered her opinion. "They've had it too easy for too long. It's time they realized how the company operates to be successful."

Lena sipped her drink while sizing up Shannon. How she came to take this job against her husband baffled Lena. Why did Bainbridge hire her? How could it not be construed as 'conflict of interest'? What made her decide that it was okay to oppose the union with her husband holding a position on the negotiating team? All week Lena had tossed around these thoughts wondering how it may affect the negotiations for both sides. The two women had spent very little time together. Lena sensed there were some other factors involved in this charade. Lena smacked her lips, the taste of her drink not being that good.

The awkwardness was broken by the waitress arriving with their appetizer. A large bowl of Caesar salad was placed in the middle of the table and then each of them had a plate placed in front. Bainbridge ordered more drinks for them and the waitress left. No one reached for the bowl.

"They better get used to the way things are going to be from now on," Bainbridge continued the conversation.

"But why?" Lena could not help but ask. "Production is very high, the employees are producing good quality, and everyone seems to be happy. Why upset everything?"

"Because it's not good enough." Bainbridge reached over for the bowl of salad.

"These people are set in their ways." Lena wasn't sure where she was going with the conversation but felt a need to justify the employees' work habits. "Taking away their picking of jobs, setting up a cell system, and eliminating getting done early will only piss them off. I don't see where the company gains by doing all this."

Bainbridge passed the bowl to Shannon and picked up his fork, aiming it at Lena. "They work for us, Lena, not themselves. We make the rules, not them."

"Rules?" Lena straightened up in her chair. "We're talking about adults here...not children. These people are doing a good job."

She stopped. Bainbridge was waving his free hand at her.

"Lena, you have a lot to learn about managing these people." He stabbed at his salad and held the filled fork in midair. "Don't get too close to them. You must be impartial in your day-to-day dealings with them. Remember, you're the boss." He nodded while eating.

Lena was dumbfounded. Shannon passed her the salad bowl, a tight smile on her face. Lena had only been on the job for a short while but had built a good working relationship with the people at BCS. Her theory of managing had always been one of cooperation instilled in her by her professors. Bainbridge was telling her differently. She took the salad bowl from Shannon and placed it back in the middle of the table. She had lost her appetite.

19

The pouring rain prevented them from playing golf, so Reece and Shawn decided to go to the 'Master Shogun Academy' to work out. Since high school they had excelled in the martial arts, winning competitions in karate, judo and taekwondo, and advancing in degrees of belts, eventually leading them to become instructors. The studio was the perfect location for Reece to vent his frustration. A few mats lay on the wide-open floor as they warmed up along the side where the punching bags were situated.

During their warm-up and stretching Reece filled in Shawn about Shannon taking on the job of legal counsel for IMP. He left out about her blackmailing the senior partners of the firm, aware that mentioning it to a police constable could cause a problem for her and put Shawn in a difficult position. Shawn had been his best man at the wedding and the only one who liked Shannon. Yet, he could be honest when talking about her. Reece trusted his judgement.

"How blind could I be?" Reece struck the punching bag with a roundhouse kick.

"You know what they say." Shawn stood off to the side, relaxing from his warmup. "Love is blind."

"Bullshit!" Reece made two quick jabs at the bag. "I should've asked for more details about her going to Toronto while I was on shutdown." He moved to the middle of the floor where Shawn was waiting.

"And what would that have accomplished?" Shawn took a ready stance, right hand lifted to his ear and left hand out front. "If she had told you that she was taking on the job, what would you have done?"

Reece pondered that question for a moment. Would he have tried to talk her out of doing it? Would he have exposed the tactic to the union? He faced Shawn, slightly bowed and took a similar stance. "I don't know what I would've done. Maybe put a kibosh to it from the start?"

"And risk her losing her job?" Shawn feigned a lunge. "I don't think you would do that to her."

Reece didn't believe that would happen with the knowledge of what she was doing within the firm. They had too much to lose by letting her go. Keeping her in the firm, they could protect their interests by having her close and under control.

Reece stepped back, rotating his arms. "No, you're right, I wouldn't." He froze in a stance. "But how does she believe taking this job would help her advance in the firm? If the union doesn't get what it wants, they can use the excuse of *conflict of interest* in the company hiring her while I'm at BCS." The union executive had already suggested that tactic if contract talks failed. Reece grimaced and attacked.

Shawn fended off the palm-heel strike with a forearm block and countered with a hard push to Reece's chest, causing him to stumble back. "You're kicking yourself for something you could never have seen. Shannon is a very determined lawyer. She would go to any length to further her career."

Reece maintained his balance, opening his stance. "What do you mean by that?"

Shawn backed off, standing with his arms akimbo. "There was talk, whispers, amongst the other officers. They heard things in the court building from some of the lawyers."

Reece stepped forward, taking up a striking stance. "Like what?"

"It was just talk." Shawn took up a defensive posture, both hands out front.

"What kind of talk?"

They began circling, bouncing on their feet, hands weaving in and out. A series of jabs by Reece were fended off by Shawn and a shuffling of the feet was a sign that the sparring was going to get more serious.

"You know what 'BBB' stands for?" Shawn had spoken about the term used to describe Shannon.

"Yeah, 'Beautiful Bitch Barrister'," Reece replied.

"There was another meaning." Shawn stopped moving around and set up in a Tiger stance. "Boss Burying Barrister."

Reece blinked, confused for a moment. He copied his Judoka partner's stance but hesitated to continue their sparring.

Shawn relaxed a moment while explaining. “Do you recall the senior partner who died earlier this year?” he asked.

Reece’s brows furrowed as he remembered Shannon going to a funeral for a colleague in the firm. “Yeah, what about it?”

“It was deemed a suicide,” Shawn continued. “We found him in his closed garage with his Audi running.”

“What’s that got to do with Shannon?” Reece was getting perturbed, his muscles tightening as he prepared to strike.

“Well, the talk around the precinct was that the man was under review by the law society for some shady transactions in the past involving money transfers from government agencies to offshore accounts.” Shawn readied himself. “The rumour has it that Shannon tipped off the RCMP about the man.”

Reece’s eyes flared and he lashed out with a series of hand strikes. Shawn blocked every blow and even sidestepped a front-elbow strike that put Reece off-balance, falling to the floor. Getting up slowly, Reece shook his arms and regained his composure. The possibility that Shannon was blackmailing this man occurred to him, but he felt he needed to defend her anyways. He opened his stance, ready to grapple with Shawn.

“Was there proof of her involvement?”

"None that we found," Shawn answered. "The lawyers in the firm refused to answer any inquiries. They denied us access to their firm which led to the RCMP getting involved."

Reece moved in to grab Shawn's Judogi. Shawn bent to the left, using the momentum of Reece's hold on his uniform, to flip him over the hip and onto the mat. Shawn backed off.

Reece sprang up and attacked, this time trying a spinning kick that Shawn blocked with his right arm and followed with a quick jab to Reece's exposed mid-section. Reece buckled over but kept his feet. Shawn, again, backed off.

Reece straightened up. "What does that incident have to do with Shannon taking on this job?" He wanted to divert the conversation away from this revelation so as not to divulge what he knew about her activity in the firm. He resumed a fighting stance.

"I'm just saying that she seems to be a very determined lawyer and that you may underestimate her contributions in the negotiations." Shawn prepared to defend. "Are you prepared to challenge her on any issue?"

"I'll do my job." Reece closed the distance between them. "I don't believe she'll pose a problem. She won't be the decision maker."

"Don't be so sure." Shawn readied. "What you must do is get through these negotiations without damaging your personal lives. She has a job to do and so do you. That's all."

"Easier said than done." Reece circled his opponent. "Being apart isn't going to help and this company's agenda will be difficult to fight. If she is as determined as you say, her contributions may finally separate us."

"You can't let that happen," Shawn urged. "Do you still love her?"

The question surprised Reece. Over the last few days, the thought of loving one another never entered his mind. It was the keeping of secrets and the deception that concerned him. He didn't reply but instead pounced.

Reece lunged forward and the two grappled, each trying to overthrow the other. They moved about the mat, grunting and locking arms and trying to knock each other off their feet. They released after a minute and when Reece attacked again Shawn was able to spin Reece and arm-lock him, forcing him to the mat where Shawn pinned Reece down face-first.

"I think you do, and you need to forgive her and find a way to get past this." Shawn's words were as strong as his pin. "Only you can do this."

20

Monday was a day of posturing and bluffing by both sides as negotiations opened. First thing the union demanded was that all issued suspensions of the previous week be withdrawn before talks began. Bainbridge refused. The union committee promptly left the boardroom in the plant where talks were being held and holed up in their office. After a morning of phone conversations and text messages between the two parties an agreement was reached whereby those suspended for more than a day would have their suspension reduced to only a day and be paid for the rest. Those with a one-day suspension would only have it on paper, again being paid for the day already served. Score one for the union team.

When the two groups re-convened in the afternoon, the meeting was constantly interrupted by employee requests for union presence on the shop floor or in the union office. This tactic was purposely concocted by the union committee to force the company to move the negotiations from the plant boardroom to an outside meeting place. The constant interruptions prevented any progress being made to getting down to business. Bainbridge had selected the plant boardroom as a way of showing that the company didn't like to waste money. It didn't work. By the end of the day,

Shannon had convinced Bainbridge to move to the hotel where they were staying, securing a boardroom for the duration of the negotiations. The union committee also requested that they be given rooms at the hotel and that their positions in the plant be replaced by personnel from the floor, namely union stewards who would act in Scott and Reece's capacity. Arrangements had to be made so the talks were delayed until Wednesday afternoon. Score another mark for the union.

After having moved into their individual rooms four floors above the company team, the union committee showed up in the designated boardroom to begin talks on a new contract. Already seated were Bainbridge, Lena, Shannon and the two junior members of the company. Spread on the table were all their materials; laptops, cell phones, binders, paper and pens ready to be used. The room was twice as large as the one at the plant and there were a couple of sofas and plush chairs along the walls. A table was set up with coffee urns, water pitchers, juices and an assortment of fruit and pastries, compliments of the hotel. The table where they all sat was wide and long affording everyone comfortable space.

The agenda for these opening talks was to deal with the language in the contract. Bainbridge made it quite clear that the union's decision to disregard his team's request for input regarding the content of their existing collective agreement led them to dissecting the book, virtually word by word. Lena handed out folders which contained all the proposed changes. The Duo-Tangs were thick. The union had one hour to digest the material and then they would start by going through the changes, section by section. Bainbridge reminded them that the changes reflected the company model. The company team left the boardroom.

Resumption of talks escalated into shouting matches. Wilson opened with the comment that the proposed changes were unacceptable, and Bainbridge countered that they were necessary for any negotiations to commence. Attempts by Shannon to bring the meeting to some sort of order were thwarted by the constant verbal jousting of Wilson, accompanied by Dunbar and Noonan, against Bainbridge. The junior members who orchestrated the changes tried to explain the points but were shouted down and even cowed into silence. During the whole fiasco, Reece rarely spoke, flipping through the pages of the handout and making notes, while Brock seemed overwhelmed, getting up numerous times to refill his glass with orange juice, not one to drink coffee like all the others. Lena kept her head down, pretending to make notes of the meeting. Shannon gave up trying to manage the situation and sat pensively wondering what she got herself into. She met Reece's stare, his face not giving away any sign of emotion, and smiled. After three hours of accusations, swearing, and threats, it was decided that the material could be reviewed overnight and that serious talks would resume in the morning.

The next few days, through the weekend, the two parties argued over every point. The company team had re-written the language affecting the entire concept of the collective agreement. On the union side, Wilson, Dunbar and Noonan seemed to conclude that most of the changes could be tolerated with the thought that giving in on these issues would lessen the need for the company to come after more monetary concessions. Reece spoke up on matters of health and safety and won on principle. Brock was relegated to taking notes. Bainbridge and the junior members hammered away at every possible proposed change to bring BCS in line with the corporate structure. They succeeded in eliminating the five-minute wash-up time at the end of the day, reducing the breaks from fifteen minutes to ten and the lunch break from thirty minutes to twenty. This increase of twenty-five minutes in productivity for the day was deemed necessary in maintaining competitiveness. The job picking at the start of the shift was replaced with an introduction of 'cells', whereby areas of the plant would be sectioned off and employees would belong to a group of jobs that they choose to work in. The union argued that they already had zones and that employees usually remained in the same zone, but Bainbridge persisted that the new system was better suited to controlling movement of personnel and creating a more productive environment. Other clauses were changed concerning the ability of an employee to transfer jobs, to exercise seniority, and to bid on open jobs. Reece and Brock argued these points on behalf of the worker's right to seek out the best possible job on a daily basis but lost the argument. Once the operations' side of the contract was completed, the company proposed more changes to the union activity in the plant. Having already agreed to reduce union time right after IMP's purchase of BCS by eliminating a full-time officer and dropping union stewards' eight hours off the job to two hours, Wilson objected to any more changes affecting the union's ability to represent the workers. Bainbridge wanted to reduce the representation down to one steward per shift from the present three and their time off the job to time as needed. Debate ensued and it was finally agreed, hesitantly, to maintain the three stewards but their time would be a half-hour of representation for any employee grievance. Score one for the company.

The effective changes concerned operations and employee rights but nothing with a monetary value was discussed. Bainbridge said that these clauses would be brought up in the context of wages and benefits. These clauses concerned overtime pay, shift premiums, holiday pay, classification rates and vacation pay. Noonan reinforced that the proposed changes that they had just agreed upon would bring huge savings to the company, implying that attempts to seek monetary concessions would be challenged. Bainbridge did not answer back. Debate over the implementation of these changes almost scuttled the progress made to this point. Bainbridge wanted immediate implementation upon ratification while the union insisted all changes would take effect after the present collective agreement expired at the end of the year. A decision on this point was left for later discussion after Shannon pointed out that an impasse had been reached and that those issues could be dealt with in final preparation to present to the membership. By mid-morning on Sunday, both sides had reached agreement on the language and Bainbridge indicated that a break was needed before they tackled the harder issue of money. Talks were postponed until Tuesday morning, allowing time to refresh and prepare. When Wilson requested a starting point in regard to the company's aim for monetary concessions, Bainbridge informed them that they already had that information. Wilson reiterated that the 'ridiculous proposal' that was floated on the shop floor was unacceptable as a starting point, Bainbridge replied that the union should look at the company's other operations to get a read on a 'starting point' for negotiations. Reece suggested that the union would walk away from everything that was already gained if the company didn't provide a proposal for their perusal during the break. Bainbridge countered that the threat didn't alter their stance to seek parity amongst their holdings and that the union be careful about their tactics. Noonan settled the confrontation by stating that they would report on the savings gained with the changes in the language for the next portion of the talks. It was agreed that both sides would resume armed with their prospective proposals on wages and benefits.

21

"May I join you?"

Reece turned to his right to acknowledge the speaker. Lena Kersey held a drink in one hand and a small wallet in the other. He gestured to the empty chair. She wore white khakis and a red t-shirt that sculpted her body perfectly, prompting him to look at her longer than he probably should have. She slid in, placing both items on the table, and adjusted the chair for comfort. They were in the back corner of the bar, the soft lighting and slow music setting a mood that suddenly made him uncomfortable.

"Do you come here often?" she asked. "Do you like the scenery?"

He laughed, adjusting his view to her face. She smiled. He picked up his beer, Coors

Light, tipping it to her. "It's not my regular haunt but the view just got better, thank you."

She took up her drink, a Bloody Mary, tapping it against his, and they drank.

"That sure was some session we just went through. It might be a while before we get this done." He tried to take his mind off her, surprised by the arousal she had stirred up in him.

Lena had her hands around her glass but moved one to face down on the table towards him. "Let's not talk shop, okay. This is supposed to be a break from that madness, so let's not ruin it." She smiled, again, and he nodded. "You're not taking the time to be home?"

"No, um"— he looked up from the table — "I let Shannon go home for a few days. She's been away for two weeks... let her do some washing." He shook his head slightly as if it wasn't what he really wanted to say. "She needed to get some things. I've only been here a few days." He shrugged his shoulders feeling he'd said enough.

"I'm sorry for the circumstances for the two of you. It must be hard." She had overheard Reece and Shannon making arrangements outside of the boardroom and felt compelled to be with him. She wasn't sure whether it was for professional or personal reasons but went with her intuition.

“Might be a good thing at this time.” He hesitated to add any more, not willing to share his concerns with Lena. The waitress appeared asking about refills, both taking up the offer. Once she left there was a lull in the conversation, either one not knowing where to go.

“Lena? That’s not a name one hears too often,” Reece resumed. “How did you come by that name?”

Lena chuckled. “That’s a long story.”

“We have time.”

“Okay, but stop me if it becomes boring.” She took a sip. “My mother and father met on a cruise ship. She was celebrating her first anniversary of marriage” — she paused, a grin on her face — “and my father was a piano player in a lounge on the ship.” She laughed at his expression of confusion, his eyes furrowed and lips pursed. “My mother spent a lot of time in that lounge while her husband was in the casino. My father sort of had a ‘karaoke’ type of program whereby the customers were encouraged to participate. My mother sang and he fell in love with her right then. That week, for her, was more exciting for the nights away from her husband than anything else. She took away more than the memory.”

She paused as the waitress returned with their drinks. They were also given menus to look over, which they put aside after the waitress was gone. Lena continued.

"Nine months later when I was born, her husband had every reason to leave her. See, my mother is white, as was her husband, and as you can tell" — she placed the back of her hand beside her face — "my father is a black man."

Reece laughed at her wittiness. "Oh, so that's how you got your tan." She laughed with him, playfully tossing a napkin at him.

"Anyways, when I was born, my mother wasn't allowed to use the name they had picked for a girl." She paused as if to reflect. "I think I remember my mom saying it was Mary or Maria, or something like that. And she obviously was going to be raising me alone. While in the hospital, she was able to contact my father on the ship, giving him the news. No cell phones or email, she just sent a telegram. He replied immediately." She dabbed at her eyes with the tossed napkin he had placed between their drinks.

"What did it say?" Reece felt awkward but also intrigued.

"I have the telegram, my mother kept it all these years. *Name her Lena. Stop. I'll be there soon. Stop."* She took a second to collect herself and then continued. "And he did show up. He stayed with us through all the mayhem and when it was all straightened out, he took us to Florida to settle down. And that's how I came to be."

Reece waited a few seconds, offering her another napkin. "Why Lena, though?"

She chuckled between sniffles. "My father's fifteen years older than my mother and he grew up listening and playing music." She gave a look that stated the obvious. "Lena Horne was his favourite singer, and he named me after her."

Reece nodded slightly while taking a sip of his beer. "Any other siblings?" He asked to keep the conversation going.

"Two brothers," she replied after dabbing her mouth. "Both younger. They live in Florida. James owns a landscaping company and Sammy works on a cruise ship." She noticed Reece trying to figure out the significance of the names. "Dad named them after singers, also. James Brown and Sammy Davis, Jr. Dad retired from the cruise line, but Sammy took it up after years of playing alongside him. Mom likes having dad home and the boys close."

"What about you?" Reece asked. "Why here, instead of in Florida?"

"I went to University of Chicago, studying economics." She replied. "I wanted to make it on my own. After graduating, I worked a couple of jobs, learning about management, then applied for BCS, on a whim, and luckily got the job."

"Are you happy at BCS?" Reece was trying to get a read on her, hoping to use it as leverage in their talks.

"Yes," Lena scrunched up a napkin. "But let's not go there, please." She wanted to avoid talking about work, or the contract talks. She took up her second drink, pushing aside the first one, empty.

They were interrupted by the waitress who asked if they were ready to order. They asked for a few more minutes, taking up the menus to show they were yet to decide.

"So, what's your story?" Lena asked from over the top of the menu.

"Not as interesting as yours." He placed his menu down in front of him. "Grew up in this area, went to university here, then right to work at BCS." He shrugged his shoulders.

"No family, besides Shannon?" she asked.

Reece put his head down for a second before lifting it up, his jaw clenched. "My father died when I was twelve, and then my mother took my younger sister, Roxanne, away from here when I was sixteen." He put up his hand to prevent her from saying she was sorry or something like that. "I stayed to go to the University of Windsor where I met Shannon, then found myself working at Border City, and ta-da, here I am. My mother lives with my sister in Haliburton…I just saw them during the shutdown." He didn't elaborate anymore.

Just then the music stopped as the DJ announced his next song. "A little something for those lonely souls who meet in the night." The music began for 'We've Got Tonight'. Reece turned to stare at the DJ, who saluted back.

Reece turned back to face Lena, a slight embarrassed smile greeting her. "I didn't put him up to this."

Lena reached over to place her hand on his. "It's okay, I know. We might be on opposite sides of these negotiations but tonight that doesn't matter. Like the song says, we've got tonight." She smiled and squeezed his hand.

22

"Where do we start?"

That was the question finally asked after two and a half hours of each side rehashing what was already accomplished to this point. The union cited numbers from their economist extolling the savings the company would reap with the changes to the contract language. They felt that the increased time for productivity and the ability of the company to control personnel movement would reduce the cost per hour per employee by at least five dollars. Bainbridge dismissed those savings as essential for the daily operation of the plant and expressed a concern that the union put too much emphasis on the value of those changes in relation to monetary gains. The company side now only consisted of Bainbridge, Lena, and Shannon. The junior members were only used to obtain the changes to the language of the contract. Wilson had finally asked the question of where they would continue the negotiations with Reece, Brock, Dunbar and Noonan prepared to challenge any attempt to reduce wages and benefits.

"How about we start with the small ticket items and proceed from there?" Bainbridge answered.

"Nothing is a small ticket when you're talking about employee earnings. We feel that the concessions already made with the language would be enough to satisfy the company." Wilson tossed the initial proposal on the table. "These numbers are not acceptable as a starting point and your reference to the other holdings of IMP for us to compare are unreasonable for many reasons."

Bainbridge took up the proffered sheet, glancing at it briefly before placing it under his pile of papers. "The company has taken failed enterprises and, with the changes, have made them profitable. It's a proven formula that we wish to exercise with Border City Stamping to make it also profitable."

"But BCS has been profitable," Dunbar spoke up. "Since the last contract changes, which the union willingly agreed to, BCS has shown increased profits every year. You may have purchased a company you thought was failing but time has shown that you were mistaken."

"We understand the competitive nature of the business and are more than willing to see BCS participate in future bidding of work." Noonan jumped into the fray. "Those savings obtained in the last session should be more than enough to make BCS competitive without having to touch the wages and benefits of its employees."

"The restructuring of many of the acquisitions that we have obtained have made it imperative that wages and benefits amongst all its holdings be relatively equal to one another," Bainbridge cited matter-of-factly. "Those savings you speak of are only a small portion of what is needed to sustain Border City's ability to quote for work and secure its future."

Reece leaned into the table, attracting everyone's attention. "You say we need to be in line with other similar operations in the IMP stable of companies, correct?" He waited for Bainbridge to acknowledge the question.

Bainbridge gave a slight nod. "Then we are in relation to one right here in Ontario." Reece opened his binder to a book-marked page. "The Aurora operation, WTW Industries, you purchased in 2018, and *you* re-negotiated a contract later that year, have similar wages and benefits that BCS have at this present time." Reece put up his hand to prevent Bainbridge from interrupting. "That operation has successfully bid for work and been profitable for the last few years. Their future seems bright as they also recently secured contracts for upcoming model years with GM."

Bainbridge had put his head down while Reece spoke. WTW Industries had sought IMP to buy them up a few years after the recession of 2008-09 because the partners, two brothers surnamed Walker and a brother-in-law surnamed Truman, had extended credit beyond their finances. IMP was interested in the wiring harnesses they produced for the automotive industry and negotiated a sale that took longer than expected to finalize, almost three years from the first contact. Bainbridge was involved in the contract negotiations with the union and was instructed to acquiesce to their demands when the existing contract expired. They maintained the WTW Industries logo with the letters now representing the term Wire to Wire Industries. The silence hung for a few seconds before he looked up and replied. "That situation is quite different from here."

"How so?" Reece smiled.

Bainbridge stared at Reece, sizing him up. "That operation doesn't have a comparable product amongst the other holdings whereas BCS will be competing with many other plants that make products along the same line. You have competition, they don't."

"But WTW was able to secure work against other competitors, not of IMP, and they're still able to have increased their profits. We've done the same over the last while, again stacking up against our competitors." Reece tapped his pen on the papers.

"But that will change now that some of our operations will be bidding for similar work at a lower operating cost than BCS presently has." Bainbridge regained his composure, accepting the challenge. "Those operations that are able to show increased profitability over another operation will get the contracts, hands down."

"Doesn't quality and productivity mean anything?" Wilson spoke. "Many of your other companies low ball a bid but end up unable to provide the quality of work that BCS has provided in the past as well as the productivity. Just look at the work that was taken from us last year and given to Motor Craft Industries. You know what's happened there and they surely are losing money for you."

Motor Craft Industries had been bought shortly after IMP was formed involving four plants spread across Michigan. The new contract forced on the employees dropped their earning potential by half with reduced benefits. The subsequent result was an unhappy workforce that produced shoddy work with poor quality, delayed delivery and discounted pricing to the customer to make up for the trouble. The product taken from BCS to bolster one plant's capacity was a rear axle assembly that had been produced for years at BCS. The customer, Ford's Atlanta, Georgia plant, received huge discounts to offset the poor performance, creating a loss for that plant.

Bainbridge sat up. "That operation is seeing increased quality in their day-to-day production and will be profitable in no time. Even with this transition period, the future profits will cover the initial start-up costs, and the customer will receive a satisfactory product on time."

The room went silent for a short while. Each team seemed to be waiting for someone to add to the conversation. Bainbridge then proposed a break.

"Let's take a half hour to get some coffee or use the washroom or whatever and come back with the intention of dealing with the next phase. We can take forever talking about the other operations, but it will get us nowhere. These talks are imperative to the future of Border City Stamping and you need to understand that we intend to stick to the mandate issued to us by our employer."

Bainbridge let that last statement hang in the air for a moment before closing with another. "The issues we collectively deal with will determine the viability of the operations at Border City Stamping." He stood up, followed by Shannon and Lena, and exited the room.

The negotiations resumed that afternoon with the company trying to deal with items such as overtime pay, personal days off, shift premiums and cost of living allowance. All attempts to reduce the amounts or eliminate the fees were met with stern opposition by the union. The day ended with no progress. The next morning the company changed tactics, putting out a full monetary proposal dealing with everything from shift premiums to a new wage structure. The union was totally against it, but Bainbridge convinced them to go through each item one-by-one. They had a marathon session of over twelve hours, not accomplishing anything, with both sides feeling they were spinning their wheels and wasting time. The next morning the union offered to look at savings through a change in the benefits package. Their thinking was that they could produce some more savings for the company that would not harm the employee as much and thus avoid talk of reducing wages. Bainbridge wanted Sickness and Accident benefits and workers' compensation qualifications' limits through Workers Safety Insurance Board (WSIB) to be included in the negotiations. The desire was to have a 'light duty policy' in effect that an employee could come to work, if able, after an injury to lessen the cost of the premiums for each benefit by having lower claims. The union agreed upon this with a provision that the ability of an employee to show up at work for light duty would be determined by an independent doctor chosen by both parties. After several changes were agreed to on the benefits and a monthly fee proposed for the employees to share in the cost of health benefits, the union surmised that the total savings to the company of all contract changes would reduce the hourly cost ratio by over ten dollars. The end of that third day saw some progress and the union requested that the company re-visit their take on the wages, coming up with a suggestion that at the least the status quo be maintained and a bonus be offered for ratification of the contract. Bainbridge recognized their contributions and promised a new offer concerning wages would be submitted the next day.

Friday morning the two sides re-convened and Bainbridge handed over a new proposal concerning wages. The union was appalled. There were cuts for every monetary item left to negotiate. Overtime was available only after an employee worked forty hours at straight time, shift premiums that had been ten percent of wages per hour for midnights reduced to one dollar per hour and five percent of wages per hour for afternoons was reduced to fifty cents per hour. Cost of living allowance would be eliminated with no roll in of the present amount into the wage, vacation pay reduced across the board by four percent or two weeks wages, holidays reduced from the present fourteen days to eleven days, and wages reduced by one third, the amount being over eight dollars per hour. This proposal wasn't much better than the original. The members of the union committee sat stunned.

Brock, who had for the most part been silent throughout the process, took up the paper in his hands and addressed the people across from him. "What is your problem with people making a decent wage?" His voice trembled, full of rage. "You don't deserve these people...they give you their heart and soul on the job...and you just want to bleed them dry."

"Like I stated at the beginning, emotions cannot be a factor in these negotiations," Bainbridge answered. "Our aim is to bring BCS in line with our overall wage structure..."

Noonan interrupted him "You are so full of bullshit, no one here believes you." He waved across the room to include Lena and Shannon. "You have no other intent but to take from these people. These haven't been negotiations; these have been ultimatums."

"I'm sorry you see it that way," Bainbridge cut him off. "For too long Border City Stamping workers have been receiving higher compensation than what the industry is paying. The company can no longer sustain that kind of imbalance."

Wilson spoke, "Lena, do you believe that we're paid too much? Do you really believe the crap that he's saying?" He pointed at Bainbridge. "I'll match our workers with anybody in the world, they're the best at what they do, and they still make this company tons of money."

Lena sat rigid, not answering or looking at Bainbridge. She sat with her hands on her lap while Shannon watched on from the end of the table. Reece sat up.

"Lena, do you not find the workers receptive to change and to finding ways to be more productive?" Reece gambled on her loyalty to BCS. "The initiatives you've introduced have saved the company money and the employees were right there with you."

Lena answered, "The employees have been very helpful in implementing cost saving procedures in the plant and have been offering more suggestions as well." she stopped when she noticed Bainbridge frown at her.

“The importance of the people is not in question,” Bainbridge interrupted the exchange. “It doesn’t matter what’s been in the past and what they are doing today is a part of their obligation to maintain their jobs. Hard decisions must be made to bring them in line with the overall structure of the company.” He stopped talking when Dunbar stood up.

“You do not hold these people as important enough to consider their worth,” Dunbar growled. “These talks are done until you realize the true value of the people who make you money. We’re done.” He grabbed up his material and walked out, followed by the rest of the union committee.

23

David Bainbridge was summoned by Max Silva. Six hours after their conversation by phone, they were sitting beside each other with about 20,000 fans of soccer at BMO Stadium in Toronto watching Toronto FC play the Vancouver Whitecaps. Bainbridge never took to the game, but his boss lived and breathed for the sport. Dressed in a home team jersey and shorts, Silva fit in with the crowd. Yet this was a man who controlled millions of dollars in industry and held the fate of thousands of people with his actions. Silva had insisted on meeting here stating it was the perfect venue to talk business. The crowd was more into the game than they were in two older men talking shop.

Bainbridge recounted the events of the day leading up to the cancellation of talks. Silva seemed captivated with the game, but every so often would ask a pointed question concerning aspects of the negotiations, especially of the people. Bainbridge concluded his report with the statement that they had achieved their goal of getting the union to reject a contract offer and that they could move forward to closing Border City Stamping. Silva did not see it that way.

"Not quite." Silva leaned over the empty seat between the two men. "It must be better than this. The membership, as a whole, has to reject the offer. The executive can say there was nothing to bring to their people and it would fall back on us to show a valid reason for closing. No, we need them to close the plant."

"How do I attain that?" Bainbridge had to wait for an answer as the crowd let out a chorus of boos to the action below. He forged on once the noise lessened. "The union won't accept anything less than the status quo with regards to wages. And the membership might accept that."

Silva ignored the hissing of the crowd. "I think you can come up with a tentative agreement whereby wage concessions are proposed to the membership" — he winked — "and which they will reject."

Bainbridge slumped in his seat. His mind was confused and befuddled. The din of the crowd didn't help with his thought process. He was used to quiet deliberation and concentration. Besides the noise of the crowd, the claustrophobic feeling of the crowd, the smell of body odour mixed with too much cologne or perfume, and the stickiness of the arms of the seat he occupied made Bainbridge uncomfortable. He then came up with an out. "Dunbar is the one who stopped the talks because we proposed wage cuts. He won't accept anything that touches their wages, let alone the others on the committee who are more closely attached to the situation."

Silva smiled as the roar of the crowd signified a play on the field. A Toronto FC player was in alone on the opposition keeper who thwarted the attacker's kick toward the net.

"See what just happened there." Silva pointed to the big screen that was replaying the missed opportunity. "That player scores nine times out of ten in that situation but" — Silva turned to Bainbridge — "it's too early in the match to go ahead. It's a game within a game." Silva tapped his head. "That player intentionally kicked the ball at the keeper. He has more at stake than winning." Silva nodded. "So, it is with your negotiations. Noonan must make it look like he's doing what's best for those BCS employees. But the union cannot afford to lose another five hundred members to another closure, so he will come back to the table to try to get something."

Bainbridge shook his head. "But the others won't agree. Wilson, Kincaid and O'Rourke won't just turn around their stance because Dunbar tells them to." Bainbridge recalled the conversation with the National Rep. "Also, Noonan agreed to stop the talks and even threatened to have the gains achieved erased."

Silva relaxed back in his seat. "I've already made Noonan aware of what's at stake. He has agreed to convince the others."

"But how?"

Silva spoke while watching the game. "There are other factors involved in these negotiations besides a contract for those workers. Those executive members on their panel have a lot to lose if we close the plant."

Bainbridge was really lost now. "I don't understand what we're trying to do here? Is it to close the plant or to keep it open?"

Silva chuckled and turned to face his Chief Operating Officer. "David, you must put yourself in their place to come up with a strategy to get them to accept a contract. Wilson and Dunbar seek higher positions in the union but can't if their place of work no longer exists. They come from Border City and therefore cannot afford to have the plant closed." He nodded and winked.

"But by coming up with an agreement," Bainbridge continued, confused, "it will be impossible to close the plant."

The crowd burst into applause as the home team scored. Silva stood, clapping along with the thousands of fans. After almost a minute of celebration, Silva took the seat next to Bainbridge and leaned over to speak.

"Divide and conquer, David," Silva espoused. "That's always been our strategy." He peered intently at Bainbridge. "That lawyer, I've heard she has some good ideas. You should listen to her."

Bainbridge was surprised. First, that Silva even mentioned Shannon Stewart, since it was his hire. Bainbridge's sole purpose behind it was to throw Kincaid off his game, but that hadn't worked out so well. In fact, he was contemplating letting her go, but now Silva was telling him she might have something to contribute to their contract impasse. Who told Silva about her ideas? Bainbridge couldn't remember any substantial conversation with her concerning the contract, his mind set on getting the union executive to reject their proposal. Before Bainbridge could question him, Silva continued, still leaning over, almost shouting.

"You work out a wage structure that the committee will accept, and the rest will take care of itself." Silva tapped Bainbridge on the arm. "She'll show you how."

"But aren't we trying to get them to reject a contract so as to close the plant?"

Silva placed an index finger to the side of his nose. "They don't know that."

"Concessionary bargaining destroys the power of a union in the same way that cancer destroys the body."

Shamus Cooke, Trade Unionist

PART 3

AUGUST

24

"You've got to be kidding?" Brock said with an exasperated look toward the three men who had just entered the union office. "After all that bullshit they handed us, you want to go back to the table?"

Wilson, Dunbar and Noonan arrived at the plant just before lunch to inform Brock and Reece that talks were to resume the very next day. Reece sat at his desk while Brock stood in the middle of the room. Wilson stood behind his chair while Dunbar and Noonan flanked him at each end of his desk.

Reece leaned forward and directed the question at Wilson. "What changed over the weekend for you to decide to resume talks?"

Wilson glanced over at Noonan who stepped forward to answer. "There was some contact made with the executive at IMP and the negotiator, Bainbridge. We hashed out some of the differences in our tactics and believe it's in the best interest of both parties if we return to the table and settle this contract."

Dunbar leaned against the file cabinet with one arm draped over top and added to the conversation. "There was some admission by Bainbridge of pushing it too far and that there had been great gains achieved up to that point." Brock attempted to speak but Dunbar put up his hand. “Brock, no matter what you feel about the man, we as a committee have a responsibility to our membership to see this thing through and come up with an agreement.”

“Bullshit!” Brock spat out. “You guys got duped. You’re reacting too fast from the decision to walk away on Friday.” His anger showed in his flushed face. “Reece and I came in early today to explain to the membership our reasons for discontinuing talks, and now this.” He glared at the three men and then turned to Reece. “Tell them they’re wrong.”

Reece stood up and came around from his desk. “Okay, Brock, I think they get the message.” He joined Brock in the middle of the room and faced the other three. “Who approached whom?” Reece watched as the men glanced at one another. “Who made the contact?” he asked again.

“They called us,” Noonan finally answered. “We met with them yesterday and believe that they are sincere in getting this done.”

“Who are they?” Reece prompted.

“Bainbridge, of course!” Noonan replied in a surly voice.

“They mean more than one person.” Reece met Noonan’s indignation with equal force, a stern reply and a piercing stare. There was something wrong here, he felt.

Noonan showed signs of impatience, crossing his arms and taking a step forward. “Silva made the initial call, but Bainbridge is the one we met with.”

Reece bent to one side, peeking around Noonan, to address Wilson. “Scott, were you there?”

Noonan answered before Wilson could reply, turning his head to Reece. “We called Scott.” The smirk on his face belied his statement. “He participated in the meeting, by phone. Everything’s on the up and up.”

Brock butted in, “Then why weren’t we called?”

Dunbar moved from the cabinet to join in, the four men almost huddled in the centre of the room. “That wasn’t necessary. It wasn’t negotiations. It was coming to some mutual respect.”

“Mutual respect!?” Brock spat out. “We’re talking about Bainbridge here. I know, he’s lying to you guys.” He stopped abruptly, looking from one man to the other. They all waited for him to continue, but all he did was let out a huff of exasperation while rubbing his bald head.

Noonan replied, “No, I believe Bainbridge realized he’s jeopardizing the gains he already achieved by not returning to the table. He can’t allow us to start all over again.”

"Why not?" Reece stared down Noonan. "That would be to our advantage to go over everything. Besides the time it would take, I feel we gave too much up already."

Noonan answered, "It's been agreed that talks will resume where we left off."

"What!" Brock was red in the face. "You mean they get to keep everything in the language the same?" He glared at the two men only inches away, holding back from punching them. "I thought they called you?"

"They did," Dunbar replied too quickly.

"Then why didn't you ask for something back before agreeing to resume talks?" Brock suggested the usual negotiating tactic.

The room fell silent. Reece sensed that they were holding something back. The vacant looks on the faces of Wilson, Dunbar and Noonan indicated they had committed an error in not pressing for some consideration of the language changes. Wilson broke the stalemate by pulling out his chair to sit and continued the conversation. "So tomorrow we reconvene at the hotel, and it has been agreed that we will be having marathon sessions to get this thing done."

"What's the rush?" Reece asked.

"The consensus is that we want to press the advantage while we have it." Noonan stepped to the door.

Brock guffawed. “What advantage? It seems to me that the company has the advantage by sweet-talking you guys to give in.” He moved over to the file cabinet, keeping some distance from them.

“We’re not giving in.” Dunbar moved across the room to join Noonan. “The company realizes that they were asking too much and that the gains they had achieved should not be lost.” Noonan opened the door to leave. Dunbar turned to Wilson. “Scott, fill them in on the details and we’ll see you guys tomorrow.” The two men left.

Reece and Brock glared at the two men departing and then turned to face Wilson.

“Make sure you bring enough clothing for the week.” Wilson fiddled with a pen while he spoke. “I believe we will be holed up until this gets done.”

Brock shook his head. “This is so stupid. I can’t believe you allowed this.” He stormed out of the room.

Reece waited a few seconds before commenting. “Now you have a split committee to deal with along with the company.” He returned to his desk.

25

"The problem then is that there is too much of a gap between what BCS employees earn and the corporate structure which you want to attain." Lena surmised after being filled in about the reopening of talks.

"I believe it can be solved." Bainbridge put his hand on Shannon's shoulder. "Shannon, would you please hand Lena the offer sheet that was created over the weekend."

Lena was summoned to the boardroom of the hotel they had previously occupied for negotiations to find out it would be used again. It was quiet, just the three of them, lunching on sandwiches, sweets and coffee. They were preparing to continue negotiations; Lena being brought up to speed on tactics to be used. While she had enjoyed the time off, the three-day weekend with the civic holiday having BCS closed on Monday, Bainbridge and Shannon obviously worked on a plan to reopen talks. She sat at one of the tables, already set with materials for each member of the negotiating teams on both sides. Shannon sat across from her while Bainbridge continued to pace.

Shannon nodded to Bainbridge and then opened a folder that had been lying on her lap. She spoke as she passed over a sheet to Lena. "This proposal would go a long way to bringing

BCS in line with other similar plants in the company without bringing undue hardship to the membership."

"This would solve two of our most pressing matters, the wages and pension." Bainbridge paced the room, a coffee in his hands. While Lena perused the paper, he continued. "By implementing this strategy, those that remain will not see any reduction in their wages while the new hires will account for the savings that this company needs to remain competitive."

The proposal was for the forced retirement of all those employees with thirty years or more of service to be replaced by new workers coming in at fifty percent of the present hourly rate. This would remove almost one-third of the workforce to date, replacing them with the lower wage worker. The employees with less than thirty years would maintain their wage structure but the pension would be wound up by the end of the year, with the money funding the pension put in escrow until their retirement. The proposal also stipulated that those on layoff would be hired first under the new wages. It constituted bringing in a two-tier wage structure for Border City Stamping.

Lena placed the paper on the table and addressed Bainbridge. "Has the union seen this already?"

"No, they haven't," Bainbridge lied. "Once we meet and secure those agreements already achieved, we'll present them this." He pointed to the sheet. "That paper is the only way forward."

Shannon leaned forward. "Lena, the present employees would not lose anything. Those eligible to retire get a full pension, something that is rare in today's industry, and that won't be offered in the future. As well, the present employees maintain their lifestyle and retain a pension that will be available to them at a future date, albeit a reduced one, that they can augment by contributing to their own retirement fund."

"What if they don't want to retire at this time?" Lena queried. "You're not giving them an option."

"But they do have an option," Bainbridge replied. "They can take their pension and apply to work for BCS."

Lena screwed up her face but didn't reply.

Shannon spoke up. "Yes, they can because their experience is valuable to us." She paused, looking up at Bainbridge who gave a slight nod. She continued. "They would come in at the new wage, almost like getting a side job at retirement."

Lena got the gist of it. "And would they retain their present positions?"

"No, they would be like new hires, starting in the lowest job titles," Shannon replied.

Lena nodded, pursing her lips. "They won't go for that. And neither will those laid off accept returning to work at that wage."

Bainbridge placed his cup on the table, leaned forward, fisted support, to answer the objection. "This type of arrangement has occurred in the industry quite often over the last few years. Even the big companies, the auto makers for one, have implemented a similar system."

Lena didn't reply and Shannon sat back, her hands on top of the folder. Bainbridge continued. "The only way to find out is to implement it. Getting an agreement is the first step." He straightened up and smiled.

26

The two sides convened in the boardroom of the hotel on Wednesday and resumed contract talks. Reece and Brock slowed the process by asking to review the previous language changes to the contract. The sessions for the first two days dealt with revisions that they were able to secure from the company, especially when dealing with health and safety issues. Reece found the atmosphere too friendly, with the company agreeing to the changes without any real objection, and Bainbridge not being as adversarial as in the past. Even during their closed-door meetings with the executive members of the union, Reece and Brock were complimented on securing better language and encouraged to seek more leverage in their review. Something didn't feel right, and Reece couldn't put his finger on it. Shannon and Lena were silent the entire time they reviewed the language, Bainbridge conducting the meeting as if the changes were already a done deal. By Friday the talks moved on to the contentious monetary issues. The discussions began with the 'minor financial items', as Bainbridge called them, of overtime, shift premiums, and COLA. To the union's surprise, Bainbridge agreed to maintain the status quo regarding these issues with a proviso that these items may be altered for new hires. When asked why that was necessary when BCS had so many members on layoff, they were presented with the new proposal.

"We believe that this proposal is the best solution for both sides." Bainbridge commented as the sheets were being handed over. "The present membership won't be affected, and the company would benefit from the new hires replacing those enjoying their full retirement benefits they so rightly deserve."

The union members scanned the sheets, taking their time to read over the proposal. Reece quickly realized the purpose of the company. They were pushing the senior workers out and replacing them with cheap labour. He looked up from the paper and sought reaction from the committee members. Wilson and Dunbar pretended to be still reading the paper, their heads down, while Noonan had his paper in his hands, not looking at it, instead eyeing Reece.

"I understand that you need time to go over this offer, as a committee, so I propose that we take a twenty-four-hour break." Bainbridge motioned to the clock in the room. "It's just after noon, so how about we break for lunch, somewhere other than this hotel" — he put up his hand in a circular motion — "and you can have this boardroom to discuss the proposal."

"That sounds like a good idea," Noonan spoke up. "We definitely need to evaluate this wage structure and retirement option before proceeding."

"Take it seriously but let me reiterate that we have accomplished quite a bit and that both sides have met with favour," Bainbridge said. "Let's reconvene tomorrow at one o'clock, here." He nodded to Shannon and Lena who started to gather up their materials. "We don't want to lose the momentum we have."

The union committee sat silent while they exited the boardroom. There were a few more minutes of silence with the shuffling of papers and feet being the only noise evident, before Noonan stood up to address the men.

"Let's go for lunch and come back here to discuss this proposal." Noonan took up the sheet. "We may be here a while."

"I don't believe it will take that long," Reece replied. "You guys already knew about this, didn't you?"

"C'mon Reece, that's unfair," Wilson said. "We got it at the same time as you."

"No, they didn't." Reece pointed to Noonan and Dunbar. He wasn't too sure about Wilson knowing of this tactic. "Gord, you were aware of this paper before we even sat down. That's why everything went so smoothly."

"Reece, you're too cynical," Noonan replied. "Why can't you take things as they are without putting some spin on it? This is negotiations and we don't get all up in a huff when given an option."

"This is unacceptable!" Brock finally spoke. "It's not worth looking at."

Noonan gestured for everyone to calm down. "Let's take a break. We have time to discuss it. Don't come to conclusions before reasoning its merits."

"But you've already come to a decision," Reece bluntly replied. "This is all a show. You don't really expect Brock and I to accept this, but we're outnumbered." Reece pointed to the three executive members. "Answer me one question, Gord? Does our President accept this two-tier wage proposal?"

Noonan baulked at replying, taking up the sheet as if to read it. Everyone else waited for an answer. Noonan glanced from one to the other as he spoke. "He understands that we are at a crossroads in our negotiations with respect to wages and benefits. We must be receptive to all possible options to secure a contract." Noonan stared at Reece. "He trusts our judgement in ensuring Border City Stamping employees continue to work for the foreseeable future."

Reece replied, "You're telling me he has backed off his declaration that this union would never entertain two-tier wages?" Reece presented his cell phone. "Maybe I should call him to verify this change of policy?"

Dunbar came to Noonan's defense. "Come on Reece, we haven't accepted anything yet. It's been advised that we consider the proposal and see if we can live with it." As soon as he ended, Dunbar realized he had implied that the proposal had been viewed by the National Office. His face blushed as Noonan shook his head and frowned.

Reece replaced his phone in his pocket. "I guess that answers my question." He sat down, taking up the proposal and ignoring the others. Brock stood, slamming his chair against the table, and exited the room without saying a word. Wilson, red in the face, followed Noonan and Dunbar out of the room, glancing back at Reece one last time before exiting. Reece watched them go, shaking his head slightly when Wilson turned, signalling his disappointment.

27

Reece couldn't sleep. It was just past one in the morning, he'd been in his room since ten, but there was no way he was going to rest. They had gone over the proposal for over six hours debating the pros and cons of it, mostly cons in Reece's estimation. Noonan and Dunbar kept bringing up similar contracts with other auto supply companies and the success that those members had gained in securing future work. Reece and Brock reminded them that they were dealing with BCS employees who were staunch in their demands for a fair contract for all of them. Wilson seemed out of his element, going back and forth on one side of the debate to the other. There were some adjustments made to the proposal but to Reece they were trivial. The group broke up for the evening with almost each one going their own way. Brock decided to go home saying he needed to be with some sane people for a bit. Noonan said he was going to his room to make some calls to the national office to get clarification on a few issues pertinent to the proposal while Dunbar offered to go to the regional office to dig up some similar agreements with other factories in the region. Wilson, confused and apparently unaware of the decisions made over the weekend, didn't say where he was going, and Reece could care less. It was clear to Reece that Noonan and Dunbar had orchestrated this reopening of talks without Wilson's approval, or his and Brock's. Reading over the papers, alone, Reece couldn't see a way to present this for ratification by the membership without scuttling the whole thing and returning to the status quo on wages. He had accepted the fact that company funded pensions were a thing of the past and that it was inevitable that BCS would wrap up theirs. The best he could hope for was that the fund would be there for the membership in the future and not lost because of receivership or bankruptcy. Not at least with IMP as the parent company. He couldn't accept the forced retirement of the membership. He got dressed and headed out the room, not really knowing where he was going.

Entering the lobby, he hesitated, trying to decide whether to take a walk outside or just go to the lounge for a late-night drink. There was one receptionist at the desk, and he could hear the music coming from the bar. His attention was attracted by a wave of a hand coming from the set of couches along the glass wall facing the front entrance of the hotel. Shannon signaled for him to come over.

"I see someone else couldn't sleep," She greeted him. Wearing a loose-fitting blue blouse and sports shorts caught Reece by surprise, causing him to catch his breath. During the negotiations she dressed appropriately in business attire, usually slacks and jacket. They hadn't been alone since the start of negotiations.

The coffee table between the two couches was covered with papers. Reece could only deduce that she had been working on a strategy for the next day. He smiled weakly and sat down on the couch across from her. Who was this woman he thought he knew so well? The secrets he uncovered and her apparent disregard for his commitment to the people he represented created a cloud of doubt about their future. Yet, he still felt something for her. What was it? He had fallen for her beauty, intelligence and wit. They were still there. The willingness to succeed at all costs is what had him concerned. Would that include forfeiting what they had?

“I don’t know if anybody involved in these talks really sleeps,” he replied.

“There is a lot at stake,” she said. “Being my first time, I feel like I’m a step behind everyone.”

“It can be overwhelming.” He believed she didn’t really have any sway with Bainbridge concerning the issues but had served a purpose of creating tension for the union committee, specifically him. “This probably isn’t the best scenario for you to break into the legal counselling of a negotiation.”

“On the contrary.” She moved forward to the edge of the couch, leaning over the table. “This experience has been terrific and,” she waited for him to look her in the eye, “thank you for not putting a kibosh to it before it even started.”

He blushed, having been caught staring at her body. But this was his wife? He tried to recover. “The strategy laid out for the company seems to be working.” He referred to the papers he had seen in Toronto. “I’m alone in the battle against you...I mean the company...without support... except for Brock.” He stumbled with an explanation of his efforts that mirrored his state of mind.

Shannon pouted, aware that he had sacrificed an advantage in not revealing to the others the company’s strategy. “Reece, you shouldn't take it to heart what we're trying to accomplish. It's not as bad as you think it is."

"Not as bad as forcing people to retire, stripping those remaining of their right to a retirement down the road, and creating a divisive workforce through wage disparity?" His sarcastic tone amplified his points.

"I believe," she caught herself. "We believe that this arrangement could satisfy both parties. Of course there is going to be some adjustment by the membership, but the company also will have a great price to pay to fulfill this commitment."

"That price will be recouped in a short time with the savings from wages and the elimination of funding retirement." He found himself practicing his arguments with her but also realized that she had contributed to the plan. "Don't for a second think that you can hide that from the membership." He stopped, not wanting to get into a battle of wits. She wouldn't be the decision maker in these talks. That would be with the others, on both sides.

A crowd of about ten people entered the lobby from the bar, laughing and talking loudly, heading for the exit. Reece and Shannon watched as the party left, the bar closing for the night. Reece returned his attention to her.

Shannon leaned forward to start arranging the papers on the table. "We're not hiding anything. We've been rather up front about our objectives and" — she glanced at him — "since my introduction, we have conducted ourselves openly." She smiled.

He wondered if she was aware of the charade over the weekend. She was in Toronto after the talks had broken off, stating that she had to report the impasse to the firm. He found that hard to believe when she could have just reported to the satellite office here in Windsor. Could she have participated? He thought not but, then again, she did keep secrets. Also, this new proposal differed from their corporate structure that Bainbridge constantly referred to. Was this two-tier wage offer Shannon's creation? He watched her gather up the papers, no longer distracted by her appearance.

"You've done a great service to the membership arguing for improvements on the concessions made." She winced after making the comment and tried to rephrase her comment. "I mean, you've improved what's offered. Don't think that this wage offer belittles that achievement."

"I don't see it that way," he challenged. "You're splitting the membership and this committee." He decided to take a shot at their team. "I believe you and Lena...umm...Miss Kersey." He blushed and fumbled to finish his statement. "You are just puppets for Bainbridge. He's calling all the shots."

She tapped a handful of sheets on the table. "Really, I've been wasting my time? You think it would have been better if I had stayed out of it and been the dutiful wife?" She smiled thinly, shaking her head slightly as she gathered up her material.

Reece felt a jab of guilt at this remark. Shannon hadn't spoken much during the latest set of talks, and he had caught her smiling a few times at him. He felt awkward with both Shannon and Lena in the boardroom. The last few weeks had been very confusing for him on a personal basis. The apparent split between him and Shannon was further complicated by the recent attention he had experienced with Lena. Since the random meeting at the hotel lounge over two weeks ago, they had been together a couple of other times. The past long weekend, when talks seemed to have ended and Shannon was in Toronto, Lena had contacted him about going to a concert. Initially he had declined the offer but she reasoned that they were no longer on opposite sides of a battle and so he agreed to go to a concert in Michigan. They stayed overnight. Returning home on the Sunday, he vowed he would not see her again but broke that vow the next day, the civic holiday, when he met her at the Sand Point Beach by invitation. What was he thinking? When he found out that talks would resume immediately, those were the first thoughts in his mind.

"You should be very careful about what you're doing." She placed the sheets in her valise. "You need to take everything and everyone into consideration when plotting your course. Don't let your conscience overrule what may be best in the long run."

Reece needed to know about what Shawn had alluded to. He looked around the empty lobby, the male receptionist being the only other person around. He posed the next question in a hushed voice.

"Did you have something to do with Don Wesley's death?" He had researched the news articles on the death of the senior partner of Ellis and Unger at the Windsor office.

Shannon froze, her eyes widened, and mouth slightly opened. She didn't reply.

"Did you have something on him that made him commit suicide?" Reece forged on, a little uncomfortable that he was resorting to this to get her off her game and reveal more about what she was doing within the firm.

"It was a mistake," she whispered, closing her eyes as she began. "He was one of the first and when I dug up the information on his illegal activity, I" — she winced — "handed it over to the wife. She used it against him."

"She gave it to the RCMP?" Reece implored.

Shannon blinked. "How do you know all this?"

"It doesn't matter how I know." Reece leaned forward, almost over the table. "What matters is that your blackmailing caused this man's death. How do you feel about that?"

She stood up. "That was not the intent. He was using the firm to line his own pockets." She bent down a bit to look at Reece eye-to-eye. "He deserved what was coming to him, even by his own hand." She gave him a slight nod, straightened up and smiled before walking away.

28

A tentative agreement was reached by Sunday after almost twenty-eight hours of non-stop negotiations. Reece was tired, not only by the marathon sessions through the night, but with fighting over every point with the company and the executives on the union committee. Brock, frustrated to the point of blowing up, refused to participate in the final session after lunch on Sunday. He left. The agenda set out by the company was virtually achieved, securing the replacement of seniority workers with new hires at over half the cost in respect to wages and benefits. The last few hours were spent going over the presentation that would be given to the membership. The company even offered financial incentives for the employees. One thousand dollars per year service would be given to those retiring, along with their immediate pension. For those employees remaining, a signing bonus of $1500.00 per employee was offered upon ratification, including those on layoff. Reece was perplexed by the company's generosity, never given to any of their other acquisitions upon a new contract, especially to a union shop. When the final agreement was ready to be signed, Reece hesitated. When he questioned Bainbridge on the ramifications of this contract with respect to the other holdings of IMP, Bainbridge replied that BCS might be setting a precedent that would be used in future contracts within the company. Reece didn't believe him. The ratification meeting was set for the following weekend.

Reece returned to work at BCS, alone. Wilson was at the local preparing for the ratification meeting. Brock, still a part of the negotiating committee, requested a few days off to cool down. It was permitted. By Wednesday Reece needed to take a break from the load of health and safety issues accumulated from the talks. Reece left the union office and headed towards the vending machines at the end of the hall. Passing by the plant manager's office, Lena Kersey called out. "Reece, do you have a minute?"

Reece stepped back to the threshold. "Sure, what's up?"

She signaled for him to enter. "Close the door behind you, please."

Reece entered. "Anything pressing from our time away?" He noticed the changes in her office; the landscape art on the walls, the two standing plants just inside the doorway and two beige cloth armchairs in front of the desk.

"Nothing like that," she said. "I just wanted to talk to you about the ratification."

"Well, to tell you the truth, anything you need you should contact Scott." Reece sat on one of the chairs. "He's down at the local arranging for the meeting and preparing the materials."

"I think he's wasting his time."

Reece was surprised to hear her say that. During the last marathon session of bargaining, she had clammed up. Reece didn't reply.

"I must compliment you in trying to defend the employee's rights during these talks. It was a difficult thing for you and Brock to do considering the opposition to your stance taken by the company," Lena paused, "and your executive."

Reece accepted the comment for its face value. Lena had told him she had come to enjoy her time at BCS and cared for the employees. "We tried to express our concerns over the direction the company's heading. This company's making money. There's no need to change it so drastically."

"There may be other factors that affected the outcome of negotiations," Lena warned.

"And they are?" Reece was intrigued.

She reached into her drawer and placed a note at the edge of her desk. "I'm not at liberty to say, but I believe you could discover on your own if you were to go there." She pointed to the paper.

Reece stretched out to gather up the note. It was an address in Michigan. He shrugged and screwed up his face at her.

"Take a day and check this out. It may answer a lot of questions about the direction this company is taking."

"Can you give me more detail?"

"Let's just say that ratification of this contract may be buying time for something else to happen." Lena paused and shook her head slightly. "See for yourself if the guarantees given by the company would be fulfilled."

Reece understood the reference to the guarantees the union sought from the company on future work being brought to BCS with ratification of the contract. The best they could secure in the agreement was a provision to bid for work. She was implying that it was an empty promise. Reece didn't ask any other questions and stood to leave.

"How are things at home, you know, with Shannon?" Lena couldn't help herself from asking.

"She's still in Toronto. We haven't had time to talk...or anything." He shrugged.

"I'm sorry, for you." She wanted to get up and console him but forced herself to remain seated. Their short time together had given her a different insight into Reece. She liked him.

He reached for the door.

"Reece, we'll talk again after your trip," Lena said as a parting gesture. "I have as much at stake as you do."

Reece opened the door and exited, leaving the door open as before. Walking back to the union office, staring at the address in his hands, he wondered what she was leading him to. A little bit of research would clarify it, but he felt she was on his side. Time would tell.

29

"We're going into enemy territory. Let's not make it too obvious where we're from." Brock explained the need to change vehicles. Reece's research into the address he was given revealed a stamping plant acquired by IMP. Its previous owners had fallen upon hard times during the recent recession and the company was gobbled up along with its satellite plants in Michigan. It was Motor Craft Industries, the company mentioned in negotiations that had received work originally destined for BCS. The latest news coming out of the local papers of Strasberg, a small town ninety miles north of Detroit, mentioned a major renovation to the plant buoyed by state government incentives. Reece recruited Brock to go with him on Thursday. Brock had suggested they stop by a fellow worker's home in Sterling Heights where they swapped Reece's Jeep for his Chevy Silverado.

"We're going to check this place out, not invade it." Reece chuckled.

"Don't kid yourself, Reece." Brock glanced over while driving. "These people aren't just going to let us walk right into their plant for a tour."

They rode into the town a few miles west of the I-75 turnoff and the sprawling plant came into view on the outskirts. Construction crews were working on the northern section, a newer steel exterior extending from the concrete walls of the original building. Passing by the front, the main offices faced the road with the employee parking lot to the left, a fence separated the lot from the building and employees entered through a series of gates. Just like BCS. Brock drove by and parked on the street a block away, in front of a convenience store. A residential area stretched out beyond the next block.

"Let's grab a couple of Cokes and go for a walk." Brock turned off the motor and opened the door. Reece met him on the sidewalk, and they entered the store. A few minutes later they strolled past Motor Craft Industries. Besides the gate, entry could also be obtained through the office which had a small visitor parking lane adjacent to it. They debated whether to try to fake their way into the plant but neither one felt comfortable about it. Nearing the end of the property they noticed an entry for the construction crews off a side street and hashed over the possibility of getting in that way. Again, they weren't confident enough about getting away with it. Finally, Brock suggested they go back into town and have lunch. They chose the 'Bull and Barrel' that served a pretty good cheeseburger platter that included home fries and coleslaw. Conversation with the waitress revealed that the tavern was a popular place for the workers on pay day. They planned on returning after the day shift ended.

Reece convinced Brock into going to the local library for more research. Using the internet available through the terminals, they were able to discover the history of Motor Craft Industries and its importance to Strasberg. It was the main employer and when it went into receivership the whole town suffered. Unemployment soared with the plant idle for over a year. When IMP purchased it, they brought work to the plant, hiring the previous workforce at half the wages. But the people were glad to have a job and returned to work. The present enterprise had been in operation for two years with expansion forthcoming. It was just past four o'clock when they left the library to return to the tavern.

Reece and Brock entered and proceeded to an unoccupied table in the middle of the place. The tables scattered throughout the main floor were filled with men and women from the factory. Some were still in their work clothes, jeans and t-shirts, while others, mostly the women, had tidied themselves up and wore shorts and tight tops, some men included. The piped-in music and the aroma of restaurant cooking filled the room, the workers enjoying their time away from work. After ordering a pitcher of beer, they noticed some of the patrons stealing a glance at them. Brock struck up a conversation with two men at the next table.

Brock spoke with an Irish brogue accent, not as thick as when entertaining at family functions. Reece could hardly keep a straight face, but it worked in getting a couple of guys talking about their work. Brock and Reece portrayed themselves as salesmen for a tool supply company having just visited the plant trying to pitch their goods. On their commenting about the expansion, a tall, wiry black kid, Arlen, spoke about how it was a boon for him having been out of work for a couple of years. His drinking partner, Tommy, not much older, freckle-faced and blonde, added that they were able to get hired because some people who had worked for the previous owners either had other jobs or wouldn't return for the lower wages. The expansion was going to guarantee work for several years enabling the two of them avoiding the unemployment line. When Reece asked about what type of work, since it would be of interest to them to pitch tools to the company, the two friends called over an older man to shed more light on the specifics. Brock ordered a couple more pitchers from the same waitress who had served them at lunch with her joining in on the conversation. They were introduced to Walter, an employee who had worked for the original owners, who had returned as a maintenance man. His salt-and-pepper hair was matched with a goatee of the same colour and his hands were large and callused. He declined the offer of a glass and seemed hesitant to talk. The two younger guys made up for his silence by describing the plans that were revealed to the workforce of the future machinery. Walter, coaxed by the two junior employees who were botching up the explanation of the type of machinery, described it as equipment that would supplement the rear axle assembly they already had, creating a frame that would be used in a multi-vehicle platform assembly plant for Ford Motor Company. When Reece pushed for more detail, Walter politely excused himself, stating that he needed to get home. He advised the other two, Arlen and Tommy, to limit the time they stayed at the tavern because they still had another day to work. Brock tried to convince them to stay for another round, but the boys declined. Reece noticed that the crowd was thinning out and that the sun was setting. The waitress came by for another order, but they declined. He and Brock discussed what they had learned while they were finishing up their beers when Brock noticed a group of men entering the tavern. Leading them was someone he had had a run-in with at Border City Stamping.

30

“You’re far from home, Brock. What brings you to Strasberg?”

“It wasn’t to see you, Ron, that’s for sure.”

Brock stood to face Ron Sturgeon, who was accompanied by five men: Walter, Arlen, Tom and two others. The burly man in dress pants, shirt and tie ambled up to the table. Their past relationship had been a rocky one as Sturgeon was a welding advisor for BCS shortly after the acquisition. Brock fought him on safety issues and employee grievances while Sturgeon was implementing a new quality control system on welding procedures. Sturgeon hadn’t stayed very long and now it seemed they were going to clash again.

“Take a seat, Brock. I want to hear what’s been going on with you lately.” Sturgeon pulled up a chair at the adjoining table. “You seemed to have lost that Irish accent from earlier today.” He chuckled, joined nervously by the other men who had spread out around the two tables. The waitress, behind the bar, blushed when Brock stared at her. There was no more music, and the only noise was the shuffling of feet by the five men still standing behind Sturgeon.

Brock sat. "We're just finishing our drinks and we'll be on our way." He downed the remainder of his beer.

"And who's your friend, or may I say, accomplice?" Sturgeon gestured toward Reece.

"I wouldn't want to sully his name by associating it with yours," Brock replied.

"I'm Reece Kincaid and I'm at a disadvantage not knowing how you two know each other."

"We used to work alongside one another, right Brock?" Sturgeon said. "That was such a long time ago." He cocked his head to one side, pretending to think. "What, last December?"

"He was there checking out our equipment," Brock addressed Reece. "The job that got taken away from us." He turned to face Sturgeon. "I bet it's here, from what I understand your men told us earlier."

Sturgeon glared at Arlen and Tom who bent their heads and fidgeted with their hands. "You obviously grilled my boys on our operation." He faced Brock. "And for what purpose?"

"We didn't grill anybody. They were more than willing to tell us about their good fortune in landing a job," Brock spoke. "Even if it's for poor pay."

Sturgeon leaned forward, pointing a finger. "Maybe you guys should consider yourself lucky to have a job, for now. I believe you two were nosing around to see what work we have and will get at your expense."

"What will that be?" Reece interrupted, anger in his voice. "No, let me guess. The new transfer line for the metal framework for Ford to accompany the rear axle assembly you presently have."

Sturgeon stood, his face flushed. "I think your time here is up. May we accompany you out?"

"I think we know our way out." Brock stood. "No need for your boys to get dirty." Reece rose to join Brock.

One of the men who had come with Sturgeon reached out to grab Brock's arm. Brock swatted him across the face. "Don't even think about it, buddy."

Sturgeon raised his hands. "Enough! Let them leave." He signaled for his men to back off.

Brock and Reece walked past the group toward the exit. Brock leaned into Reece. "What did I tell you? Are you ready for some fun?" Reece nodded.

They stepped out into the night, the sun barely showing above the landscape. Their truck was parked in the next block to the right, but they turned left to the adjoining parking lot. The six men followed. Once they were in the middle of the lot, the two newcomers to the group blocked off Brock and Reece's path. Brock turned around to stare down Walter, Arlen and Tom. Sturgeon stood on the sidewalk. "I think you need to learn a lesson. You mind your own business around here."

Brock and Reece backed into one another. "Can you handle those two while I get these ones?" Brock whispered to Reece.

"I'll help you when I'm done," Reece replied. Brock chuckled.

The first guy to move was one of the strangers, a muscle bound heavy in jeans and t-shirt. He lunged toward Reece who sidestepped him, and delivered a chop to the big man's neck, dropping him to the ground. Brock didn't wait for his opponents to move, taking a few steps and bear-hugging Walter. He crushed him up against a pickup, head butting the older man. Walter slinked to the ground. Reece meanwhile took up a defensive posture, Kata, in between his foes. The other man was just as big, and clumsy. When he charged, Reece spun around delivering a kick to the midsection, doubling over the man while the first attacker tried to counter with a punch. Reece blocked the blow and returned an open hand thrust to his attacker's side. The two ruffians regained their feet and prepared to attack. Brock turned to face Arlen and Tom who were both wide-eyed. They attacked together, putting up their hands in a boxing pose. Brock fended off their feeble blows with his arms and just bulldogged his way into them. They both fell to the side. Arlen got up and tried to kick Brock, who gripped his leg and twisted it around. A loud snap was followed by a harrowing scream by Arlen who dropped to the ground and clutched his knee. Tom scrabbled from the ground and saw what happened to Arlen. He feigned an attack that Brock snarled at. “Beat it kid, before I break you into pieces.” Tom stared at the crying Arlen, scared out of his wits, and turned to run. Reece met his combatants head on. They both charged. Reece knelt on one knee and, with both arms, chopped at the men’s waist and lifted, flipping both in the air and over him. They landed on their backs with a thud and a gasp of air escaped their lungs. Reece turned around and lunged with both hands at their chests. The quick jabs took out the remaining fight in them and they lay moaning on the ground.

Brock and Reece met back in the middle of the parking lot and looked upon their handy work. Four men down, one gone, and their leader nowhere in sight. Sturgeon had abandoned his position. Sirens could be heard in the distance.

“Let’s get out of here before we have to answer too many questions,” Reece said.

Brock harrumphed and they dashed off to their truck.

31

"We're sealing our own fate if we sign this deal," Reece tried to reason. "Closure in a couple of years."

The five men, huddled in Dunbar's office at the local, were debating over the tentative agreement they were to present the next day to the membership. The cluttered shelves and desk, papers and books scattered in disorder, seem to compliment the disjointed conversation. Reece and Brock had filled the others in about their trip to Strasberg. During the ride home Reece had concluded that IMP had no intention of keeping BCS open for the long haul. He was now trying to convince the others, namely Wilson, Dunbar and Noonan.

"You're jumping to speculation based on incomplete information," Noonan retorted from behind Dunbar's desk. "You guys didn't see anything or get specifics on their work. For all we know it could be just other work that has no effect on us."

"Do you always have to be drawn a picture?" Brock rebuked. "Everything those guys told us points to the work we lost earlier this year and the work that was destined for here now going there." He was having a hard time controlling his temper, his legs bouncing as he sat in one of the chairs in front of the desk.

"The details you want are here." Reece, sitting beside Brock, handed over a folder to Wilson sitting along the wall. "There are newspaper articles stating the specifics of the parts they produce now and an overview of the expansion with reference to the parts that will be produced." Wilson flipped open the file while Reece continued. "They got the whole framework for the Ford Edge and its hybrid model that we had bid on and won but" — he stared right at Noonan — "was taken away right after IMP purchased us."

There was silence in the room while the folder was passed along to Dunbar, sitting beside Wilson, and then to Noonan. Brock seethed with contempt over the apparent disregard these executive members seemed to have over this new information. He wanted to tear up the highlight booklets that were printed up to distribute to the membership and force the company back to the table for a fairer deal. The problem was that these guys needed to agree with him and Reece.

Noonan handed over the folder back to Dunbar. "Regardless of what this shows, we need to provide some savings to the company to ensure that we can bid on future work. This contract will do just that."

"No, it won't." Reece replied while stretching out his arm to prevent Brock from lunging over the desk. He shook his head slightly, getting a grim expression in return from

Brock. He stood and retreated a few steps before turning back to confront Noonan. "By agreeing to this contract, which I may remind you have no guarantees of future work, all we're doing is allowing IMP to clear wages off the books. In my mind they have no intention of replacing those forced to retire with new hires..."

"Wait a second, Reece," Wilson interrupted, "you have no justification to say that."

Brock erupted, "Are you that stupid, Scott!" He shot up from the chair and stepped to the middle of the room. "Can't you see what we're trying to tell you?"

Wilson rose and stepped forward to challenge Brock. Dunbar appeared in-between and spoke. "Okay, guys, we're not getting anywhere by arguing. Let's cool down and talk this thing over."

"Reece, I don't understand how you come to that conclusion," Noonan calmly said while still seated.

Reece waited for Brock to return to his seat and then turned to face the others. "That expansion is huge. There is more room than what is needed just for that operation." He pointed to the folder. "I believe that the company plans on having us continue operating well below capacity by taking more work out of here or not replacing work that will expire next year." He referred to contracts that were coming up for renewal on new models that everyone in the room were aware of. "By doing so, they create an untenable situation for BCS in becoming inefficient and unable to compete with the other facilities for future work. Bainbridge continuously brought up numbers that showed the cost ratio being too high in relation to the other IMP plants."

"We addressed that matter by stating they created the problem by taking work out," Dunbar spoke.

"Exactly!" Reece stated. "And that's what I believe they'll do again." He gestured for the others to hear him out. "We ratify this contract, by the New Year the seniority people are gone; one third of the workforce. Before then, how many contracts are expiring?" They all knew the number. "Service parts are all that is left to produce on those expiring contracts and that doesn't take much manpower. They continue to operate with the remaining employees, producing less at higher labour costs, and becoming less efficient."

"You paint a bleak picture," Noonan commented. "But let me do it one better." He leaned on the desk. "We don't ratify this contract, and the company declines to return to the table and at the end of the year we're without an agreement. What does the company do?" Noonan raised his hands, palms upward.

Reece had thought of that scenario but didn't believe the company would let it go that far. He suggested a strategy. "We do the same as WTW. We strike and force them to settle a fair agreement or face the consequences with our customers."

Noonan shook his head. "They won't bend to that. Are you willing to gamble on the workers' livelihood in that scenario?"

"Why not?" Reece answered. "That way we control our fate." He recognized the doubt in the faces of Noonan, Wilson and Dunbar. "At least propose that option to the membership and let them decide." He thought of another way to scrap this tentative agreement. "Or you can cite 'conflict of interest' with Shannon representing them as an out that the union executive mentioned when we began this."

"That's not an option anymore," Noonan answered. "We've gone beyond that."

"What?" Brock shouted. "That should've happened from the start. Why not now?"

Reece watched as Noonan bowed his head, avoiding their intense stares. Reece wondered why the union had changed its mind on using this option to avoid an unfavourable outcome.

Noonan took up a highlight booklet and lifted his head to glare at Brock and Reece. "This is the best we can get. The plant is old and really has gone way beyond its shelf life." Noonan had compared BCS to many other plants that had closed in the last fifteen years as being one that had extended its life expectancy beyond normal. "By offering this contract we allow everyone to benefit. The plant will become competitive, and we'll be able to revisit these issues in future contracts."

"There won't be any future contracts!" Brock shouted.

"That's it!" Noonan replied just as loud. "We're not debating anymore. This is what we've negotiated and it's what we're presenting to the membership." He slapped the highlight booklet on the table, ending any more debate.

32

"There's no way I should have to retire. This is bullshit." The first speaker, a slim man with a receding hairline, yelled into the microphone, followed by shouts of agreement from the crowded room. The air conditioning did little to cool the temperature in the room, or the tempers.

The hall at Local 123 was overcrowded, its capacity beyond its lawful limit. Reece wondered if this lack of foresight could be used to delay the vote. Was he strong enough to make the call and have the room cleared? There was something about this whole proceeding that just didn't sit right with him. His thoughts the last twenty-four hours had been conflicting, going from accepting that Noonan was right, to an innate fear that by ratifying this agreement they were doomed to regret it. The crowd seemed to be coming out of its stunned mood with the first objection to the tentative agreement just read by the committee. Wilson was at the lectern trying to calm the crowd.

"Bill, the pension is going to be stopped at the end of this year, anyway. You may as well take it while you have it," Wilson's answer was condescending.

"That's bullshit too." Bill Henderson had just made thirty years seniority and hadn't reached fifty yet. "It's not fair to all the others who planned on having a pension to retire on. Now you want us to agree to have it stopped?" He huffed while waiting for a reply.

"It was the one item the company said was not negotiable. They no longer want to fund retirements. The legacy cost is too high." Wilson was botching the question-and-answer session of the meeting. Noonan replaced Wilson, trying to reduce the damage.

"You all have to understand something. Company funded pensions are a thing of the past." Noonan's words elicited boos and catcalls from the crowd. He waved to silence the crowd.

“Let me speak.” The crowd quieted. “The industry, as a whole, is eliminating this type of retirement option. At Border City Stamping you are fortunate to have one that is still in place after its recent takeover. By getting the company to acknowledge and fund it to the end of this year, most of you will have at least some pension.” Smatterings of insults were shouted but Noonan continued. “With maintaining the wage structure, you’ll be able to augment that pension with your own contributions and those who have a full pension will enjoy the benefits for the rest of your life.”

“But I’m not ready to retire.” Bill still stood at the microphone. “I have a young family to feed, and a pension won’t do it.”

The crescendo of voices drowned out any attempt to continue the debate. Noonan conferred with Wilson and Dunbar. Brock and Reece were at the other end of the head table, uninvited to the discussion. It was strongly suggested that they not participate in the presentation of the tentative agreement, afraid that their views would hinder the outcome of the vote. Dunbar changed places with Noonan.

“Everybody in this room is aware of the factories that have closed recently. Many of them were affiliated with our local and I was involved with the processes that resulted in their unfortunate closure. The common denominator in every instance was the excessive legacy costs these companies said they could not sustain.

These include pensions and retiree benefits that have become prohibitive for the companies to stay competitive in today's market. The failure of each unit to address this concern led to their death." The crowd stirred with rumblings. "We don't want that happening to Border City Stamping. By offering to suspend company funded pensions, yet fully funding to the end of this year, we're able to keep BCS viable for the future. Your future is secured by bargaining to maintain your high standard of living in respect to wages and benefits. It's a trade-off. But it's one that will prevent this plant from closing." Dunbar returned to his seat to be replaced by Noonan.

The crowd was quiet, almost as if trying to comprehend what was just implied. Reece took it as a threat. Where did he hear that before? His mind sorted through his memory banks to find an instance where that same scenario was mentioned. The debate continued with the membership.

A petite, short-haired brunette stepped up to the microphone. "How do you expect me to live on these wages when I return?" Judy Ferris held up the highlight booklet. "Why did you agree to this wage for those laid off? We deserve to come back at the wage we were earning." Her comment was buoyed by a chorus of cheers.

Noonan grasped the lectern with both hands. "We tried our hardest to include those of you laid off to return at your present wage and benefit package, but the company fought us on it. They didn't even want you to be hired before people on the street. That's how difficult it became to bargain for you to be hired first, without interviews, with a benefit package better than a new hire and maintaining your seniority status." Noonan's smug expression conveyed that they'd won on this point. "Let's get you people back to work and we'll improve those wages in the next contract."

"But I can't live on that wage," Judy lamented. "I have three teenagers to raise on my own and the wage I'd come back to is barely more than what I'm getting on unemployment. How will I make it?"

"Don't worry, Tim will help you." Someone shouted from the back of the room. A wave of laughter rose, and Judy turned toward the back. "Fuck off!" she shouted and that spurred more laughter.

Noonan glanced to his right at Wilson and Dunbar, who had smiles on their faces in reference to the shop floor romance. They both shrugged and Noonan returned to address the crowd. "I know it'll be difficult, but the main thing is to get you back to work."

There were others who chose to speak but Reece zoned out of the meeting. The mention of a closure had been brought up before in conversations. Never during negotiations had it been raised but individuals had implied the possibility. Noonan expressed that opinion during the debate yesterday and Reece remembered Shannon warning him that the alternative to this contract could be worse. Why would they even bring up the possibility when there had never been the threat of it in talks? Did they know something the others didn't? Reece was trying to figure it out when he felt a tap on his knee. "Reece, they're asking for you," Brock interrupted his thoughts. "They want you to speak."

Reece rose, grabbed his bottled water, and walked toward the lectern. Noonan met him halfway.

"Stress the importance of keeping BCS viable." Noonan held Reece's arm. "They have to understand that a closed plant does them no good."

There was that inference to a closure, again. Reece was bothered by the implied threat. "A good portion of these people are being asked to call it quits. I don't think that possibility will sway them."

"Their pensions depend on BCS continuing, remember that," Noonan replied. Reece didn't believe that because the money was already there for those eligible now. Noonan leaned in closer to Reece. "This committee endorses this contract. We must show solidarity."

That last sentence struck a chord with Reece. That was it. He smiled warily and moved to the microphone. "Nick, I'm sorry, I didn't hear what you said."

Nick Campo repeated his question. "Reece, I just asked for your opinion on this deal. You and Brock are closer to what happens at the plant than the others, and I believe the people here value your opinion."

"Thanks, Nick, for that compliment...um...I appreciate it." His thoughts were clearer than they had been for a few days. But he was afraid of how to phrase it properly. "The negotiations were very difficult, as you know, and...um...there was a stalemate halfway through. The sticking point was the big-ticket items of wages and pension commitment. They were determined to lower them." He paused, taking in the scene before him. For a packed house, the silence was eerie. "Without rehashing everything you've been told, this was the best package they would offer."

"That's not what I'm asking, Reece," Nick cut in. "As fellow workers" — he spread out his arms to indicate the membership — "who will have to live with this contract every day, whether on the job or retired, do you feel it's one that we should vote yes for?"

Reece decided right then what he was going to say. First, he bent over to whisper to Wilson seated next to the lectern. "We owe them representation in their best interests, not ours." He straightened up, took a sip of water, and then moved the microphone to calm his nerves.

"If you ratify this contract, then the person working beside you may well be earning less than half doing the same job." Reece felt a welling up of emotion. "If those who're being forced to retire ratify this contract, you're agreeing to reduce your earning power, not of your choice. If those of you who've been laid off ratify this contract, you do so without any guarantee that the company's even going to hire people to replace those retired." The crowd was beginning to buzz with excitement. "I was just reminded that we have to show solidarity." He glanced at Noonan. "This contract would divide us, the membership, today to choose between those who will maintain their standard of living and those who will see it reduced, significantly. That is not solidarity." Reece paused, a rising of emotion spurring him on. "For those who work side by side, for those who came before you, and for those who will come after" — he stole a peek at Brock who nodded his head — "I say no to this contract."

The crowd burst out with shouts and whistles, and the clapping of hands. The membership stood, from the front with a rising wave to the back, cheering wildly. Reece stepped away from the lectern toward his seat. Brock met him with a handshake and a hug.

33

"You'd think the vote would be in by now?" Bainbridge stopped his pacing to look at the clock over the file cabinet. It showed 4:11. Shannon and Lena sat watching him pace.

In Lena's office, the three of them had been waiting for the outcome of the ratification meeting since just after one in the afternoon. Lena sat at her desk with a laptop opened while Shannon sat in one of the plush chairs swiping away at her cell phone. They both ignored Bainbridge, who for the umpteenth time made a remark about the waiting. He and Shannon had arrived from Toronto where they had been since the tentative agreement had been made the previous Sunday, poring over the details of the deal. Lena had worked all week.

"I'm sure the union needed a lot of time to sell the contract to the membership." Lena offered up, closing the laptop and leaning back in her chair. "The mood on the floor was mixed," she paused, not having mentioned this during the last few hours, "with probably the majority against the agreement."

Shannon jerked her head up from scanning the cell phone. "How can you say that when they'd only have seen it today?"

"Because it made it on the floor." Lena smirked. Shannon's stunned expression brightened Lena's face. Bainbridge observed the two women, ready for a cat fight. He was not surprised by the revelation. In fact, he had orchestrated the appearance of the paper on the shop floor showing the highlights of the agreement. Being uncomfortable about the proposal being acceptable to the union negotiating committee, he sought to infuriate the membership. Hearing the plant manager say that they were unhappy about the deal eased some of the tension, but not all.

"Why can't they see that no one loses with this contract?" Shannon stood and started pacing, her hands exploding from her head. "I considered every scenario when I came up with this version to avoid taking something away from them."

"Forcing people to retire" — Lena counted with her fingers — "bringing back those on lay-off at half the wage, stopping their retirement plan." Lena held up three fingers. "That's not taking something away from them?"

Shannon turned around sharply to reply but was held back by Bainbridge stepping in front of her. He had doubted the proposal when first presented to him as one that would be workable but was convinced by Silva that it was exactly what was needed to divide the membership. Now he was being told that it would be defeated. He couldn't let on that's what he wanted.

"That agreement is similar to many others in the industry over the last few years." Bainbridge turned to face Lena, standing with arms outstretched, blocking Shannon. "The Big Three have adopted the same principle even though they don't call it two-tier." He was referring to the new wage structure the Big Three, Ford, Chrysler and General Motors, had adopted after the recession. Citing the elimination of two-tier wages, they implemented a progressive wage for new hires, starting at a lower hourly rate than those senior employees, increasing each year until they reach full pay scale within ten years.

Lena stood and came around the desk. "It won't work here because it affects everyone, no matter whether they stay, go, or return." She leaned back against her desk, hands on her desk supporting her and legs crossed. "You alienated all that had a stake in this. I'm sure you're going to have to go back to the table." She shrugged. "Just my opinion."

Shannon stepped out of the shadow of Bainbridge. "They won't get anything better than this. The only other option is getting what the other plants have. D'you think they'll go for that?"

Bainbridge leaned up against the file cabinet watching the two women verbally spar. Going away from the corporate structure had been a gamble. What scared him was that the membership would accept this alternative. Especially with the incentives, those forced to retire could reap a large payout with their pension, those on layoff would get a huge signing bonus, and those maintaining their wage have nothing to lose. If the contract was accepted, closing the plant would be almost impossible. He hoped Silva was right.

Lena's cell phone chirped before she could reply. She reached back to fetch her phone off the desk and swiped the face. A smile formed as she read the text. She looked up at Bainbridge and Shannon. "They voted it down."

34

The euphoria of the ratification meeting didn't last long. Reece's return to work was met with slaps on the back and handshakes from many of the employees. Brock, who had returned to the midnight shift, greeted him in the union office, but that's pretty well where the celebration ended. Scott Wilson reported to the office only to assign Reece his duties for the week while he spent time at the Local and Regional Offices trying to repair what Reece had caused. No one was assigned to cover Reece's duties, leaving him alone in the office, and there wasn't much to do. Taking advantage of the free time, Reece pored over the tentative agreement that had been turned down, making notes of changes he would propose when they resumed talks. By Wednesday afternoon he sought a break from the solitude of the office and wandered around the shop floor, his second tour of the day. The people's mood had changed. Rumours spread like wildfire, and they were beginning to question their decision. Some were afraid, others angry about the possibility that the company would punish them for their actions. The gossip ranged from stricter disciplinary action being taken for missing time, or being late, to the ultimate penalty being running out the present contract and being locked out in the New Year. Reece spent most of the day assuring them that none of that would happen. His confidence waned when he spoke with Scott about any progress in resuming talks and was told that the company hadn't responded to any overtures by the union. Heading home at the end of the day, Reece felt despondent about his role in all of this.

Pulling into the driveway beside Shannon's Mustang, Reece prepared to deal with personal matters. She left for Toronto right after the tentative agreement had been reached and had only texted him during her absence. His posed queries about their future were answered with clipped responses of 'We'll talk'. He passed through the gate to find her relaxing on the lawn alongside Hurley. His breath was taken away at the sight of her wearing only a halter top and shorts, stretched out on a lounge chair, soaking up the sun. She raised her arm over her head, pointing back to the patio.

"There's a cooler full of beer. Grab me one, will you?" She eyed him above her sunglasses.

Reece stepped up to the deck, opened the cooler and grabbed two bottles of Corona. He saw the cut limes in a baggie amongst the ice, taking two out. He popped the caps and inserted the lime in the open neck of the bottles. Returning to Shannon, who had sat up on the lounge chair, an empty beer bottle lying on the ground, he offered her one and moved a lawn chair over to the shade of the elm tree right at the edge of the sun.

"No better way to get reacquainted than with a couple of beers." She saluted him before pushing the lime down the neck of the bottle and taking a sip.

Reece pushed his lime down, placed his thumb on the opening, and tilted the beer over while he collected his thoughts. Where to start?

He returned a weak smile to her gesture, remaining silent.

"Reece this isn't going to be easy so don't give me the silent treatment." She took off her glasses.

"Where do we begin?"

"Good question." She brushed away a strand of hair from her face. "How about we start by talking about work? How are things going?"

"No, I don't want to talk about that." Reece avoided her eyes by looking at his beer foam up. "We both know what's going on and I'm more concerned about us right now." He peered over at her.

"Okay, then what do you think we should do?" She said, gesturing with her hand for him to start. "You ask the questions, and I'll answer." She tilted the beer to her mouth.

With the uncertainty of the resumption of talks, he didn't want to get into a debate about the outcome of the vote. He also wasn't sure about her plans with her law firm. The importance of their relationship superseded any of that, at least to him.

"Do you still value our marriage?" He couldn't use the word love.

"Of course I do. There was never an issue about you and me."

"But a marriage can only last with honesty. Can I trust you to be honest with me about what you do?" This was the moment of truth for him.

She took a swig of her beer. "I admit that was a mistake, and I'm sorry. There was never any intent to deceive you or hurt you." Her sad expression, puppy-dog eyes and frown, seemed genuine, he hoped.

"You never expected me to discover what you were doing?" He tested her. "Need I be suspicious of everything you do?"

Shannon cracked a wry smile. "Need I ask you the same?"

Reece was startled and blurted out a response. "What does that mean?"

"C'mon, I'm not blind." She teasingly bent down to place her beer on the ground. She stretched out her legs and leaned forward, smiling as she continued. "Lena is a very pretty woman. Intelligent, too. I could easily see how her charm could win you over."

Reece felt warm and it wasn't because of the summer heat. "There's nothing there. I won't lie to you, we spent some time together, but there's no interest in carrying it any further." Hurley had ambled over to him. He petted the dog, keeping his eyes on Shannon.

Shannon raised her eyebrows. “I’m not blaming you. I’m just pointing out that you kept secrets, too.”

“It was totally different circumstances.” He tried to reason. “You had intent, a purpose, which you kept from me.” He defended. “Ours was a moment of loneliness that we both shared, that’s all.”

“Don’t be so sure about her intent,” she remarked. “We women can tell when another is smitten with someone.”

Reece wanted the conversation to steer away from Lena. “It doesn’t matter what you think, I’m telling you she means nothing to me.” He prepared himself to gauge her response, whether truthful or another lie. He stopped petting Hurley. “Tell me the same thing about your intentions with respect to what you were doing.”

“I don’t need to do that anymore,” she whispered as she reached for her beer.

“What do you mean?” Reece asked, sweating even though he was in the shade.

Shannon took a long gulp before replying. “I quit Ellis and Unger and accepted a position with International Metal Products.” Reece was startled for the second time in less than five minutes. He didn’t know what to say.

“Bainbridge and Silva were very satisfied with my work,” she pressed on, aware she had shocked him. "Even though an agreement wasn't reached, they felt that the options I provided were something they could use within their company. They have always used lawyers from corporate firms in the cities where they purchased a facility or negotiated a new contract." She paused, taking a sip of her beer. "They believe it's time they had their own lawyer to deal with the factories they own. That's me." She smiled.

"What about Ellis and Unger?"

"I met with the president of the firm and handed over all the files on those lawyers who hadn't complied with my first attempt," she said. "It's his problem now."

"What about us?" Reece returned to the matter at hand.

"I figured you could join me in the New Year." She stared at him.

35

The three semis pulling flat-bed trailers loaded with moving equipment drove into the shipping driveway of Border City Stamping on Thursday afternoon. Reece was awakened by a phone call early Friday morning by Brock alerting him to a meeting being held with the membership. Reece was able to get there a few minutes before it started.

The cafeteria had been set up with rows of chairs now filled with employees from the midnight shift and those early for the day shift. Many men opted to stand along the wall where Reece and Brock were situated. Bainbridge and Lena entered the room and proceeded to the lectern set up just inside the doorway. After a few seconds of conferring with each other, Bainbridge stood at the microphone.

"This meeting will be short and there won't be any questions to follow." He laid out a paper on the lectern. "Due to the recent rejection of an offer for a new contract, Industrial Metal Products has decided that the future of Border City Stamping is unstable and threatens to disrupt the production of auto parts to our customers in the future. The decision has been made to move equipment from this facility to other similar facilities in the corporation to satisfy the future production requirements of those customers. During this transition time, it is expected that BCS employees will abide by their present collective agreement and maintain required production standards as is necessary. The time frame set out to accomplish this feat is to coincide with the expiration of the existing collective agreement. The company will coordinate with the union the requirements necessary to achieve the closure of this plant."

Bainbridge folded up the paper, smiled at the stunned audience, and then exited the room.

The crowd burst into loud chatter, some directing their questions to the union representation in the room, Reece and Brock, and some to Lena, who stood at the lectern trying to calm them. Scott Wilson hadn't shown up, too busy at the local to be present. They were able to dismiss the crowd with a promise of more information on the surprise announcement. Reece and Brock left with Lena to discuss the matter.

"What the hell were you thinking dropping a bombshell like that without consulting us first?" Scott Wilson's face was red with fury. Bainbridge hadn't even sat before he met with the onslaught of anger.

"That was uncalled for and unnecessary," Dunbar weighed in on the matter. "That threat won't work to get us back to the table."

Bainbridge calmly took a seat at the middle of the table in the boardroom. Lena was already seated at one end of the room, having come here with Reece and Brock directly from the scene in the cafeteria. Wilson and Dunbar showed up around a half hour later and immediately called Bainbridge to join them.

"That wasn't a threat. It's the direction the company has decided to take considering the setback." Bainbridge sat sideways from the table facing the four men still standing. "There was no need to consult you. Your opportunity has come and gone."

Dunbar stepped in front of the others. "You can't be serious about this? There's still time to come to some agreement."

Bainbridge frowned and shook his head. "No, we made it quite clear that the offer was the best we could do. You decided."

"Bullshit, Bainbridge!" Brock tried to lunge forward but Reece held him back. "You planned this all along."

"What do you mean, 'planned this'?" Bainbridge toyed with them all. "I planned to have your membership vote no?" He chuckled. "I'd like to hear how I was able to do that?"

Reece moved past Dunbar. "You had no intention of keeping this plant open. If the agreement had been ratified, it would just have taken a little longer for you to close it."

Bainbridge smirked. "That's what made you speak up against the committee's consensus?"

Reece was taken aback by the comment. The other men turned their attention to him. "A visit to Motor Craft Industries convinced me. Their expansion plans seem to include work from here or destined for here."

Bainbridge leaned forward. "I heard about your little foray. Whatever happens there should have no bearing on the operations here."

"That's not what we were told," Brock growled.

"Are you denying that the work that they're preparing for isn't work we already perform here?" Reece cut in. "And that work that we bid on and won a contract for, is slated for there, also?"

Bainbridge tapped his fingers on the table. He looked around at everyone before continuing. "Every job we have goes through a process of evaluation that determines the highest return. If a larger profit can be realized producing the product elsewhere, then that's where the product will go."

Dunbar interrupted, "Bainbridge, don't hand us that bullshit. We're smarter than that." Bainbridge arched his eyebrows. "That work was bid on years ago and is determined where it's produced long before now. Border City Stamping won the bid and produced parts today because they are profitable. Any change in the allocation of work comes because of some other reason. Just tell us."

Bainbridge sat up. "Okay, let's see if you understand. The rejection of the contract that we believe could have brought Border City Stamping in line with our overall structure has caused senior management to fear a ripple effect on the other operations. If we were to re-negotiate, obviously a more costly agreement, then the other plants would seize that as an opportunity to seek similar contracts. We'd find ourselves with an internal battle instead of competing against our rivals, thus affecting our ability to secure more work. We're not prepared to go down that road. The alternative is to cease operations here and maintain our corporate structure."

"Wow, you guys really spin a story," Brock gushed out. "You use the excuse of a 'corporate structure' to suck your workers dry."

"Regardless of how you feel about it, it's how we run a profitable enterprise," Bainbridge stood. "We've had success running our company under this corporate structure and we don't intend to change it."

"Even if another proposal would come up with the same savings as the last?" Reece asked. Less than twenty-four hours after Shannon had implied about the plant closure ending any chance of negotiations resuming, he sought to reverse that decision.

"Any proposal other than the one rejected would mean we acquiesce to give in to you." Bainbridge stepped to the door. "That's not going to happen." He opened the door and left.

36

"Can they close up shop within four months?"

Brock asked his father with concern in his voice. They sat in the living room of the house he grew up in. Not much had changed. The two-storey wartime house still felt like home and showed it. Brock sat on the brown leather couch that was bought about a year before he left. Gil was in the familiar recliner adorned with crocheted arm sleeves that covered the cigarette burns. The weekly maid service maintained the home, but Brock noticed the piled-up dishes in the sink of the open concept kitchen from the living room. He'd have to remember to ask his wife, Margaret, to come over. His sister Bonnie lived in the city but didn't seem to visit that often. Other than that, he assumed the other rooms were clean. The two bedrooms upstairs hadn't been used in a while. Bonnie had left home first, then when Brock moved out, his room was taken up shortly after by Reece. It was used for about five years; the time it took Reece to graduate university. That had been over ten years now, Brock thought. His parents' bedroom was on the main floor but had only been used by his father the last four and a half years since his mother had passed. He couldn't imagine what mess was in there. He turned his attention to what his father had to say about the situation at work.

"It's been done before." Gil was wearing a jogging suit even though it was over ninety degrees inside. The windows were open but didn't offer much relief. There was no air conditioner.

"But we're making money for them. How can they think of closing it up?" Brock was trying to keep cool by drinking cold beer.

"I've seen it happen to the best of outfits," Gil said. "When they decide it's time, profitability is not a factor in their decision."

"Then how do we stop it?"

Gil frowned. "It's difficult to do today. They've made it impossible for the union to fight back with the language in the contracts. You must abide by the current agreement and from what you've told me, they'll be closed before you can strike."

Brock felt drained by the situation. The sudden announcement had caught everyone off guard and the discussions by the union executive had concluded that there was nothing that could be done to prevent IMP from following through with the closure. He had come to see his father for advice.

"Unfortunately, the union had bargained away our only tool," Gil continued. "When I first got elected to a union position at BCS we used to walk out for everything. That was way back in the seventies."

"What do you mean 'walk out', Pop?" Brock hadn't heard the phrase used.

"During those times we had to fight for all sorts of things." Gil counted his fingers, "There were safety issues in the plant, and there were health concerns over types of chemicals and solvents being used, and then there were times we fought to get people hired full-time over the company using temps," he paused while holding his fingers. "And then there were disciplinary action taken against employees that sparked walk outs. Someone would be suspended, and the people would just walk out, wildcat we used to call it, to show support for that person. It happened all the time."

"What about a situation like a closure? Did they walk out for that?"

"There weren't many of those at that time," Gil reflected. "A couple, I recall, we formed up a bunch of people to stage a wildcat to prevent a closure but in those cases, most of the workers in the affected plant got another job elsewhere and we never really cared about the company going belly-up. By the mid eighties and into the nineties the auto industry was riding high and there was work for everybody." Gil grimaced and huffed. "But that's when they got us."

Gil held out his empty bottle. Brock took it, and his own, into the kitchen where he replaced them with two others from the fridge. He returned to the living room, taking his seat after handing over one to his father. Gil swigged before continuing with his reminiscence.

"The companies were making money, and we were securing pretty good contracts for the workers. By then I was at the local and heavily involved with negotiations for the units."

"I remember you being gone a lot when I was in high school." Brock recalled those tumultuous years. "Mom had to come to the school quite often without you."

"I know you got short changed, son," Gil replied. "But you turned out okay. It toughened you up."

"Thanks Pop." Brock saluted his old man with his beer and took a gulp.

Gil followed suit, placing the bottle on the side table amongst his pill bottles. "Where were we?"

"Something about the company got an advantage on you in negotiations, I think?" Brock replied.

"Yeah, sort of. They gave us almost everything we asked for; raises, benefits, pension increments, you name it we got it. But they wanted something back." Gil pointed at his son. "They wanted improvements on the language in the collective agreements. This included work arrangements introducing cells which limited seniority rights when selecting jobs and the most important issue for them, the condition that disrupting production was no longer acceptable. They bargained to outlaw strikes during negotiations, ban illegal walkouts, sit downs or slowdowns within the plant that would affect productivity. We agreed to it all in good faith believing there was no need for them anymore because we had built a partnership with the companies in their future success. Man, did we ever get taken."

"How did that hamper your power to negotiate?" Brock was confused. "You would think the companies wouldn't feel threatened and would find the process more favourable in coming to a fair agreement."

"We thought so too, but just as I was retiring, things changed," Gil said. "After September eleventh, the economy began to falter. Companies were claiming losses and couldn't afford the contracts they had signed, so they say. Negotiating became difficult and they used that provision against us."

"How so?"

"We couldn't hinder production while negotiating, a tactic we used in the past when fighting them, because of the language," Gil paused. "They would stretch out the talks almost to the end and just before it, they would lock us out instead of us going on strike."

Brock was really confused. "But that's the same thing, isn't it?"

"No, it isn't, because they were preparing for it!" Gil's smirk indicated doom. "They would stockpile inventory by working overtime, Saturdays, and increase production rates and we couldn't do anything about it because of the language. They got what they needed to lock us out for a time knowing that most workers couldn't survive without that paycheck every week. They outlasted us. Concessions became the norm, supposedly helping these companies through hard times, but really it was just to bring us down. Those that wouldn't bend closed. You've seen that happen the last ten to fifteen years, Brock."

Brock realized what his father was saying. The union had been duped with short term gains only to lose in the long run. Border City Stamping could become one of those statistics.

"How do we reverse it, Pop?"

"I don't know if we can, son. I think it would have to take a miracle to get them to return to the table." Gil shook his head. "Too bad we didn't know their true intent before negotiations. It might have changed Reece's mind."

"I should have seen it coming," Brock spoke under his breath.

"What's that, Brock?"

"Nothing, Pop." Brock shook his head. "I know what needs to be done."

37

"Uncle Reece!" The excited squeal could only have come from one person. Reece caught up Gillian, who had raced by the throng of people in the park, to jump into his arms. Brock, Margaret, and the twin teenage sisters, Evie and Jackie, followed. Even though he wasn't blood kin, Reece had always been considered an uncle to the girls. "Have you been on any rides yet?" Gillian hugged him around the neck.

"No, I haven't, yet." Reece swung Gillian to face the family. "Hi, Margaret, girls." The girls resembled their mother; tall, slim, tanned complexion, and flowing blonde hair. He nodded to Brock.

Gillian giggled and leaned into Reece. "Daddy almost threw up on the Tilt-a-Wheel.

But I loved it." She glanced beside Reece. "Who are you?"

Reece placed Gillian down. "This is Lena." He blushed introducing her.

Lena knelt. "Hello, Gillian. You love coming to the carnival, I bet?"

Gillian smiled. "It's the best part of the summer. I get to do everything at one time." She waved her hand to indicate the surroundings. The Tecumseh Corn Festival was one of the last of the county's fairs of the season. They met at the entrance to the *Carter Shows* section of the festival.

"I guess we'll have to try some of those rides then." Lena pointed to Gillian. "Which ones do you think we should try?"

Gillian clung to Reece, staring up at him. "Where's Aunt Shannon?"

Reece cracked a smile. "She had to go away for a few days." Shannon was in Toronto looking for an apartment and setting up in her new office. He sought help from the others by arching his eyebrows.

"Lena works with me and Uncle Reece, Gillian." Brock carried a green stuffed frog Gillian had picked when he won at the *Shooting Gallery* booth. "She's never been to the Corn Festival before. What ride do you think they should go on?"

Gillian screwed up her face trying to think of one. Before she could answer, Evie spoke up. "Maybe the *Tunnel of Love* would be appropriate." The two sisters grinned. They knew about Uncle Reece's situation.

Gillian shook her head. "No, I think Uncle Reece would like the bumper cars." She tugged his hand. "You always have a hard time riding Daddy's four-wheeler. You could practice with the bumper cars." Everyone laughed.

"How are you enjoying the festival?" Margaret directed her query at Lena.

"There's a lot to see." Lena rose, matching Margaret's height. The cut-off jeans and Miami Dolphins muscle shirt helped to display her attractive features. "After checking out the rides, we're going to stay for the concert. Are you taking it in?"

"No, we're just going to get something to eat." Margaret wore a sundress. "The girls love the corn here and this guy" — she playfully punched Brock in the shoulder — "needs his pulled pork and poutine."

Gillian reached out for her father. "Come on before the corn's all gone."

As they parted ways Brock reminded Reece. "Don't forget I'll be over to get Hurley in the morning." The O'Rourke's faded into the crowd.

“Who’s Hurley?”

“My dog.” Reece explained as he’d never mentioned Hurley or had Lena to the house for her to know. This weekend was the first opportunity they had to get together since the long weekend in August, with Shannon being at the house shortly after the rejection of the tentative agreement. Reece had purposely avoided contact with Lena, even at work, not wanting to encourage a relationship. But, when Shannon left mid-week to Toronto, Reece let it slip out during a meeting with her concerning a safety issue in the plant. The next day, Lena had mentioned the Tecumseh Corn Festival during a chance meeting in her office, stating that she lived nearby, and that the town was very crowded with visitors to the event. Before he knew it, he offered to show her around the fairgrounds, the Lacasse Park being the location. “Brock thinks I’ll neglect him next week because I’ll be so busy at work. They’re going to their cottage for the week and want Hurley to keep their dog, Rufus, company.” He shrugged his shoulders. “I’m sorry.”

“Nothing to be sorry for.” She took his hand in hers. “They’re a nice family.”

Lena was happy to be seen with Reece, embarrassed as he was, believing there were some mutual feelings between them. She had enjoyed their brief time together, wanting to explore the possibility of nurturing it further. She wasn’t sure about what was going on with

Shannon, but just the fact he was with her now gave her hope that something could come of this. They continued their walk to the rides. "Why're you going to be so busy?"

"I'm alone in the union office next week." He appreciated her nonchalant attitude. "Scott's at the local preparing for next week's Labour Day festivities and I'm left holding the fort."

"Good thing it's only a four-day work week. I'm looking forward to getting away next weekend." She noticed his puzzled expression. "I'm going to Chicago to visit some friends...but I'll be back." She nudged him, getting him to smile.

"Look, I promised you a good time and instead we're talking about work and," he glanced over his shoulder, "that awkwardness...um..."

"Forget it, Reece." She leaned in to peck him on the cheek. "If you're not comfortable here, my place is only a short walk from here." She squeezed his hand.

"There are a lot of people who aren't too happy about how the union executive has handled the justifiable anger of the workers…and are throwing their support behind the most militant leaders in the plant."

Quote from a union steward at Ford, 1952

PART 4

SEPTEMBER

(LABOUR DAY)

38

Reece Kincaid marched alongside thousands of others in the Labour Day Parade, but he may as well have been alone. Marshalling began at nine in the morning with Reece joining those affiliated with Local 123. He was always amazed at the turnout for this day of union labour celebration. It didn't only involve autoworkers. Every sector of the labour movement was represented in this march. Nurses, electricians, plumbers, civil service employees and more joined in the event each year showing solidarity for their unions. Even the police officers who lined the route, blocking the side streets from traffic interfering with the parade, showed their support for the union movement by displaying their unit flags and handing out candy to the many children who participated with their parents in the parade. There wasn't any conflict during this event, only recognition for each other's union and its struggles to maintain a standard of living for the members. This was the one day of the year that union solidarity was truly displayed.

There were not many people from BCS attending, as in years past, and he attributed that fact to the recent failure in getting a contract. It was easy to blame the union, their protest being non-attendance in this function. For Reece, not only did it seem those fellow workers who did show avoided him as if he had the plague, but the Local executive hadn't even asked him for assistance. Previous marches saw him helping organize the marchers and being a volunteer for one of the booths at the Fogolar Furlan Club, the eventual destination of the event. Not this time. The march set off on time, ten o'clock, making its way south on Walker Road to the E.C.Row Service Road heading west to the Italian club hosting the event. Reece was just like one of the ordinary workers showing his support for the union. The weather cooperated with a balmy 23 degree Celsius with a slight breeze making the trek enjoyable for all the participants. Banners, flags and hand-held signs bobbed its way down Walker Road for the forty-five minutes it took to complete the journey. Reece used the time to think about all that was happening in his life.

The long Labour Day weekend not only signified the end of summer but, for Reece, the end of a relationship. Shannon had returned on Friday from her search for an apartment and borrowed his truck to get a U-Haul trailer. He helped her pack up all the things she was taking; boxes and bins of her clothing, the complete bedroom set, a couch and lounge chair newly purchased and delivered that morning from Leons, and one small box of kitchen items. She tried to talk him into going with her, for a few days, not only to help her unload, but to show up at the Faculty of Education at the University of Toronto on Tuesday in the hope that an opening was available. He declined. His heart wasn't in it, he said. It was only now, during the march, that he realized he meant being with Shannon, not the idea of going to teacher's college. He couldn't come to terms with her activity within Ellis and Unger, the blackmailing of fellow colleagues. He also could not, in good conscience, be associated with IMP if he stayed married to Shannon. There was no way he could abandon his loyalty to BCS and all the membership. She gave a parting comment that maybe four months apart would be a good thing for them. They could sort out their feelings for one another and come to some conclusion, like a separation. She even suggested that he would be welcomed in the New Year. They parted with a promise to keep in touch, with her returning his Jeep the following weekend.

Reece wandered around the grounds of the Fogolar Furlan Club with the many tents housing food booths, stands displaying free items like water bottles, t-shirts, hats and pins, that displayed the union logo, and play areas for the many children in attendance. It had been a long time since he was able to do this having manned any one of these booths in the past. The main stage was set up near the soccer nets at the north end of the field with volunteers putting out folding chairs in front for those wanting to hear the many dignitaries prepared to speak. Reece found himself strolling that way when he met up with a couple of BCS workers.

"Hello, Paul." Reece shook hands with Paul Fields, wearing long jeans, t-shirt and safety boots. Reece nodded at the other man. "Nick, how're things going? I didn't see you guys in the parade?"

Nick Campo had his hands in his jean pockets. "We just got here. Parking is ridiculous...we found a spot almost at the mall." He cocked his head in the direction of the Devonshire Mall. His hair hung down to his shoulders, touching the black t-shirt emblazoned with the band 'KISS' logo, its four members painted faces adorned across the letters. He wore safety boots, also.

"You two came together?" Reece figured Nick had come alone, being single and a loner. He wasn't sure about Paul. "Paul, I saw Cherise and the kids in the parade."

"Yeah, they walked in the parade." Paul craned his neck as if searching the crowd for his family. "I had some things to do."

"Yeah, we were too late to join the march." Nick shuffled his feet, almost turning away from Reece. "We needed to pick up..."

"I helped Nick move," Paul interrupted, cutting off Nick. "He got another apartment."

Reece found it odd that Paul would be helping Nick. The two weren't known to chum around. Nick had his head down while Paul continued the conversation. "They're around here somewhere. The kids are probably playing some games."

Reece nodded his head and asked. "Have you guys seen Brock?"

Nick blurted out, "You mean here?"

"Yeah," Reece squinted at the two men as Paul nudged Nick ever-so-slightly. "Unless you've seen him somewhere else?"

"No, no, we haven't seen Brock." Paul feigned looking over the crowd.

Reece was wary of their nervousness. "It's just that he never misses this parade. For that matter, I haven't seen Gil either." He sensed something amiss. "What's going on, boys?"

"What do you mean, Reece?" Paul adjusted his glasses. "Just like you, we're here to celebrate the labour movement. Are you hanging around to hear the speeches?"

"Yeah, I am," Reece replied, trying to read their body language. "How about you?"

"Well, I got to find the girls but, yep, I hope to hear what they say." Paul took off his ball cap and wiped his brow with his forearm. "I should go find them so I can get back in time." He pointed to the stage.

Reece turned to see men setting up chairs and a microphone on the stage. Off to the side, a number of dignitaries mingled about, preparing to make speeches. Reece turned back to see Paul whispering something to Nick before Paul waved at Reece.

"I gotta go." Paul disappeared into the crowd.

Nick grinned. "Do you think they'll mention us, you know, our situation at the plant?"

"I don't know, Nick." Reece noticed beads of sweat on Nick's upper lip. "What's wrong Nick? You and Paul looked out of sorts?"

"Nothing, really." Nick finger-brushed his hair back. "Just interested in what they have to say about our plant closing."

Reece replied, "I talked with Scott before the parade, and he said there was nothing on the slate concerning Border City Stamping." He looked away towards the stage. "I believe there is nothing going on to re-open negotiations." Reece didn't want to reveal that the union had given up trying to re-open talks. Instead, they were planning on approaching the company, IMP, for a closure agreement. The national office sent out feelers to IMP's President, Max Silva, about settling the matter concerning the pension, a benefits package and a buy-out agreement. There hadn't been a response, yet.

"We'll see about that," Nick said under his breath as he made his way through the crowd, away from Reece.

Reece was suspicious of the encounter, the two men's appearance together giving him a weird sensation that something wasn't right, their body language feeling forced and reserved. He shook his head, erasing any concern over the chance meeting, and walked toward the chairs set up in front of the stage.

39

Labour Day evening

Lena had just returned from the long weekend in Chicago visiting friends from her college days and had finally settled down to open the laptop. She had left the Windy City after having lunch with her computer friend who had unlocked the Surface Pro laptop she had discovered in the file cabinet belonging to the previous manager Theo Epstein. She was embarrassed when he told her the password was ‘Negotiations’. The four and half-hour drive along with a stop at the Meijer store in Ann Arbor, Michigan to stock up on groceries had her not arriving home until after eight in the evening. By the time she squared everything away she finally sat down at the kitchen table with a glass of wine to open the laptop. What she had so far seen in the last three hours only confused her more when her cell phone rang. She hesitated to answer when she saw the caller's identity.

The security guard at the plant, in a panicked voice, informed her of the takeover of the plant by the employees. He told her that the gates were blocked off, the turnstiles locked and that a couple of the employees involved were loitering on the grounds inside the fence and had told him they were taking over the plant to force the company back to the negotiating table. Other employees, showing up for work and locked out, were setting up picket lines at the driveways. The guard didn't know what to do but to call her. She told him to do nothing until she got there. After hanging up, she mulled over what to do. She decided not to call Bainbridge or Wilson until she saw for herself what was happening. She put away the laptop, the information forgotten for the moment, the present crisis taking precedent. She dressed up in a more formal attire than her shorts and tank top and hurried out of the apartment. It only took eight minutes to get to the factory where she found out that everything the guard had told her was true.

Lena finally made a call, ringing up Reece.

The chaos was evident as Reece parked the Mustang on the side of the road in front of Border City Stamping. The darkness of the night was illuminated by the strobe lights flashing from the two police cruisers, butted bumper-to-bumper facing each other, in front of the employee entrance, already blocked off by the workers of the midnight shift surrounding the steel barrels lit with fire. He stepped out of the car and noticed further down the road another group manning another lit steel drum in front of the shipping driveway, the smell of burning wood heavy in the air. Heading toward the police cruisers, Reece recognized Lena Kersey and Scott Wilson huddled with four constables. As he neared them, Scott broke away to meet him.

"Have you made contact yet?" Reece spoke to Wilson. During their telephone conversation Wilson had indicated that no one had answered the call to the offices.

"Nothing." Wilson stepped aside pulling Reece with him. He lowered his voice. "I haven't been able to get a hold of Brock."

Reece winced. "Did you try the union office?" Brock was back to work on the midnight shift.

"No answer. Same with his cell."

"You can't assume Brock's a part of this," Reece defended, not believing it. "Have you asked any of these people?" He indicated the throng of employees around the pickets, a low hum coming from their voices breaking the silence of the night. The crackling of the fires sent sparks in the air.

Wilson didn't answer so Reece stepped around him and posed a question for Lena. "Has anybody contacted the company?" She grimaced and shook her head.

Reece separated from them and approached the closest party of picketers at the employee entrance. The midnight shift consisted of only fifty employees: a scaled down crew due to the lack of work to sustain a full three shifts. There seemed to be about thirty of them, equally distributed at the two picket lines, around the burning drums. They told him that the turnstiles were out of order when they arrived for work and that they were milling around, wondering how to get in, when an old guy in a red pickup truck pulled up with the barrels and wood. He instructed them to set up the barriers and that they would be doing it to help save their plant. None of them knew who he was. Reece feared he knew. He strolled over to the other barricade at the shipping driveway only to learn the same thing. These people hadn't been at BCS long enough, mostly low seniority people were assigned the midnight shift, to know who Gil O'Rourke was. Reece took his time returning to the police cruisers and the others waiting for him. He made a phone call only to get the message service. He left a plea to contact him. Finally rejoining Wilson and the others, he asked them what they planned to do. He didn't tell them what he knew or feared.

"I've made a call to Bainbridge and left a message," Lena seemed nervous. "I don't expect to hear anything until daylight."

"I called Brad about the situation," Wilson added. "Hopefully he can speak with Bainbridge before things get out of hand. We need to find out who's in charge of this and stop it right away."

Reece sensed panic in Wilson's voice. "Scott, what we need to do is calm down, find a way to get in touch with those inside, and find the purpose behind their action." Reece noticed the police officer hovering outside of the group. "Officer, what is the intention of the police in this matter?"

"We're here just to keep the peace." The constable waved his hand toward the plant. "We haven't received any instructions concerning what's happening inside."

"I pointed out to them that I'm the plant manager and wasn't prepared to lay any kind of charges, yet," Lena spoke; a wry smile escaped her face. "I don't know how long that will last, though?"

Reece appreciated her delay of action. "Okay, I'm going to walk up to the fence trying to get their attention." He broke away from the group.

"I'll join you." Lena fell into step with Reece. The two trudged past the picketers, through the parking lot partially filled with the picketers' vehicles, and toward the fence.

"You know who's in there, don't you?" Lena had waited until they were far enough away to ask. "What do you think he's doing?"

"I have an idea, but I'll let him say it." Reece stopped at the turnstiles. He tugged on the bars, locked into place, then peered through the darkness at the light in the employee entrance. A shadow cut across the window. Within a minute his phone rang.

"Hello, Brock. What's going on?" Reece answered the phone, on speaker for Lens's benefit.

"Reece, it had to be done." Brock's voice echoed. "Now listen to what I want you to do."

40

"What does he think he's accomplishing by doing this?" Lena asked as they walked away from the fence back toward the police cars. "Bainbridge will use this to close the plant sooner." She concluded, waving her hand back to the occupied factory.

"That's what I'm afraid of," Reece answered. "I don't know what I'm going to say to convince him to end this."

They were crossing the grass before the parking lot when Lena stopped, turning to look back at the building. "How'd they get in?"

Reece stopped, turning back to her. She was looking along the fence, at the turnstiles and then at the entrance to the office parking lot. He tapped her on the shoulder, getting her to turn around, then motioned with his head toward the shipping driveway.

"They crashed through there." He stared at the mangled gate, illuminated by the glow of the fire from the barrel.

"Why is the jitney there?" Lena noticed the jitney backed up against the door of the guardhouse, on the inside of the fence.

"They're blocking any way to get in," Reece stated. Lena glanced back at him. He nodded toward the other entrance, to the visitor/office parking lot. "They blocked that guardhouse, also." Lena intently stared at that gate, the same eerie flame lighting up the gate and moving crane. Reece continued. "They put the crane there to prevent opening the gate." The mechanically operated gate swung to the inside. "I have to hand it to them, they thought of everything." He moved on. Lena stood for a moment more, stunned by the action taken to secure the plant. She had never experienced a takeover of a facility and was at a loss for words. They were serious.

The early morning darkness was giving way to a daylight glow in the east. More employees had shown up for the day shift, rather early, adding to the congestion on the road. A few more police cruisers were positioned at both ends of the street directing traffic for the other businesses whose employees were reporting to work. Replacing the officer of the night was Shawn Bennett.

"Good morning, Reece." Shawn offered his hand. "What's the situation?"

Reece shook hands and faced the others. "Brock is inside. He has some demands."

"What the hell do you mean he has demands?" Wilson barked out while skirting the group to come face to face with Reece. "You get on the phone and tell Brock to lead his people out of there. This is an illegal..."

Reece grabbed Wilson by the arm and pulled him aside. "Shut up, Scott. You're not helping matters by spouting off." They moved away from the group to the rear of the cruiser. "What Brock has done can't just be undone. All those inside are serious about their actions. We must support them."

"But Brock's a union representative and his action will reflect on us." Wilson was very agitated, his eyes wide and his complexion red and moist. "It could be taken that we condone this...this... takeover."

“No, it won't be, Scott. It is what it is. A bunch of employees took it upon themselves to protect their livelihoods. You’ll see, come on.” Reece led Wilson back to the others.

Shawn was leaning back on the cruiser’s hood with Lena facing him, discussing the situation. Reece approached them and brought up Brock’s demands. “Brock wants me to go inside and talk with him. Alone.” Reece directed his attention at Lena. “Have you been in contact with Bainbridge?”

“Yes, just now.” She grimaced. “He wants to send the police in to clear out the trespassers. I convinced him to wait until you returned.”

“Thanks.” Reece took a deep breath. “I’m going back there, and, in the meantime, Brock wants you to see something. Let Bainbridge know, too.” He took out his cell phone and showed it to the others. “Use whatever you can, cell phone, laptop, whatever. Go to ‘YouTube’ and type in “Wildcat’. You’ll see what their purpose is.” Reece nodded with a tight smile, turned, and left to return to the fence.

The picture was shaky and blurred, showing only darkness. Then the video focused on Brock standing in front of an automated press, its yellow painted surface a contrast to Brock's appearance in jeans and a black t-shirt. The shirt was emblazoned in white with the words "We Stand Together" along with the national union logo.

My name is Brock O'Rourke and I'm an employee of Border City Stamping situated on Patillo Road in Lakeshore. Along with several brothers and sisters we have occupied the building, shutting down production while we fight for our livelihoods.

What brought us to this action? The company's disregard for the contributions of the workers to the success of the company and instead its intentions to close the profitable operation by year end. A tentative agreement was rejected by the membership because it sought concessions, forced members to retire, and proposed a divisive two-tier wage structure on the employees. Within days of this vote the company brought in moving equipment and announced the closure of the plant by year end. We had to act. Not just for ourselves but for many of you, too. We stand together against this obvious corporate agenda of attacking workers' rights for a decent wage, benefits for our families and the promise of retirement of our own choosing. We, the employees of Border City Stamping, have stood beside many in our community in their time of need in the past. We were there on your picket lines when you fought for a fair contract. That's what we're fighting for, too. We were there when your place was threatened with closure and stood arm in arm protecting your jobs. We're doing the same by taking over this plant until a fair agreement can be reached.

All we ask is that you support us as we've done for you. Come stand with us against the corporate greed that erodes away our standard of living. Together we can stop this agenda of concessionary demands on the workers while the profits soar for the corporations.

The video zoomed in on the logo on Brock's shirt, 'We Stand Together' and after a few seconds ended.

41

"This is better than expected. Now we can move our timetable ahead for the closure."

Bainbridge was pleased with the development of the takeover and had just finished filling in Silva on the details. They were in Silva's office having coffee while the dawn brightened the room. Unlike Silva's private room on the other side of the door to the right, this office was small and sparsely furnished. Besides the desk, which took up the centre of the room, two armchairs occupied the front of the desk, to complete the seating arrangements. The walls were adorned with certificates showing Silva's education and accomplishments, here in North America and in Europe. There was a bookcase to the left of the desk that held binders of each facility acquired by IMP. The entrance to the office from the lobby was guarded, somewhat, by a secretary just outside of the door. The whole purpose behind the inexpensive appearance was to let visiting clients believe that IMP was not in the business to squander their wealth. It was all a charade.

"It won't be as easy as that, David," Silva spoke for the first time since their greeting. "We need to get that facility back up and running. Our customers will not appreciate having their production halted due to a supplier problem." His expression was very serious. "No, this isn't a good scenario, and we have to avert any setbacks immediately."

Bainbridge was deflated and confused by his boss's comment. "Surely, they can see that this illegal takeover of the plant favours their ultimate desire for the demise of that operation. They must expect a little inconvenience to achieve their goal." He sat in one of the armchairs, holding a coffee. His own office was similar, the reason why he rarely used it, spending most of his time on the road going to those facilities under their ownership. Rooming and working out of hotels was more comfortable.

Silva stood up and walked around to the front corner of his desk, leaned on it facing Bainbridge. "You're mistaken about whom your scheme is for. I assure you our customers could care less about Border City Stamping's future except where it affects their receiving parts."

"Did I not understand that these three companies were interested in seeing them eliminated from the supplier chain?" Bainbridge had assumed he was plotting on the behest of Ford, Chrysler and G.M.

"I never told you that." Silva crossed his arms, a stern expression directed toward Bainbridge. "This action was unexpected, as you have stated, and needs to be rectified before too much damage has been done to our relationship with them. All three are just recently recovering market share lost during the pandemic and can ill afford an interruption in their production."

Bainbridge was getting perturbed about the ambiguity over who he was working for. "Then whom am I trying to please?"

Silva bounced off the desk. "Industrial Metal Products, of course." He stepped away toward the window. The Toronto skyline was welcoming a new day.

Bainbridge stood and followed. Stopping a few feet behind Silva, he pursued clarification. "Max, what's going on here? Don't you trust me with your confidence in knowing who I'm working for?" Not being involved in the purchase of BCS had kept him in the dark too long.

Silva turned around. "David, you have done an admirable job working for *us.* You have succeeded in your task without knowing the identity of those that requested it. It's in your best interest, as well as theirs, that it remains undisclosed." He held up a hand preventing Bainbridge from interrupting. "Now, this disruption needs to be rectified, quickly. How are you going to do it?"

Bainbridge was dissatisfied with the reply but could tell by Silva's demeanour that any further probing would be fruitless. The direct query to the situation was more of an order than a question. "I'm not sure? There was very little detail from Kersey." He reminded Silva of the conversation with the plant manager. "She asked me to wait until there was more information before requesting police intervention."

Silva moved back to the desk, taking his time to reply. Bainbridge only turned to watch. Silva finally pointed at him. "You need to get down there and take control. I'll arrange for you to fly out immediately." Silva paused. "I'll try to assist you by seeking an injunction to have the authorities move in and disperse the trespassers." He reached for his phone.

Bainbridge recognized the meeting was over. Striding to the door he was halted by Silva's voice.

"David," Bainbridge held the door open while looking back. "You're doing an excellent job. Get that plant back running and we'll deal with the other stuff after."

42

Everything was slipping away from him. Shannon's revelation that she had taken the position with IMP had started the dominoes effect of events. The announcement by the company confirmed her hint at the ending of his career at BCS. The backlash he experienced from the union executive for his role in the rejection of the contract and the subsequent decision by the company to close the plant weighed heavily on his mind. Now Brock's action seemed like the 'final nail in the coffin' for the end of Border City Stamping and Reece didn't know what to do. He walked slowly to the turnstiles with a sense of doom and foreboding about the outcome for the workers, both inside and out, as to their future. He felt a huge responsibility to set things right. He pushed against the turnstile, the system unlocked to let him pass. Once inside the fence he heard the turnstile re-lock. He glanced up at the camera on the wall, then made his way to the entrance.

"Hi Reece, not exactly how you thought you'd report to work today, is it?" Paul Fields greeted Reece inside the employee entrance.

"No, it isn't Paul. I never thought I'd be coming into an illegal takeover of the plant."

"It's not something the union would have agreed to." Paul patted Reece on the back. "You've already shown your concern for us. Brock took it upon himself to act." He cocked his head to the shop floor. "I'll take you to him."

The two walked past the change rooms into the plant. Proceeding up the left aisle, they passed workers milling about one of the comfort areas of the zone. The aroma of bacon lingered in the air as breakfast was being cooked on barbecues. Music was coming from a boom-box placed on top of a locker and there were sleeping bags spread out along the floor. Continuing toward the offices, Reece noticed employees at the exits and an unsettling mood from those who acknowledged his presence. There was very little talk and suspicious glances from people who normally chatted away every time they came in contact with him during a workday. There were employees from all three shifts, not just the midnight shift, taking part in this illegal occupation of the factory. How many there were he couldn't tell, aware that some were in other parts of the plant. He followed Paul into the offices, making their way past rooms to the boardroom where Brock sat at the far end.

"Reece, I'm glad you're here." Brock jumped up and extended his hand.

"Brock, what're you doing?" Reece held onto Brock's hand and grabbed his shoulder, squaring off face to face.

Brock smiled. "Right to the point, eh." He braced Reece just as hard. "It's okay, Reece. I couldn't tell you before because you would've stopped me. We're on the same side, you know. Take a seat." His smile remained as he released Reece.

They separated with Reece pulling up a chair along one side and Brock returning to his seat at the end of the table. Paul remained standing at the door.

"Reece, what you did was right by us," Paul spoke up. "This company's action has shown us they don't care about us. We didn't know what to do, so we asked Brock."

"I'm not good with words, Reece, like you, but I know what to do when someone threatens me," Brock said.

“You sounded pretty good in that video,” Reece commented. “That was smart, appealing for outside support for your stance. I never would’ve thought of that.”

Brock smiled and pointed to Paul. “Not my idea... his.”

“You know you’re not the only one with a university degree here.” Paul moved to a chair along the wall. “We figured we needed public support and hope this works.”

Reece acknowledged their strategy but needed to know what they sought. “Support for what? What is the aim for shutting down the operation?”

“We want them to get back to negotiating a fair contract,” Brock said. “They’re going to receive pressure from the Big 3 the longer we stay out, so we want you to convince them to go back to the table” Brock knocked on the table twice. “In here.”

Reece was shocked. “In here? You mean you want them to negotiate in here while you occupy the building?”

“That’s right. You get everyone back here, except Shannon, to sit down and hammer out a contract that would be acceptable,” Brock replied.

“They won’t go for that,” Reece answered. “Hell, Scott won’t agree to hold negotiations while the membership conducts an illegal strike."

"They have no choice," Paul spoke up. "We pay them to represent us and we're demanding that they do their job and get us a fair agreement."

"They'll have no bargaining power with you holding production up." Reece was trying to make them understand the precarious position the union was in. "How can we ask the company to return to negotiations by use of force? They'll refuse just on principle."

"The company will show up," Brock was smug with his comment. "You tell Scott if he and Dunbar don't show" — he pointed to Reece and himself — "we'll negotiate without them."

Reece closed his eyes and shook his head. "Brock, even if I convinced them to come in here, there's no way Bainbridge will."

"Reece, we know Lena's on board with getting an agreement," Brock paused. "Bainbridge will come, too.'

"How can you be sure?"

Brock sat back. "Tell him I said we can finally meet in the plant. He'll come."

43

Reece walked out of the plant an hour later to bedlam. The crowd had grown to a multitude of people carrying flags, signs and banners that stretched out in front of the plant, across and down the street, blocking all traffic either way. There were more police cruisers and officers trying to maintain order. It was a peaceful demonstration in support of the workers inside the plant. 'Enough is Enough – No More Concessions' was one of the phrases seen on placards and t-shirts throughout the crowd. Flags of other locals fluttered in the air and hand-made banners were raised above the crowd pronouncing the slogan 'We Stand Together'. The video had worked.

Reece weaved his way through the people, receiving high fives from fellow workers and being asked about the ones inside. John Prentice stopped Reece while sitting on his motorcycle to ask if any more employees could join them inside. Reece said that wasn't possible. He had been given a tour of the plant, finding that there were quite a few employees involved. How Brock had selected those to join him had Reece concerned. Many of them were considered 'trouble' by management, even by the union, who would not hesitate to cause havoc if they didn't get their way. Yet, there were some Reece was surprised to see, like

Paul, who had a good head on their shoulders. Could these people keep those troublesome ones in line? A camera crew from one of the local television stations tried to question him but he ignored them and forged his way to where he had left the others. Reece found Lena and Scott waiting for him by a police command trailer where Shawn was joined by a commanding officer.

"Reece, this is Captain Mallory." Shawn introduced the officer who offered his hand. He stood as tall as Reece, grey hair that was cut short with a stern face that came with his firm grip. "He's taken over command of this situation."

"Do those people know what they're doing?" Mallory asked. "I don't want to have to go in there by force."

Reece took exception to his comment. "They know what they're doing. They're protecting their interests."

"This wildcat has escalated to an illegal rally that could get out of hand." Mallory had obviously seen the video. "I'm not about to let that happen."

"Then don't," Reece replied. "Take care of the crowd and we'll take care of inside." He stepped past the officer and approached Lena.

"They want negotiations to resume." Reece shook Lena's hand in a friendly way. "Inside."

The gleam in her eye told Reece she understood. “Bainbridge is on his way. He should be here soon.”

“I can’t allow anyone else to go in there,” Mallory interrupted.

Reece snapped back. “Look, officer...”

“Captain,” Mallory retorted.

Reece matched the animosity. “Captain, unless you have orders to break this up, we’re going inside to settle this thing, peacefully. Your job is to control this assembly, peacefully.” Reece waved his hand to indicate the crowd.

The two men squared off, a time bomb ready to go off. The short sound of a police siren broke the tension, and a police cruiser rolled up to the command centre. Bainbridge stepped out of the back.

“I’m glad you’re here, Captain.” Bainbridge strode up. “This has gone on for too long. What action can you take on these trespassers?”

Reece intercepted Bainbridge. “Wait a second, Bainbridge. They have every right to be in there. You forced this on them.”

Bainbridge chuckled. “I forced this on them? That’s ridiculous.” He turned back to the Captain. “When can you clear them from the plant?”

Scott entered the fray. “Only when you have judicial orders to move in can the police intervene.”

“That’s correct,” Mallory confirmed. “Do you have that, sir?”

Bainbridge glared at Reece. “Not yet, but that property belongs to us, and those people have entered illegally.”

“They entered their work of employment,” Reece countered. “They own as much right to that property as you do, maybe more.”

“I can’t act unless I receive an injunction stating cause for police involvement,” Mallory stated. He turned away to enter the command trailer.

Reece watched Bainbridge steam up, waiting for the opportunity to state the demand. Bainbridge moved within the circle of people, glancing at Wilson, then Lena, before settling on Reece. “Okay, Kincaid. I understand you went inside. What’s the scoop?”

“You know what the scoop is.” Reece needed to direct the blame onto the company. “They had no choice but to take over the plant to save their livelihood. You gave them no other option.”

“They chose when they voted down your agreement.” Bainbridge stood firm.

"An agreement you knew wouldn't fly. You were counting on it being turned down." Reece gambled on his intuition. "Well, this is what it produced. We can stand here all day arguing about the past, but it won't solve a thing."

Bainbridge wondered how long he could wait before Silva could get an injunction. "What do they want?"

"To reopen negotiations," Reece answered.

"Not going to happen," Bainbridge replied.

"I think it would be in the company's best interest if they did," Lena spoke.

Everyone was surprised by her comment. They all wanted to hear more.

"I believe Mr. Silva will be satisfied with an agreement instead of a confrontation," she continued. "Bainbridge, I think you should call him to get instructions."

Bainbridge looked perplexed. He walked away with his cell phone in his hand. Lena gave a curt smile to the others. Nothing was said for a few minutes while Bainbridge conferred with Silva. He returned to the group.

"How soon can you get your people together?" Bainbridge directed his query to Wilson.

"It's getting Noonan here that will take up time," Wilson answered.

"He's not needed," Bainbridge replied. "He'll keep in touch through the phone and with Silva."

"Then you have everyone here. Dunbar can make it from the regional office within a half hour." Wilson was sweating.

"Maybe we should go there?" Bainbridge suggested. "I assume there is a copy of the agreement at those offices."

"No, he needs to come here," Reece spoke. "We're negotiating inside." He indicated the plant by a jerking of his thumb.

"What?" Bainbridge exclaimed. "No way!"

"That's the condition they put on it," Reece said. "Brock said you can finally meet in the plant." Reece shrugged his shoulders like he didn't know what that meant. He noticed Bainbridge flinch.

Bainbridge ran his fingers through his hair. He turned and walked away.

44

Lena wasn't sure what she had found on the laptop. What she read confused her and scared her. Bringing it along, she hoped to decipher its meaning and possibly avert any further trouble with this plant takeover. The only problem was who she could share this information with and trust that it would be used properly. She had taken the liberty to call Max Silva and imply that she knew about Epstein's attempt to stop the sale of Border City Stamping. She hadn't let on to Silva that she didn't know why.

Lena trusted Reece. Their last time together, the evening of the Tecumseh Corn Festival, he had confided in her. Staying overnight at her place, they talked till the wee hours of the morning. He reasoned that Shannon working against him, for IMP, in the contract talks played a huge part in their separation. Now, her taking the position with IMP sealed their fate, in his mind, as being the final straw to ending their relationship. Lena sensed there was more to the matter than what he was telling her. She didn't press him for further explanation. Now, this wildcat had put an extra strain on him, feeling guilty that his role in the rejection of the tentative agreement had led to this. She wondered how she could show him what was on the laptop without Bainbridge finding out. She had to wait it out.

The five waited for the turnstiles to be activated from inside. It had taken most of the day to get organized; packing clothes for the stay, gathering all the contract material and conferring with their respective higher authorities about the issue. Bainbridge had asked her what she had over Silva, but Lena wasn't comfortable with him. She stated that Silva was concerned about holding up production and left it at that. She could tell Bainbridge didn't believe her. They were escorted by Captain Mallory and Constable Bennett. The crowd had grown and there were three television stations recording the events. As they passed through, a roar of approval rose from the crowd. Paul Fields met them inside the employee entrance, before the shop floor.

"Welcome." He held out a small wicker basket taken from the office. "Could you please put your cell phones in here?"

"What's this?" Bainbridge complained. "You're taking away our phones?"

"They won't be needed since everyone will be face to face," Paul said. "We don't need any distractions from the outside."

Reece placed his phone in. Lena complied and spoke. "Come on Bainbridge, you don't need it. I think you've already been given instructions."

Bainbridge huffed and reached inside his pants pocket for his phone. The others provided their cell phones and were escorted inside where they were met by Brock.

"I'm glad you agreed to talk."

"Did we have any choice?" Bainbridge retorted. "Don't think for a moment this weakens our stance. We're negotiating under duress. It better be good what you propose."

"Anything will be better than what you offered." Brock had stopped their progress into the plant. "I'm sure you've been in tougher spots than this. We're just looking for a fair agreement." He smiled, waved his hand for them to follow, and led them into the plant.

As the group entered the shop floor from the entranceway they were met by a group of employees, armed. They halted their advance. Two men passed by them carrying hunting rifles to guard the employee entrance.

"What the hell is this?" Wilson was the first to respond to the surprise.

Reece grabbed Brock by the arm. "Brock, what're you doing? Why the guns?"

Brock stepped away from the grip and faced the group. "We're not giving up this place without an agreement or a fight. It'll be upon you to make the choice."

"Are you nuts?" Dunbar approached Brock. "We can't condone this activity and negotiate in good faith."

"You can negotiate in good faith." Brock eyed Bainbridge. "This is just insurance against any other plans." Everyone turned toward Bainbridge.

"This really puts us at a disadvantage." Bainbridge had dropped his belongings. "We're now forced to come in as hostages to negotiate a more expensive contract. Talk about fair."

Reece moved forward to speak with Brock, taking him aside and whispering. "Brock, you got your point across. You got us to come in here. There's no need for this."

"You don't know Bainbridge," Brock replied in a whisper. He moved past Reece to address the others. "If you feel uncomfortable about this, then you can go back, but we're not giving up this plant until an agreement is reached."

Everyone looked around at each other waiting for someone to reply. To everyone's surprise Lena stepped forward, heading to the offices. "I don't think we can negotiate on the shop floor. I'm going to the office." She walked past Brock and Reece down the aisle.

For a few seconds the others stood frozen. Brock was inspired by her courage and followed. The others trudged on with Bainbridge bringing up the rear. All along the aisle, workers watched the procession, some armed with rifles or shotguns. Lena sensed their hostility and fear. There wasn't much time. She heard Reece and Brock behind her.

"Brock, why didn't I see this before?"

"If you had, would you've agreed to come in here?"

45

The two sides met in the boardroom a little after eight in the evening. They took up familiar positions on opposite sides of the table. Bainbridge felt helpless. He had never been so undermined before in negotiations as he felt now. Besides not knowing who the interested parties were who requested the demise of BCS, he now had to deal with Lena Kersey holding some power over Silva. Bainbridge had been instructed to entertain a proposal by the union. The only chip he had in his favour was that Silva had obtained an injunction and that it would be acted upon soon. The possibility that the standoff would come to an end before an agreement was reached would enable him to deal with Kersey and Silva separate from the negotiations and clear up this mystery.

"We're not starting all over again, are we?" Bainbridge opened the debate.

"Not necessarily," Brock replied. "Reece has some suggestions to modify the present proposal."

"Who am I negotiating with, Reece now?" Bainbridge smirked.

"The union committee is who you are negotiating with," Dunbar spoke. "We think Reece's points are reasonable and beneficial to both sides." Wilson was nodding his head while Brock smiled.

"I have seen his proposal, and I believe it's workable," Lena said.

Reece opened a file folder, taking out stapled sheets, and distributed them to everyone. Bainbridge ignored the sheet in front of him.

"Part of negotiating is allowing time for the other side to read over any counters before discussions," Bainbridge pointed out.

"You mean instead of ramming it down your throat and saying it's the best offer you can get?" Brock sarcastically replied.

"Much like at gunpoint?" Bainbridge retorted.

"Okay, okay," Reece blurted. "Arguing is getting us nowhere." He stared down Brock before turning his attention to Bainbridge. "Of course, you'll have time to read it over. The points are cross referenced to sections of the tentative agreement so that you can easily compare. How much time do you think you need?"

Bainbridge peered over at Lena who replied, "I think if we had an hour we could reply to your proposal."

Dunbar stood up. "Then we'll leave you alone and return" — he looked at his watch — "at ten." It would allow ten minutes more than an hour.

A phone rang. Brock retrieved his cell phone from his pocket. "Yeah"

Excited chatter could be heard from the phone. Brock's face flushed and his eyes sought Bainbridge. "Hold'em off, I'll be there in a minute." He swiped off and glared at Bainbridge. "You bastard! The cops are moving in."

46

Brock raced out of the room, followed by the others. Busting through the office doors into the plant, Brock hurried toward the shipping drive side of the plant. Reece tried to keep pace, weaving by the machinery, as Brock tried to short-cut his way to the action. The others lagged behind, shouting coming from different areas of the plant. The commotion heightened at the sound of gunfire. Clearing the corner of an automatic three-ton press Reece sighted Nick Campo at the side exit firing into the fading light of day. Return fire caused Nick to duck, sending bullets ricocheting inside the plant. Reece dove for the ground as he watched Brock reach the doorway where Nick lay. Nick again returned fire with Brock joining him with a pistol of his own. Reece turned to see the others kneeling in the aisle as more bullets pinged off the walls. Reece ran to Brock.

"Stop firing!" Reece pushed Brock's gun down. He peeked outside to see three police officers retreating along the driveway to the fence. They disappeared through a gap in the fence and the silence enveloped the plant. He punched Brock in the shoulder. "Is this what you wanted?"

"They're not getting in here without a fight." Brock held his pistol down while he glared at Reece. "I told you not to trust Bainbridge."

"Reece!" A scream pierced the air. Reece turned around. In the aisle, Dunbar, Bainbridge and a few employees were huddled around a body on the floor, Lena kneeling beside the body. Reece ran back. Wilson was on the ground as Lena performed CPR on him. She was furiously pumping his chest and then leaning over to check for a breath. Reece instinctively reached for his cell phone but remembered it had been taken away. He turned to Brock, just arriving at the scene. "Call for help!"

He knelt and took over from Lena. "C'mon Scott, you bastard, you're not getting out of this that easy!" Reece furiously performed CPR. Wilson didn't move. He had suffered a major heart attack brought on by the excitement of the gun battle.

"There's an ambulance just outside the gates," Brock said.

"Get 'em in here, now!" Reece yelled during a pause, while Lena leaned over checking for a breath from Scott. She grimly shook her head.

The ambulance drove up the shipping driveway after the cement blocks were moved by a jitney and the lock was taken off the gate. The police didn't move in. The employees were armed while clearing the way and stood guard while the paramedics went inside. They tried to revive Wilson but to no avail. In the meantime, a discussion by the union representatives and the people involved with the takeover ensued about the continuation of the occupation of the plant.

"We're sorry about Scott, but we're staying." Brock was backed up by many of the others involved in the takeover. "If we leave this plant, we may as well close it now."

"The police aren't going to stay out now that there is a death involved," Dunbar reasoned. "This is an illegal strike, and they have an injunction. We can't fight that."

"Maybe you can't but we will," Nick answered.

"There might be another attempt to end this takeover that could result in injury or death. Do you really want that, Brock?" Dunbar was pale. "Let's walk out of here. You've proven your point, and we'll go back to the bargaining table."

"No, that won't work. If we leave, they'll just continue with their closure," Brock replied. "Scott was willing to get an agreement. His death will mean nothing if we don't stay and get one."

"Are you serious?" Dunbar replied. "We have no bargaining power while you hold this plant. We're not staying under these conditions."

Brock, grim faced, walked past the group toward Bainbridge and Lena. They were watching the paramedics put Wilson on the gurney. Reece followed, the others just turned and watched.

"Bainbridge, you still up to the task?" Brock allowed the paramedics to push the gurney to the opened doors of the ambulance. Two men with rifles followed close by, having a careful watch on the paramedics, afraid they might be undercover police.

"Under these circumstances?" Bainbridge gestured toward the ambulance.

"Brought on by you, I'm sure," Brock challenged.

"None of this would've happened if your people weren't armed," Bainbridge confronted Brock, pointing at Brock's pistol tucked in the front of his pants.

"You could've called it off when you entered."

"I didn't have a phone," Bainbridge smiled.

Brock almost lunged but Reece stepped between the two men.

"That's enough! This isn't solving anything." Reece's arms spread out to prevent a fight. A crowd formed around the men and cooler heads prevailed. Reece continued. "How are we going to settle this?" he questioned both men. After a few seconds of silence Reece asked Bainbridge. "Will you negotiate another contract outside of here?"

Bainbridge hesitated to answer, looking around the crowd. "No, I'll do it here."

Everyone seemed shocked. Nobody spoke but there was a rumbling from the employees on the edge of the crowd. Bainbridge continued. "Let's get this over with. I'm willing to stay and look at your counter."

"I don't think we can," Dunbar spoke. "I'd prefer we take it outside."

"We don't need you; we'll work it out," Brock replied.

The mumblings grew from the employees.

"I'll stay here, Brad." Reece understood the predicament the union was in with this situation. He gave them an out. "You can leave." He turned to face the employees. "Anybody here who wants to leave can also go. Now would be a good time when the ambulance is leaving." He turned back to Dunbar. "We'll keep in touch with our progress and any final agreement will go before the national for approval."

There was a shuffling of feet and more murmuring as the group dispersed. Reece spoke with Dunbar before he headed to the exit. A few employees followed, expressing their fear to the others about staying. The ambulance drove out of the plant toward the gate while the employees walked along the driveway, accompanied by the two men watching the paramedics. The cloud covered night was illuminated by the many lights aimed at the plant, from police cruisers with their coloured strobe lights to the camera lights of the news stations hovering along the road in front of the plant. The gate was opened, the ambulance passed through, while those employees leaving, apologizing to those staying, passed the gate. The gate was re-closed, wrapped with the chain, and padlocked. The two men checked on the repaired fence, the gap closed by another chain tightened around the clipped fence. The procession was watched by the crowd still lingering at the front of the plant and the constables stationed along the fence.

Reece was alone by a work centre when he felt a hand on his arm. Lena appeared by his side. "Reece, you have to come out with me."

"Why?" Reece thought she was staying to complete the talks. Her wide eyes warned him of something else.

She kept her voice low. "I may have found a solution, but I need some confirmation."

"Confirmation on what?" He leaned in closer, also whispering.

"I can't tell you here because I don't have all the details." She squeezed his arm. "You're the only one I think I can trust, and I need help in tracking someone down." She gave him a pensive look.

Reece was torn about his duty, getting a contract and seeing these people safely out of the plant. She decided for him.

"Bainbridge won't settle now. He's just buying time." She tugged on his arm. "We don't have much time."

47

"You knew what you were doing!" Bainbridge punctuated his statement by throwing down the counter proposal on the table.

Brock fumed while standing at the door of the boardroom. They were alone. They hadn't accomplished anything since returning from the incident in the plant. Instead, they had argued about their past relationship. It was agreed that they'd wait for Reece to return from his duty of informing Scott's wife of his death.

"It wasn't to help you close this place," Brock growled back. "I understood that my reports would be used to eliminate needless jobs making BCS more efficient."

"I didn't need you to tell me that," Bainbridge replied. "The foremen know what's going on. No Brock, you knew your reports would undermine the union's stance in negotiations."

Brock shook his head and sat down on a chair along the wall. This confrontation over the role he played the last year informing Bainbridge on employee activity hadn't turned out the way he'd hoped. He had to admit to himself that some of the information he'd passed on could be perceived as traitorous to the union. It wasn't meant that way. He did it to preserve his future and that of most of the fellow employees who still had years to work. Bainbridge used the information during negotiations to point out excesses in the daily operations of the plant. High seniority jobs were discredited as being wasteful where they were shown being non-productive, down time was cited in areas throughout the plant that could be remedied by adding tasks to existing work, and productivity could be increased with the implementation of an eight-hour day to replace the present hourly rate standard that was being produced in lesser time. Brock reported on this environment in the hope that changes would improve the efficiency of the plant and allow for future work to be secured ensuring longevity for employees. The reverse happened.

"And I imagine the money came in handy," Bainbridge continued.

Brock raised his head to sneer at Bainbridge. "I didn't do it for the money."

"Brock, everyone has a price and you're paying for it now," Bainbridge kept turning the screws tighter. "You were so easy to buy off just like the others." He gave a knowing expression. He had a snitch on each shift. "Don't give me that story about solidarity and doing what's best for the membership. It's a dog-eat-dog world out there, I understand."

"It was a mistake on my part," Brock mused out loud. "I'll correct it by getting an agreement." He pointed to the counter proposal on the table.

"Trying to make amends for your disloyalty is the reason for this wildcat?" Bainbridge teased. "What would the membership say if they heard of your contributions?"

"I don't care about that. That contract was no good," Brock toned his voice down. "I realized that when I went to Michigan. Reece was right when he said you had no intention of keeping this plant going."

Bainbridge chuckled. "Yeah, he really helped. Without his speech, I really thought you guys were going to ratify that contract. That would've caused a problem with our plans."

"Why?" Brock sought the truth. "Your plan all along was to close a profitable company? That doesn't make any sense."

“There are other factors,” Bainbridge caught himself before he revealed any more. “The corporate structure...”

“Fuck off!” Brock exploded out of the chair. “Don’t hand me that shit. What other factors?” he approached Bainbridge.

The two men were a foot apart. They stared each other down, hands clenched and stance firm. Bainbridge spoke. “I’ll tell you. It’s not going to make a difference now.” He sat down. “You guys make too much and influence the contracts others seek. You are pushing the industry out of Canada with your demands. We won’t be a part of that.” Bainbridge hadn’t been told by Silva who the interested parties were, but he had figured it had to do with the auto industry. Border City Stamping would be the sacrificial lamb for the next generation.

“Then why did you stay here if you have no intention of negotiating?”

“To talk you out of this nonsense before,” Bainbridge smiled, tapping his fingers on the table.

Brock realized the truth. “You’re expecting the police to try again.”

“It’s just a matter of time, Brock,” Bainbridge explained. “You really think your people stand a chance?”

"You underestimate their will power." Brock stepped toward the door. "They'll defend this place."

48

"That was hard to do."

Reece finally let out a breath as he carried two coffee cups from the counter to the tables of the cafeteria at Metropolitan Hospital. Lena followed, carrying a large handbag over her shoulder. They had just consoled Rita Wilson over her husband's death and Lena had told Reece that they needed a private area to discuss what she had discovered. The cafeteria suited their needs. With the darkness outside, the track lighting and pot lights did little to brighten the cafeteria. There were very few people in the seating area and Reece chose a round table off to the left corner of the room. As they walked to the table, he glanced out the big window to the road lit up by streetlamps and feared what Lena had to tell him. The only other time he was in this room was the night he was told of his father's death. He recalled that fateful evening.

Mom was making supper while we were doing our homework at the kitchen table. There was a knock at the door and Mom went to answer it. There were voices, hardly heard, before Mom came back into the kitchen followed by a police officer. Me and Roxanne were hurried out with Mom to the police car and taken to the hospital. Mom went to the emergency, and a female police officer took us to the cafeteria. It was getting dark. I held my sister's hand the whole time, the doughnuts on the table untouched. Mom and Mr. O'Rourke appeared to tell us the devastating news. Roxanne was bawling, Mom trying to console her, while Mr. O'Rourke stood by me, his arm draped over my shoulder, the weight feeling like I was holding him up. I didn't understand what had happened to my father.

"You were very gracious in telling her." Lena's voice snapped Reece out of his trance. "She took it well, considering." Lena placed her oversized bag on the chair beside her. She tried to ease the tension but knew it was going to get worse.

Reece sat across from her and pushed across the coffee for her. He cradled his cup as he prepared himself to hear what she had to say. "You didn't say a word on the drive here. How bad is the news?"

"I still don't know what I've found, but" — she reached inside her handbag to retrieve a laptop and placed it on the table — "I wasn't sure you were ready to hear it then, you know, with all that happened."

"Well, let's hear it now."

As she flipped open the laptop, she continued. "I found this in the personnel files during our summer shutdown when I was overseeing the changes to the plant." She gave a weak smile and tapped on the keyboard. "I had to send it to a friend to break the sign-in code." She tapped some more, "I didn't see what it held until just before this crisis." She looked away from the screen and stared at Reece. "I don't understand why Mr. Epstein didn't put this information on a flash drive?"

Reece gave a short chortle, placing his coffee down before replying. "Theo was an old-fashioned guy. I never saw him on a computer, laptop or even a cell phone. I'm surprised he had this." He pointed to the laptop. "His assistant manager took care of all the reports, emails and personal contacts and then would print up a report for Theo."

"He had an assistant?" Lena's raised her eyebrows at this revelation.

Reece shrugged and took another swig of his coffee.

Without replying to her question, she got the hint to continue. "Anyways, did you know that Mr. Epstein owned a share of Border City Stamping?" Now it was Reece's turn to raise eyebrows. "And that he tried to stop the sale of

BCS to IMP?" She slid her chair around the table to sidle up beside him, moving the laptop to face him. "He used this as a journal, recording every detail in the negotiations for the sale. The beginning shows how he had obtained the shares of BCS from his uncle, Benjamin Rollins, one of the original owners." The screen showed the opening entry, dated over two years prior.

"That's about the time we heard that the plant was up for sale." Reece pointed at the date.

She scrolled down. "Epstein was given half of the company back in 1995 by Mr. Rollins and the other half was owned by Mr. Ermler until his death in 1999 where his shares were passed on to his sons, Eli and Isaac Ermler."

"Yeah, those were the sons you heard us talk about during negotiations who drained the money out of BCS." His eyes were glued to the screen.

"So, when I read this, I began to see Mr Epstein doubting the validity of the sale and his interest in researching IMP." She closed the Word document and opened another file. "He did extensive research on the other acquisitions made by IMP and their history." She tapped the screen, opening different files pertaining to other companies.

Reece quickly read the documents for each one of the companies IMP purchased and finally glanced over at her. "He probably was trying to get the best price he could." The documents he read seemed to be standard offer sheets and agreements with the amounts highlighted on the bottom of each page.

"That's what I thought at first," she brought up the Word document. "But the tone in his journal is more like suspicion, like... he suspected 'foul play', for lack of a better phrase." She left the journal entry open as Reece read it.

August 21

There is a lot of pressure from E&I to sign the deal but can't because of the questions of the make-up of IMP. Not enough info on how they came to be, where the money came from, who is in charge, the purpose of IMP.

Reece gave a slight nod to Lena, and she scrolled down some more.

August 26

While in TO doing research at main office ML showed me some files. Financial records bouncing around from one bank to another to another...none of it makes sense. Didn't have the privacy to review it further but ML agreed to copy files and will go over them at a later date. This puts the deal on hold.

Reece read the entry again and without taking his eyes off the screen said. "Who's ML?"

49

"He never really says," Lena answered as she held her finger over the laptop waiting for Reece to finish reading. He nodded and she scrolled down some more. "He continues, but now he starts using short forms as if he's trying to hide something." She stopped the page.

August 27

...E&I came in today pressing me to sign...S called too. waiting on reply from BPN in It. and from BoV from Mal. about $ trans.- seeking ties to Bru. – how do they figure in this?

Reece leaned back and rubbed his face. He sat back up and spoke. "Too bad Theo isn't here to tell us." He placed his hands on top of his head and spoke. "Did you know he died last year in a car accident?"

Lena worked on the laptop. "Even that seems suspicious." She paused while bringing up another page. "In his last entry he states that he wasn't going to the cottage last year but was meeting with ML in Toronto. She points to the entry.

August 30

Cancelling the weekend in SSM... Sheila ok with it...she'll do shopping in TO while I meet with ML

Reece noticed the date was just before the Labour Day weekend last year. "If I recall, Theo and Sheila were found in their car up north?" Theo and Sheila Epstein were found in a ravine just north of Owen Sound.

"I looked up the newspaper report on their deaths," Lena replied. "Do you know whether they usually went up to their cottage by that route?"

Reece was confused by the question. "What do you mean?"

"Well, I would assume if they had a cottage up by Sault Ste. Marie that they would go straight up through Michigan to get there instead of all the way around the lakes," Lena stated matter-of-factly.

Reece remembered something Theo had told him. "Yeah, they would, or they did." He shook his head to focus his thoughts. "Theo mentioned having to show ownership of his ATVs at both border crossings every time they went. He said it was a hassle and eventually he just left them up there at the cottage." He shrugged. "Maybe that time they decided to go after he got what he wanted in Toronto and headed straight up from there?"

Lena shook her head. "They were found early Saturday morning of that long weekend," she paused. "It was reported that the accident occurred sometime Friday. Do you think they would have had enough time to see ML in Toronto and drive up to Owen Sound where the accident occurred?"

Reece sat quietly for a while reading the last passage in the journal. He was thinking what all this had to do with the present situation. It finally dawned on him what they needed to do.

"Shannon."

Lena's eyes widened at Reece's response. "What about her?"

"She's in Toronto. She's at the head office," Reece reasoned. "Call her." He indicated to Lena.

"Why me?"

"She was part of your team. Tell her everything, about Scott, about Theo, about this situation we're in," Reece eyed the laptop. "Give her the initials," Reece urged.

"But she won't divulge anything about the company now that she works for them." Lena stated the obvious.

"Do it now." Reece gambled on Shannon sensing something illegal in the make-up of the company and wanting to correct it. He nodded to Lena, who just shook her head, rose and went to the other side of the room.

Reece didn't want to reveal that Shannon had warned him about this exact scenario, but he hadn't heeded the hint. Now he needed her to help them. He wasn't sure she would respond to his request and hoped Lena would be able to convince her to help. This whole situation was getting complicated by the minute and Reece was upset at himself for not suspecting it. He planned on checking something else that had gotten past him, after this phone call. Fifteen minutes later Lena returned.

"She recalls a name but wouldn't tell me." Lena slid into the chair. "She mentioned client confidentiality, but she suggested I look up the company's website and scroll the department heads." Lena showed Reece her phone, the Industrial Metal Products website queued up. "The lady works in the accounting division of IMP. Not payroll, but in finances and investments. I found a cell phone number and sent a text." Lena paused, putting the phone down, then looking Reece in the eyes. "I told Shannon everything. She asked about you."

Reece was surprised and intrigued. "What did you say? That I messed everything up and caused this problem?" He could imagine Shannon gloating.

She reached over to place her hand on his. "Reece, you did no such thing. Brock acted on his own, reacting to the company's action. There's no way you could have seen this happen."

"We're going to find out." He stood up. "Let's go. We've got someone else to see."

50

Brock walked throughout the plant inspecting all the exits. He had to get away from Bainbridge before he exploded and was wondering how long he had before another attempt was made by the police to intervene. Starting down the office side, he came upon the remaining people in the plant. Twelve people had decided to leave after Wilson's death leaving fifty-four willing to protect their interests. The plant was all lit up like it would for the midnight shift. The only difference was the silence that prevailed. Two people were assigned to each exit at a time to watch for any further police incursion. The others were bunked out in different comfort areas of the plant trying to sleep. Not too many were. He had designated four-hour shifts for the sentries, right after the incident, and urged those others to get some rest. He needed everyone to be alert at their posts. Bainbridge had basically told him there was going to be another attempt to regain the plant. How much could he ask these people to risk? Their lives? How could he avoid any bloodshed? A settlement now seemed out of the question. He was tossing these ideas in his mind as he made his rounds.

"Quite a show, eh?" Paul Fields, smoking a cigarette, pointed out the window of the employee entrance door.

At the front of the plant, Brock peeked outside to see the flashing lights of the police cruisers which had increased in numbers. Huddled around the lit barrels at the two entrances were a congregation of people, thinned out from earlier in the day, in support of the strike. Would they prevent the police from moving in? Brock couldn't count on it. There were also lights from camera crews of television stations glaring in the night as they waited for the next newsworthy piece. How soon would they get it? Then an idea crept into his head. He decided to finish his tour before seeking Paul's advice. "Paul, meet me at the office in about fifteen minutes." He had to think it all through before presenting it.

Brock made his way to the shipping drive side of the plant. Nick was still at his post, talking excitedly to his partner about his fending off the police. The smell of marijuana permeated the air. Brock tried to calm him, worried that the next time Nick's action could prove fatal.

"Relax, Nick." Nick's wild eyes and constant fidgeting scared Brock. "Maybe you should bunk down for a bit."

"No way. I'm not leaving this post, uh-uh."

"I don't need you to incite them any more than you already have."

"Then you need to do something about it because if they try to come in here again" — Nick's mischievous smile was accompanied by a pistol-shaped hand — "I'm not going to shoot over their heads."

Brock scanned the group nearby for their reactions. One guy was circling his finger at his head while staring at Nick. "I'm working on it. Just be patient and don't do anything stupid."

Making his way to the shipping area Brock met with Judy Ferris and Tim Poulter sitting at one of the comfort areas.

"Brock, when will Reece and the others return?" Tim, a short thin man with thick greying hair, was munching on a burger. "They must be working on a deal, right?"

"Yeah, yeah," Brock lied to allay any fear. "I expect to hear from Reece any minute now."

Judy rose from her seat next to Tim, wringing her hands as she spoke. "We came here with you for support, and we'll stay as long as it takes, but…" Her face blushed and her eyes blinked back any tears.

"Everything will be okay, Judy." Brock laid a reassuring hand on her shoulder. "I don't believe it will be much longer."

"I'm sorry about Scott." She paused, looking around, avoiding Brock's stare. "I just don't want a repeat of that." Tim had risen, wrapping his arm around her. She gave a weak smile and turned back to the picnic table with Tim.

Brock moved on, coming up to a group of men and women camped out in the middle of the shipping floor. There were sleeping bags spread out in a circle, with coolers in the middle, almost like an old western wagon train perimeter. A barbecue with a propane tank stood off to the side closest to the five loading docks.

The automated loading doors, large garage-type doors called ZIP doors, were open to allow the smoke out. Moe Gizmet was manning the barbecue and Brock headed over to him.

"They got you on cooking duty, Moe?" Brock extended his hand.

"Just like old times with your father." The black man held out his hand. "He'd be so proud of you." Being the maintenance man on the midnight shift, he came up with many odd ways of fixing things in the plant and earned the nickname 'Inspector Gadget' from the employees. Brock was pretty sure Moe was close to thirty years seniority and sixty-five years old. Still well built and as tall as Brock, the only sign of aging was the grey hair that graced the man's head. He'd gone to battle many times with Brock's father. Brock was sure glad that Moe had decided to join the group in the takeover and stay. Brock was relying on the resourceful man for support and guidance.

"I'm not so sure." He appreciated the comment but wished for more. "I should've brought him here, too."

"He's here with us." Moe pointed first at Brock's head and then lowered his hand to Brock's heart. "Everything you've done is exactly what he would've done." Moe winked and returned to the barbecue.

Brock moved on to the back of the plant where two men were sitting on lawn chairs at the open ZIP doors. "How are you boys doing?"

"Just enjoying the night air." The burly lift-truck driver from midnight shift, Ted, blew out cigarette smoke. "Too stuffy in there." He waved into the plant.

Brock looked beyond them to the back tarmac where corrugated bins and plastic boxes were stored outside. Before he could reply, the other man, Samir, an inspector on his shift, spoke up in his South African accent. "A bit of a storm is rolling in." He pointed outside. "That should discourage any more action from them." The clouds were heavy, blocking out the moon, and there were flashes in the distant sky.

"Just be on the alert, anyways." Brock couldn't ignore Bainbridge's subtle warning.

"We should be more concerned about the rats getting in here," Ted replied. "I'm sure they smell all that cooking going on." He chuckled while Samir nodded.

Brock moved along the wall toward the other side coming up to the door to the old boiler room. He tugged on the padlock on the door and stopped in his tracks. Should he post someone here? There was one exit out this wall to the open field and forest. The exterior door to this unused power plant was also padlocked, from the inside, which shouldn't pose a threat for entry, he thought. Brock looked back to the shipping area one hundred feet away and then to the other ZIP door a similar distance the other way. He tugged again at the lock and moved on.

51

"Brock told you he was going to do this, am I right?"

Reece leaned forward on the couch facing Gil seated in his lounge chair. Lena had gone into the kitchen to make a pot of coffee. It was going to be a long night.

"Of course he did." Gil wore fleece jogging pants and a stained white t-shirt. The television was on the local news station that had just shown their report on the earlier incident at Border City Stamping. "He figured you guys did the best you could and now it was time for action. I agreed with him."

Reece had lived in this home during his last year of high school and university years and had come to respect Gil O'Rourke for his dedication and loyalty to the working man regardless of whether they belonged to a union or not. Many a time he offered his home for meetings amongst groups seeking solutions to labour related problems or to debate social and political issues of the day. Reece had also witnessed stubbornness in the man that could produce anger that was hard to defend against. His son, Brock, carried the same traits.

"Great! And you two didn't think of telling me?" Reece clasped his hands out front, his elbows on his knees.

"You already did your share of the work, and he appreciated it," Gil replied. "You spoke up, told the people the truth about that deal and Brock felt he hadn't done a thing. He wasn't one for words." Gil pounded on the arm of his chair "But when the company announced the closure, he acted, and maybe it's time that was done again."

Lena returned and placed a tray filled with cups, sugar bowl, milk and the coffee pot on the table at the end of the sofa. "Don't get yourself all worked up, Mr. O'Rourke. We just need to help Brock get out of this situation." She indicated the tray. "What do you want in your coffee?"

"Just black," Gil gruffly replied. "And it's Gil, young lady." He smiled as he accepted the cup.

"Okay, Gil." She handed Reece a cup and sat beside him. "Tell us why you think this wildcat will solve our problem?"

Gil answered, "Because they will only listen to force, not words. That's why they took away our ability to strike because it worked in the past to get them to settle an agreement. Now, without it, they control the negotiations without fear of a stoppage." Gil's face was grim. "I learned a long time ago that action speaks louder than words."

"But Gil, this wildcat favours the company, not us," Reece tried to reason. "Public opinion will portray the union as a bunch of ruffians while the company reports that we turned down a contract."

Gil wagged his finger. "That doesn't matter, public opinion. Showing them we mean to fight back does."

"How?" Reece's voice rose as he put up his hands. Lena placed her hand on his knee. Reece glanced at her and then sat back on the couch.

"Reece, I'm going to tell you two stories that will make you understand what needs to be done, okay?" Gil waited while Reece sighed. "This first story I've never told anyone." He stared up to the ceiling recalling that fateful day so many years ago. "When I was a young boy, I saw a man beaten to death because he was trying to get his fellow workers to join a union. That's what companies did in that day to control the workplace." Gil pursed his lips for a second before continuing. "My father was the thug hired to beat that man. He didn't intend to kill him but, it happened, and that was that."

Reece and Lena stared in disbelief. Neither one spoke.

"Now, that man's brother started a business and invited the union to organize his workers." Gil's eyes gleamed. "That was Benjamin Rollins, and he created Border City Stamping."

There was an eerie silence in the room. Reece and Lena stole a glance at one another before returning their attention to Gil.

"Now, this next story will hit closer to home for you, Reece," Gil warned. "When I was at the local as president, your dad was my right-hand man. He headed up our flying squad, the group of men and women who would organize for any strike action in our union. We had the ability to strike in those days, and it was an effective tool in negotiations." Gil's eyes moistened. "During one of those instances where the flying squad was used, the company tried to move scabs into the plant. Your father stood in front of a convoy of trucks, blocking their way into the plant. There were others with him, and it seemed to have worked until" — Gil wiped his eyes — "one truck tried to break through, and your father was knocked down. He hit his head on the pavement but refused any medical help. They stopped the attempt, and we settled that contract but at a great cost." Gil leaned forward in his chair, his outstretched hand shaking. Reece bent forward to grab hold of the hand. "You were young at the time, and it was reported as a car accident that caused his death." Gil placed his other hand on top of Reece's. "But your father was heading home that night of the incident and apparently lost consciousness while driving."

Reece was stunned. Gil kept a firm grip, their eyes met, both moist, and there was an understanding between them.

Gil let go, relaxed back in his chair, a burden lifted from his conscience. "I'm telling you these stories to show you how the companies will do whatever they can to get their way. They'll do illegal activity if it meets their agenda. They don't care and, in most cases, their actions are not put out there for public opinion. We can't be swayed by public opinion. We must do what we can to protect our rights. Brock is doing that."

The three of them sat in silence for a few minutes, each with their own thoughts. They were interrupted by Lena's phone ringing. She rose to retrieve the phone from her purse on the kitchen table. Reece and Gil faced one another.

"Reece, I'm sorry to have told you about your father but I feel it's the right time."

"I understand," Reece replied. "But now, what do we do to help Brock?"

"You get an agreement," Gil said. "Brock told me you have some ideas to make the contract more acceptable for the membership?"

"I do, but Bainbridge won't want to listen to them. He'll hold out."

"No, he won't." Lena leaned over the back of the sofa holding her phone out for them to see. "That was the lady from IMP." She eyed Reece. "We got to go."

52

Reece was confused and angry. Driving back to the plant on E.C. Row Expressway, Lena filled him in on the conversation she'd had with Maria Lipinsky, the lady who worked in the Finance Department of IMP. The more he heard the angrier he got. Details would be forthcoming as Maria was copying whatever files she had found and sending them to Lena's cell phone. The information would determine a plan of action.

The truth about his father's death caught him by surprise. As a young boy he accepted the reasons for the absence of his father at many of his events or just not being home. He grew to admire his dad's dedication and the times they spent together Reece would ask his father about his job. The answer would always end up the same. If he didn't do it, who would? Now

Reece understood his mother's argument over his desire to stay in Windsor with the O'Rourke's when she decided to move away with his sister. She didn't want him to be like his father, yet he did. Deep down he wanted to follow in his father's footsteps but didn't realize it until his last year in university while working summers at BCS. Now, so many years later, he was at a crossroads. How far would he go to adhere to his father's maxim?

Reece was also disturbed by Gil's story of his witnessing a death in his youth. Could that mentality still be present today? Would companies go to that length to get what they want? Was Theo Epstein killed to keep him silent? Lena related the conversation with Maria Lipinsky, specifically concerning Theo Epstein. They were to meet on the Friday, BCS being closed for a four-day Labour Day weekend, in Toronto, away from IMP. Theo never showed. When she read that he and his wife were found dead in the ravine, the timeline seemed suspicious. She believed it wasn't coincidental. Reece didn't want to believe that could be but everything he'd learned over the last few hours pointed to that end. Now the question was would he have the strength and conviction to do what his father would do?

"Making it public would really tie their hands," Lena's words after a few minutes of silence brought him back to the present. "Bainbridge would have no choice but to settle." She made it sound like a done deal.

“It won’t be that easy.” Reece turned onto Patillo Road. “Going public might do more harm than good.”

Driving up toward BCS, the road was blocked by the crowd and a police barricade. They parked the Mustang and got out to walk the rest of the way. Reece was recognized by a few protesters as they weaved their way to the two police cruisers positioned across the road. They were stopped by an officer from passing through.

“I need to get in the plant,” Reece told the constable. “We’re part of the negotiating team that had come out earlier. We need to go back in.”

“Sorry sir, our orders are to let no one pass.” The officer stood between the vehicles.

“Is Captain Mallory still here?” Reece asked. “Tell him Reece Kincaid and Lena Kersey request permission to get past.”

The officer stepped away talking on his two-way radio clipped to his shoulder. After a few moments he returned. “Captain Mallory is on his way. Please wait.”

Reece noticed that the crowds had been dispersed from in front of Border City Stamping. The two entrances had been cleared of protestors and the barrels. Several police cruisers parked in the employee lot, their blue and red lights flashing constantly, while the command trailer was joined by another large panel truck on the road. Across the way there was another barricade of two police cruisers preventing traffic, vehicular or pedestrian, from advancing to the plant. A lone figure approached them.

"Captain Mallory, we need to get in there," Reece stated as the officer appeared.

"No way, Mr. Kincaid. No one else is entering that plant." The commanding officer looked worn, his uniform tie loosened, and his eyes bloodshot. "We've taken every precaution to ensure no one else gets hurt until this situation is resolved."

"But we can do that. We have," Lena was stopped by Reece's hand squeezing hers and his stern face shaking slightly at her.

"Sorry, Miss Kersey, but we have everything under control and hope to resolve this situation shortly," Mallory stated matter-of-factly. "Please abide by our orders and stay away. I need to get back." He turned around and walked back to his command centre.

Reece stared at the back of the departing officer and understood what was happening. He grabbed Lena's hand and led her back through the crowd toward the car. "Let's go." He waited till he cleared the demonstration to speak. "There's another way in. You drive. I've got to make a call."

53

Bainbridge sought out Brock, finding him in the lobby with Paul Fields. He needed to convince them to give this up, soon. Silva was acting fast, stating that the police were preparing to end the wildcat. There wasn't much time left.

"You've proven your point," Bainbridge commanded. "Now let's walk out of here before anyone else gets hurt."

"Are you willing to agree to the amendments to the contract?" Brock challenged. When Bainbridge didn't answer right away, Brock replied. "I didn't think so. That means we stay."

"You guys have lost your advantage," Bainbridge said. "Bringing guns in here, Wilson's death, and your union executive abandoning your cause has weakened your stance in the public's eye. The authorities are not going to let this go on for very long."

"How much time do we have?" Paul asked. "We know you or your boss is pulling the strings, so tell us how long we have to make our case?"

Bainbridge didn't want to tip his hand, but he also didn't want another shootout. "Look, just tell your people to lay down their guns and walk out the front. I'll lead them out so nothing will happen to them."

“You’re so thoughtful, aren’t you?” Brock criticized. “You’ll get the publicity for saving the day. Well, that doesn’t fly with us.” He deferred to Paul. “We’ll appeal to the media for government intervention.”

Paul took up the conversation. “We’re going to make another video, but this time we’ll send it to those television news crews outside to air. You saw how our last one got the public behind us. Now we’ll see if the government will be urged to act.”

“Ohh, they’ll act, but not the way you think.” Bainbridge took a seat on one of the lounge chairs. “To them, your wildcat strike is almost like a terrorist’s attack. Asking them to intervene under duress won’t cut it. If anything, they’ll prompt the police to act quicker.”

“We’ll agree to leave the plant, peacefully, if they agree to appoint an arbitrator for contract negotiations,” Brock pleaded. “That provides a simple solution where a neutral party decides the outcome that both parties can live with.”

“They won’t interfere in negotiations, especially when they’re told that you guys are breaching an existing contract with this action.” Bainbridge posed another difficulty in their plan. “Besides, how long before a politician sees this video of yours? Daylight? Mid-morning? You don’t have that much time.”

“Getting it out to the news now and telling them that the police plan to storm this place will buy us that time,” Brock said. “It won’t look good for the police having news crews film them attacking us.”

“Are you even sure there are crews still here?” Bainbridge saw the surprised expressions on the two men. “By the time your message gets heard, they might be reporting on a bloodbath. Do you want that?”

Brock huddled with Paul behind the receptionist’s desk. After a few moments Brock came around to continue talking with Bainbridge while Paul was on his cell phone with men at the front of the plant. “Okay, Bainbridge, you seem to have all the answers. For the last time, I’m telling you, we’re not giving up this plant until a contract is reached. You get on your phone and tell whoever it is that’s running the show out there that’s our plan. We’re ready for whatever they throw at us.” Brock wasn’t bluffing like he believed Bainbridge was. “We’ve got nothing to lose. This plant is our life.”

54

"Slow down," Reece instructed Lena. "Turn in here."

It had taken under four minutes to complete the circuit. Driving the Mustang back the way they came in, Lena turned east on Highway #22 and travelled just over a kilometre where Reece directed her to turn right on Wallace Line. She sped down the gravel road that split the corn fields, the headlights giving off an eerie reflection off the rows of corn, flying over the railroad tracks and onwards toward the next highway. She veered right again, heading back west on Hwy. #42 until she came upon Patillo road once more, this time from the south side. Racing north, they re-crossed the railroad tracks, where Reece indicated she turn onto a dirt path, basically two tire tracks in the weeds the farmers used to access their fields. Lena stopped before reaching the woods.

During the quick journey, Reece was on his phone with Moe Gizmet inside the plant. Reece remembered Moe was amongst the group of employees who decided to stay and now he needed him to help them get in. The plan was to gain entry through the old power plant. When Reece was living with the O'Rourkes, Gil would take Brock and Reece hunting deer in the woods behind BCS. To get a break from the winter cold, Gil would take them to the old boiler room to warm up. When the company modernized the plant in 2004, they didn't want to spend the money demolishing the old powerhouse and instead left it standing but closed.

"Why didn't we just tell the captain?" Lena couldn't understand the need for secrecy.

"The less people know about it, the better for everyone." Reece opened the glove box to get a flashlight. He shone the light at her. "Lena, can't you see the ramifications of making this information public?"

"No, I can't." She brushed aside his hand.

"It's not just BCS we're protecting here." Reece wanted her to figure it out for herself. He still wasn't sure about the details, but the damage that could be done to the industry by revealing their intent could be devastating. "Put yourself in their shoes if we went public with it. What would they do to protect themselves?" He reached over to turn off the motor. "Get the lights." He stepped out of the Mustang.

Lena sat in the darkness for a minute before getting out and joining Reece at the front of the car. "You really think that would happen?"

"They'd be forced to close everything. It would take years in the courts before anything was settled and where would the workers be.

Out of work." Reece reached out for her hand. "We need to bargain with them using this information, as a chip, that we'll keep private. Let's go."

"What's your plan to deal with Bainbridge?"

"I don't know," Reece answered. "I haven't gotten that figured out yet."

They started for the forest. The beam from the flashlight cut their path in the darkness. The moon was obscured by the cloud cover making the trek through the woods more difficult. Reece was counting on his recollection of the direction they needed to go. The small forest spread out along the railroad tracks for some distance and jutted into the fields. The northeast corner lined up with the back of BCS. There were two other buildings, a warehouse for tires and an auto body repair shop, before BCS, and the large tract of corn that made it impossible for them to cut across to the plant. Reece recalled a furrow between the fields running from the corner of the forest right to the old boiler room. They needed to get there.

They skirted the edge of the forest for as long as they could before the corn fields forced them to trek into the woods. Reece weaved his way through the trees, using one hand to point the flashlight in their path and the other hand to lead Lena. Glancing off to his left he could make out a faint glow of red, white and blue in the sky from the police lights flashing in front of the plant. He was getting his bearing when he was surprised by an onrush of light from the trees.

"Freeze! Don't Move!" Shouts burst out as Reece's leading arm was grabbed, the flashlight falling to the ground, and his hand released from Lena as it too was grasped by the attackers. Lena let out a short scream before she was silenced by a hand over her mouth. Reece couldn't fight back as he was pinned to the ground and his wrists shackled.

"All right, all right. Get'em up!" The command resulted in Reece being hauled up on his feet by his arms. He came face to face with a police officer dressed in SWAT gear, the small headlight from his helmet shining in Reece's face. "Reece, what the hell are you doing here?"

"I guess I'm not the only one who remembered this way in," Reece replied to his friend's query.

Shawn Bennett flicked off his light and put his hand down indicating to the others to lower their guns. The four members of the SWAT team obeyed but still held on to their prisoners.

"I should've known it was you," Shawn said. "Un-cuff him and release her." He commanded the others. "You two shouldn't be here."

"Neither should you." Reece rubbed his wrists. "I'm afraid to ask what you're doing."

"You're not going to like what you see." Shawn turned to walk away. "Follow me."

A minute later the group came upon other SWAT members at the edge of the forest. There were over twenty more policemen geared up. Shawn went directly to one man, the commander of the force, who he talked with for a moment. The leader stepped to Reece and Lena.

"Reece Kincaid, I'm Sergeant Thompson of the tactical squad." The officer had a ball cap on instead of a helmet. "What is your purpose for coming here?"

"Looks like the same as yours." Reece answered while pointing toward their mutual target. "I need to get in there."

"I can't allow that. We're just about to execute an operation," Thompson paused, realizing how his statement sounded. "I can't involve more civilians."

"Sergeant, you don't want to do this," Reece pleaded. "I can get those people out of there without confrontation."

"We're not expecting any confrontation, sir," Thompson said. "Our operation is aimed at containment without opposition."

"You're fooling yourself if you think you can get in there without opposition. They've already shown that they will defend the building," Reece raised his voice. "Don't do this, let me in there!"

Shawn interceded, "Reece, what do you have that's going to bring them out?"

"We have some information that will convince those inside to give up the plant, peacefully." Reece knew that wouldn't fly without a further explanation that he wasn't willing to give. "Trust me, let me in there."

"What's this information?" Thompson asked the obvious.

Reece swayed on his feet. "It's more complicated than I can say. The company negotiator, Bainbridge, is there and when he sees what we have he'll agree to a contract, I'm sure.'

Thompson wasn't convinced. "That's not enough for me to let you go.'

Reece ran his hand over his face. He didn't know how to proceed. Lena showed up beside him, running her hand along his arm. She spoke to Thompson.

"Sergeant Thompson, I'm Lena Kersey." She smiled at him. "I'm part of the management team and I'm telling you that we cannot deny a contract with this information." She paused for only a second. "But this is what I want you to consider. How would it look if you went in there and met resistance that resulted in injuries, possibly fatalities, and you had the option of letting us go in there to settle this thing peacefully?" She held everyone's attention as she paused again. "You decide, Sergeant, but remember...the stakes are human lives."

55

They made their way along the furrow as the rain began. They didn't talk as they made their way toward the factory. Reece was fuming mad at Shawn for not giving him a heads up about the police action. Reece led the way, stopping just before the irrigation ditch running lengthwise for the entire field. It was four feet wide but dry. Reece carefully traversed it, putting out his hand for Lena. Shawn helped her from behind and they proceeded up the other side and to the door of the old power plant. Before Reece gave the signal, he turned to Shawn to remind him of the deal that was made.

"You remain in the boiler room until I call you." Reece put out his hand to shake on it.

Shawn grasped the hand. "Reece, Thompson's only giving you an hour before he moves in. No negotiating, okay. Tell your people in there and get them out."

“You make sure he doesn’t jump the gun.” Reece tried to read his friend’s face. “He didn’t seem too keen on this arrangement.”

“Can you blame him? He’s overriding Mallory’s orders.” Shawn pointed at the door. “Let’s get this over with.”

Reece knocked three times on the door, waited a couple of seconds, and knocked another three times. The door swung open, and Moe Gizmet appeared. “Hello, Reece. Miss Kersey.” He blocked their entry when he saw Shawn in SWAT gear.

“It’s okay Moe,” Reece assured him. “Remember Shawn, my friend?”

“He’s police... you didn’t tell me they were coming?” Moe tried to reach for the door handle.

Lena stepped forward, placing her hands on the older man’s arms. “Moe, he’s just here to ensure we got in without police intervention.” She managed to get him to back off. “Besides, I'm getting too wet out here.”

They all entered the boiler room. Shawn closed the door behind them, and they all stood in the eerie illumination of the room. There were only two light bulbs providing lighting for the area, giving off more shadows than clearness. The huge storage tanks and rows of electrical panels took up most of the space while stacks of boxes lined up the walls allowing only a narrow pathway for them to stand in. Moe stood in their way.

Lena gently turned him around. "Lead us out of here. This place gives me the creeps."

Moe weaved his way around the piles of materials until he came to another door lit up by a red exit sign over top. He halted the group, guarding the door. "I don't think Brock will appreciate him being here." Moe nodded at Shawn.

"He's not coming with us into the plant." Reece clapped his hand on Moe's shoulder. "He's staying in here until we clear things up." Reece reached for the door, but Moe grabbed the handle before him. Slowly he opened the door, peering out into the aisle before stepping out. Reece followed along with Lena. Shawn peeked out.

"Reece, remember, you have less than an hour. Make your case and get them out."

"I understand Shawn. Thanks." Reece closed the door on his friend. He held onto the handle for a few seconds, his ear to the door, and then turned to Moe. "Padlock this door and place something to block it. That will buy us some more time."

Sergeant Thompson and his team didn't wait in the woods. They crept along the furrow a few minutes after the three others had left and lay in wait about thirty metres from the plant. He sent out a reconnaissance of the perimeter of the plant while the other SWAT members settled in amongst the corn trying to stay dry. A few minutes later the returning scouts indicated a movement of machinery at both ends. Their reports were similar in that containers were being moved by jitney toward the front of the plant to act like a barricade. Mallory was right when he said that they would attract the attention of the strikers allowing the rear of the plant to be free of opposition. The scouts also reported that the ZIP doors were left open. Thompson saw an opportunity to move in but remembered his word was given to Kincaid to wait. He positioned his men at the edge of the tarmacs on both ends, protected from detection by the remaining bins. Time seemed to drag on.

56

"Reece, how'd you get in here?" Brock stared open-mouthed at their arrival.

Reece entered the lobby with Lena and Moe. "It doesn't matter how. What needs to be done is to get this settled once and for all." Brock and Bainbridge were on opposite sides of the receptionist's desk. "Where's everybody?" Reece indicated the shop floor because they hadn't seen any other employees on their way through the plant.

"I had Paul move everyone to the front to show the police we intend to stay," Brock said. "They set up a barricade that should discourage the police from trying to move in."

"It's not those in front you need to worry about," Reece informed Brock. "There's a SWAT team waiting in the fields behind here to disperse you guys." Reece stepped up to Bainbridge. "But I think we can avoid that from happening once Mr. Bainbridge here sees what we have.'

"Reece, before you start," Lena interjected, her eyes shifting to one side at Moe.

Reece moved over to Moe. "Moe, thanks for your help. Could you make sure no one else comes in here." Reece walked Moe to the doorway heading into the offices. "We need to talk to Mr. Bainbridge without any interruptions. Call me if you need something." Moe left the lobby area.

"What do you have now, Reece, another version of a counter proposal?" Bainbridge stood firm, arms crossed.

"We have better than that, David." Lena waved her cell phone in his face. "We know your true intent."

"What's this? You've jumped sides?" Bainbridge said sarcastically. "I'm really at a disadvantage here."

Reece gently grabbed Lena's arm, moving her away from Bainbridge. "It was Theo Epstein who led us to this information. He understood, more than anybody, your true intent to close this place. I'm sure if he were here we wouldn't be in this situation." Reece stood a foot away from Bainbridge. "You can give up your 'corporate structure' excuse. The gig is up."

Bainbridge guessed they found a memo or note that stated their strategy for dealing with the union. "So, you fell right into my plan and now that you figured it out you expect me to change it?" He gave a brief guffaw. "I told Brock here the same thing."

"Did you also tell him that the power behind Industrial Metal Products is our competitors, and they intend to eliminate us and other companies who stand in their way?" Reece was trying to feel out Bainbridge. He couldn't believe that Bainbridge, being the lead man in these negotiations, didn't know. "Going public with this information wouldn't be something they'd like to see happen, would they?"

"What are you talking about, competitors?" Bainbridge stood firm. "We have always said each plant is an entity of its own, competing for business with the other subsidiaries of the company."

"It's not those plants we're talking about," Reece almost shouted. "That's just a cover up for their plan. These big three want to control the market and create an environment in which they can eliminate unions and undermine the workers' ability to earn a decent living."

"Why would Chrysler, Ford and GM care about competition amongst auto suppliers?" Bainbridge's smug smile was irritating. "They want that, so they can get the lowest price for their parts. You guys are wrong to believe they would design to disrupt that."

"We're not talking about them." Reece was getting flustered by Bainbridge's tactic. "Don't try to hide it any longer. We have proof of their identity and their purpose." Reece paused to calm down. "We don't have much time, so agree to our conditions and we won't reveal their identity."

Bainbridge was confused and showed it by shrugging his shoulders and putting up his hands. His eyes darted from Reece to Lena and then to Brock, without speaking.

"He doesn't know what you're talking about," Brock said. "And neither do I?"

Reece and Lena exchanged glances, with Lena showing her phone. Reece nodded.

"David, are you aware of who financed Industrial Metal Products?"

"Of course, the Italian firm Bruggi created Industrial Metal Products to expand into North America," Bainbridge answered.

Lena smiled "Not exactly. Let me quote something for you first." She scrolled on her phone before continuing.

"The parties agree to equally fund this enterprise for one billion dollars each, US currency, to use for the expansion to North America in the automotive supply market with the sole purpose of buying up financially troubled firms at a percentage of their actual worth. To this end, these firms will be re-organized under one venture, Industrial Metal Products, with the intent of lowering labour costs by implementing wage and benefit concessions. Also, the elimination of unions in the make-up of this venture should be of paramount importance to the eventual end of creating a workforce independent of outside influence in determining future labour costs."

She glanced up from her phone at Bainbridge.

"So, an agreement was made to rein in the high cost of doing business," Bainbridge stated matter-of-factly.

Lena interrupted, "Do you want to know who these parties are?"

He shrugged and she handed him her cell phone. Bainbridge read for a while, his face taking on a pale complexion. He stole a glance at Reece as he continued to read. Before he could say anything, Brock spoke.

"Don't keep me in the dark?"

Reece grimaced. "Brock, as long as you understand it doesn't go public unless we say so?"

Brock shrugged. "What doesn't go public?"

Bainbridge interceded. "Where did you get this?"

"I think you can figure it out," Lena replied.

"What?!" Brock shouted. "You guys haven't told me anything yet!"

Reece stepped over to Brock. "Relax, Brock, it's complicated and we'll explain it soon enough, but we need Mr. Bainbridge to understand the complications it could create if it got out." They all stared at Bainbridge.

"I need to make a call."

"That's right, David. Call Silva."

57

Battle lines were drawn on either side of the fence. The employees on the inside were behind their make-shift barricade that stretched across the width of the fence. Behind corrugated boxes, jitneys, the huge machinery mover, stacks of plastic bins, and all their vehicles, the men and women were armed with shotguns, hunting rifles and pistols. The police, on the other side of the fence, spanned across the width of the property, in formation, adorned in riot gear complete with clear shields, helmets and Kevlar vests. The light rain was lit up by the headlights and flashing lights of the police cruisers aimed at the occupied plant while spotlights from the jitneys were pointed back at the police. Paul Fields stood at the fence facing Captain Mallory.

"Put down your guns and leave the property," Mallory said for the third time in the last five minutes. "This injunction has been issued by the courts and your people are obstructing justice by remaining on the premises."

"And I'm telling you that you'll have to come in to remove us and I'm not sure you'll want to do that with them watching." Paul indicated the TV crews set up across the street on another property. He had contacted them with their appeal for government intervention and had reported a possible police action.

"You're making it very difficult for yourselves to avoid breaking the law and finding yourselves being detained," Mallory tried to reason with Paul. "Do you or your people really believe it's worth it?"

"Yes, we do, Captain." Paul spread out his arms. "We're protecting our livelihood just like your men would defend theirs if they were at an impasse in negotiations. They may not have the option to go to this extreme, but they are union brothers, and I believe they understand our position."

"They have a duty to uphold the law, and they will act if forced to."

"We're not forcing anything," Paul replied. "We're just holding out until those inside agree to a contract."

Just then an employee broke from behind the barricade to charge at the fence. Paul raced toward the disturbance.

"Nick, back off!" Paul yelled as he approached Nick Campo who was waving his rifle in the air. Two officers were yelling back, urging Nick to lower his gun while they held up their shields and brandished their firearms. Paul placed his hand on the rifle, lowering it, while trying to calm Nick. "Are you crazy pointing that gun? We're not going to be the ones responsible for starting a shootout."

"He called us intruders! Said we didn't have the right to be here!" Nick pointed a finger at one of the police officers. "We have every right to be here!"

Mallory had signalled to his men to back away from the fence. He glared at Paul. "See how close a situation can get out of hand."

"Nick, calm down." Paul pushed Nick away from the fence. "Get back behind that jitney."

They made their way back to the barricade when Paul's cell phone chimed. Reading the text from Brock gave him a start but he concealed his surprise and spoke calmly to Nick.

"Take a break, Nick." Paul led him up the shipping driveway toward the back. "Cool off in the back and make sure the Zip doors are closed, okay."

Nick lit up a cigarette as he made his way. Paul was right about not being the cause of a confrontation, and he needed to tone it down. Slowly walking in the rain, he relaxed and remembered why they were there in the first place. A showdown with the police would only damage their ability to secure a good contract.

Passing the docks and rounding the corner of the building, he noticed the Zip doors were open. The drivers bringing the boxes and bins must've opened them manually and forgot to close them because otherwise automatically they would have closed. Stepping inside the doorway, he turned to flick his cigarette outside when he noticed some movement around the remaining bins in the yard. Trying not to show alarm, he casually went to the power box and pushed the down button for the Zip door. He stole a glance as the door dropped, raising his rifle in defense. There was someone behind those boxes.

Shawn wasn't comfortable waiting in the boiler room. The eerie silence was too much, and he took a moment to check outside. The rain was getting harder, making it difficult to see in the corn field. The others weren't in sight, but he was sure they were there. Returning to the inside, he went to the interior door to steal a glance. It wouldn't open. He tugged at it a couple of times and became worried. Why would Reece do that? He hurried back outside while getting out his cell phone. It vibrated before he could make his call.

"Bennett, we've been detected," Thompson announced. "We're moving in."

"Wait, you can't get in here," Shawn responded. "The door has been blocked." He saw the team appear out of the corn field.

"We're heading for the side entrances before they can react from the front," Thompson replied. "Assist those men going to the north side. Enter through wherever you can. Use force if necessary." The command ended the conversation.

Shawn ran to his left joining the men who had jumped the irrigation ditch and travelled along the wall toward their target.

58

"Put him on speaker."

Reece demanded Bainbridge put his conversation with Silva for everyone to hear. The speaker button was pressed on the receptionists' console.

"Who am I speaking to?" Silva's voice was clear over the speakers.

"Reece Kincaid, Lena Kersey and Brock O'Rourke," Reece answered.

"O'Rourke?" Silva's tone was sharp. "The O'Rourke who engineered this illegal activity?"

"That's me, all right."

"Then you'd better be calling to tell me you've given up this nonsense and returned that plant for production," Silva stated. "David, is that the situation?"

Bainbridge hadn't had time to fill in his boss about the discovery. "No, not quite Max. There's a complication that has come up."

"What complication?"

"We know who is behind Industrial Metal Products," Reece spoke, more loudly than he needed to. "I believe it would be in your best interest if their identity is not revealed."

There was silence on the line for a few seconds before Silva spoke. "Who are you talking about?"

"Do you want names?" Reece asked. When there was no immediate response, he nodded to Lena.

"Thomas Wilkes, the third, Herman Stouts and William Johnston are the signatures on the letter of intent in this document," Lena read off. "Are you familiar with these names?"

Again, there was silence. Brock was agitated and burst out. "No, I'm not familiar with those names or what the hell you guys are talking about?"

"Would you like to enlighten Mr. O'Rourke about the significance of those names, Mr. Silva?" Reece wanted to hear Silva's acknowledgement of the conspiracy.

"David, is this document authentic?" Silva's voice was almost a whisper.

"I guarantee it's authentic," Lena answered for Bainbridge. "As well as the files on financing." She glanced at her phone. "A paper trail was left of moving money from the U.S. to the Bahamas then to Malta and eventually Italy to set up your venture."

"What gives?" Brock shouted. "Enough with the mystery. What are we dealing with?"

Reece moved over to Brock, clapping him on the shoulder and smiling. "Brock, since Mr. Silva seems to be at a loss for words, I'll explain it to you." He paused for a second, directing his next comment at the phone. "If I make a mistake, correct me, Mr. Silva."

There was no reply, so Reece began his explanation.

"Those three names are the people who own the three biggest auto supply conglomerates in North America. Thomas Wilkes owns Trans-Motors Industrial, Herman Stouts operates Railman Automotive, and William Johnston runs North American Machinery and Gears." He noticed Brock recognized the company titles. "They got together some years ago and devised a plan to set up another company, Industrial Metal Products, to buy up companies as you heard Lena quote. IMP was created in collusion with one another," Reece paused. "Is that the right terminology, Mr. Silva?" Again, he paused and looked over at Bainbridge. "Mr. Bainbridge, am I correct in using that phrase?"

Trans-Motors Industrial originated in England as a builder of motors at the advent of the automobile and set up in Toronto, Canada after World War I. Railman Automotive started as a manufacturer of parts for trains over two hundred years ago, switching to cars at the turn of the twentieth century. Their birthplace was St. Louis, Missouri but their operations spread across the United States and Canada. North American Machinery and Gears began as a producer of bicycles but expanded to the supply of gears and parts for the auto industry when that mode of transportation boomed. They operated out of Detroit, Michigan with subsidiaries throughout North America.

When neither man confirmed Reece's request, he continued. "Brock, in layman's terms, they agreed to join forces under another company for the sole purpose of reducing labour costs by attacking the working man's wages and benefits. They also targeted the unions with the intent of eliminating them from the field. Eventually their goal, once they had purchased all the competition, was to sell off IMP to each other, in parcels. Did I leave anything out, Mr. Silva?"

"What do you want?" was the response from the speaker phone.

"You don't deny the explanation?"

Before an answer could be made, Brock spoke, "You mean to tell me that these three companies are in cahoots with one another to control the industry?"

"That's a simple way of saying it, but yes." Reece smiled. "Would you like to elaborate, Mr. Silva or Mr. Bainbridge?"

Brock's phone chimed. Everyone in the room watched as Brock answered. His face contorted as if in pain and he spoke with anger.

"The police are moving in."

59

The infiltration was coordinated and timed between the two forces of police. At the front of the plant smoke bombs were tossed in front of those strikers lined up along the barricade and officers scaled the fences, adorned with gas masks and wielding batons. Paul Fields ran up the line yelling at his people to retreat into the plant or down the outside of the plant. He was the first person taken down, tackled by an officer, and restrained. Other strikers lay down their weapons as they choked on the smoke and were detained by the police. Some made it back into the plant.

The SWAT team on the shipping side of the plant got lucky. The pedestrian door alongside the Zip door was unlocked, avoiding the need to rip through the canvas covered Zip doors. They threw in a smoke bomb before advancing on the building. Nick Campo was making his way toward the other side when Shawn and his team appeared. They too had luck on their side as the Zip door was opened and unguarded. They entered without the smoke diversion but met with the first resistance. Nick shot in the air at them. Shawn tried to warn Nick off, yelling at him to drop his weapon, but Nick retreated in amongst the machinery of the plant.

Brock led the group from the offices onto the shop floor. The sound of gunfire prompted him to run toward the back of the plant. Reece and the others stopped just outside of the guard rails of the office. Reece took out his phone.

"Shawn, what's going on?!"

"Reece, tell your people to put their guns down," Shawn responded to the call. "The order is to secure the premises."

"I'm not near anyone to tell them." Reece was furious. "Tell your men to back down and I'll try to get our people to surrender peacefully. You didn't give me the time."

"It's too late, Reece, and besides one of your men already took a shot." The sound of officers yelling commands could be heard on his phone.

Reece hung up and scanned the shop floor. Lena, Moe and Bainbridge stood beside him. From the front of the plant several employees were running up the aisle.

"Moe, go to the front and tell those people to put down their guns." Reece pointed in that direction. "Have them sit down at one of the eating areas. We can't have any casualties." He clapped Moe's shoulder as the man raced down the aisle.

Let's go find Brock." Reece led Lena and Bainbridge to the back.

"Shouldn't we just stay here instead of adding to the confusion?" Bainbridge said.

"You can stay but we're going to try to prevent anybody from getting injured." Lena glared at Bainbridge. She followed Reece who was already weaving his way through the plant.

Bainbridge hesitated for a second before joining them.

Nick sidled up alongside a punch press peering back where he'd just come from. The fear from the initial confrontation was now replaced with anger. There was no way they were going to take away his livelihood without a fight. He knew this place better than they did and would use it to his advantage to outsmart them. Bring it on, he scowled. Nick cradled his rifle as he sneaked past the lockers that surrounded an eating area. Where was everyone else? Too bad all the lights were on, he thought. It would have been easier for him to hide in the dark and surprise them. Still, they were in his place, and he knew how to move around.

Brock cleared the welding cell to cross the aisle to the press cell. Chatter from radios, obviously the police, broke the silence off to his right. He scurried onward away from them hoping to find any employees before they did. The gunshot was from a hunting rifle, he was sure of, meaning there was someone he was responsible for engaging the police. They were following his orders, and he needed to be there with them. Brock felt for the pistol at his side. The Colt .45 had been used only at the gun club and was specifically registered for that purpose only. He hoped he wouldn't have to use it otherwise. Inching his way now by the huge three-ton automatic press, the one he stood in front for the video of their takeover, Brock detected movement by the smaller punch presses on the right. There were police dressed in riot gear searching the area. He was going to withdraw when he noticed Nick peering over the lockers at the lunch station on the left side of the aisle. They were on a collision course.

Reece was trying to think what to do next. Zigzagging through the equipment and trying to find Brock was only making things more difficult for him to concentrate on coming up with a solution to this chaos. White smoke was rising to the ceiling near the shipping area, and he thought he may have passed where Brock had gone. Lena and Bainbridge showed up a moment later.

"Did you see Brock?" Reece realized it was a dumb question just after he spoke. "We must've passed him. Let's go this way." He grabbed Lena's hand as he made his way to the centre of the plant heading to the back. Bainbridge shook his head but followed.

60

Reece and Lena scurried around the machinery heading toward the press cell. Shawn's team had entered from the field and reported being shot at. That's where Reece was going. Just as they crossed the aisle dividing the welding cell from the press cell Reece spotted Brock advancing past the automatic presses. They were about a hundred feet apart. Reece ran.

Brock moved quickly to cut off Nick from the police. The lockers surrounded an eating area that had been set up with a barbecue and coolers by the strikers. Nick had positioned himself on the other side of the lockers, in hiding, aiming his rifle over the top at the oncoming police team. Brock was forty feet from Nick when he saw two officers appear from among the tub cell in the open directly in line with Nick. There was no time to stop Nick, except to divert his attention. Brock dropped down on one knee, grabbed his Colt, and aimed. He fired at the propane tank of the barbecue. The explosion lifted the barbecue in the air causing Nick to duck and the police to hit the floor. Brock got up and ran toward them.

Reece and Lena were racing down the aisle when the blast occurred. They shielded themselves with their hands, stopping in their advance while they watched Brock sprint across the aisle. Two policemen appeared on the right, in a firing stance aimed at Brock. Reece ran waving his hands.

"Don't shoot! Don't shoot!"

The barrage of gunfire brought Brock down and then the firing was directed toward Reece. He dove to the ground as the bullets pinged by him. More police officers appeared from both sides of the aisle yelling commands. Nick was apprehended, forced down to the ground, while Brock lay prone. Reece crab-walked quickly to Brock. The two officers advanced on them with arms outstretched and yelling commands. Reece ignored them as he got to Brock.

"Brock, you idiot, see what mess you've gotten into." Reece tried to joke with his fallen friend. He held him up. Lena appeared beside them.

"Is Nick okay?" Brock grimaced. "I had to prevent them from shooting him down."

"Nick's fine, you did good." Reece put his hand on the red blotch of Brock's shirt. "Hang in there, you'll be fine too."

"Tell Margaret I had to do this." Brock's eyes fluttered. "I had to make up for everything I did wrong." He gave a weak smile. "Tell Pop his son tried to live up to his standards."

"Shut up, Brock." Reece's eyes watered as he braced Brock. "You can tell him yourself."

Brock shook his head slightly. "No, Reece. Tell him for me." He coughed up blood. "Get these people a good deal, Reece." He reached over with his hand to grasp Reece's shirt. "We won, right?" Brock smiled as his head lolled to one side.

Reece hugged Brock fiercely as the police circled him. Lena sobbed as she bent down to embrace both men.

EPILOGUE

EIGHT DAYS LATER

David Bainbridge felt betrayed. Having held the position of Chief Operating Officer for all these years and to be deceived about its true intent was one thing, but then to be made out to be a puppet and be on the sidelines of negotiations was taking it too far. Driving away from Border City Stamping on his way to Toronto, he figured he could convince Silva to reverse the decisions made over the last few days.

First, the revelation of their collusion in creating Industrial Metal Products had taken him by surprise. Theo Epstein had discovered the collusion and, with his journal, had directed the union to finding the information. With assistance by Lena Kersey, Reece Kincaid used this in the subsequent dealings with the investors that produced an agreement that virtually destroyed Industrial Metal Products. Those men were more interested in protecting their individual companies and reputations than following through with their plan.

The agreement that was settled gave the workers of Border City Stamping everything back, their wages with raises, full benefits, and the continuation of the retirement plan with increased values. On top of that, Kincaid was able to get an arrangement whereby Industrial Metal Products would be dismantled, piece by piece, to independent buyers at a bargain price. Furthermore, these newly formed firms would be required to be unionized. This was to be done within a twelve-month period with Border City Stamping being the first one to receive this action, immediately. There was already a local buyer proposed with the reins of the company in the hands of Lena Kersey. Even Shannon Stewart was involved. When she learned of the collusion, she quit IMP immediately and offered her services to the union in the dismantling of the company. They declined. The three entrepreneurs of the auto supply conglomerate and Max Silva agreed to all these conditions without a fight. Bainbridge had been left out of the one-sided negotiation. The final signing was to occur within the next two days.

Then, he was humiliated even more when he was forced to attend the funerals of Scott Wilson and Brock O'Rourke on behalf of the company. Sitting amongst all the workers listening to the eulogies making these men martyrs for their cause only infuriated him. If everyone knew about the contributions these two men had in the original failed negotiations, would they be honouring them? But that was a moot point now. Bainbridge pressed down further on the gas pedal of the rental car, a Dodge Challenger SRT, as he headed east on Highway 42.

But he had a plan to reverse their decision. All the parties were to meet at the head office in Toronto to sign the agreement. Putting aside his feelings about the deception, Bainbridge believed that the creation of Industrial Metal Products and its intent was ingenious. He was determined to convince these founding partners to follow through with their plan. Collusion had occurred in other industries and those involved had stayed the course, paid the penalties and continued to strive in the enterprises. He felt so confident about succeeding that he even thought of threatening them by exposing their collusion to the press if they went ahead with the deal.

Turning onto the Puce Road heading to Highway 401, Bainbridge devised a plan on how to approach those men with his proposal to reverse this action. The day was bright and sunny, and the road was clear. So was his mind. He believed in his plan.

Bainbridge pushed the car faster on the straight road. In the distance a red pickup truck veered onto his lane. He flicked his lights and lay on his horn. The vehicle was approaching fast. Bainbridge steered onto the other lane but so did the truck. Bainbridge stared at the driver, recognizing the old man just before they collided head on...*O'Rourke!*

Acknowledgements

Writing is a lonely occupation. The author spends endless hours creating a story. There are the characters, the plot, and the setting that the author lives with, alone. But to bring this story to life for the reader, the author needs support. Mentors, readers, editing people and book preparers help to bring this novel to reality. So, with that being said, these are the people who've supported me along the way to create WILDCAT.

The journey began over 15 years ago with the Odyssey Project, a creative writing course, taught by Vanessa Shields. Her classes, including those at Gertrude's Writing Room, were very instructional and inspirational. Her devotion to her students is unprecedented.

To the many readers who offered criticism. Without your input this story could not have taken shape. Thank you, Sue & Richard Nantais, Carol Milner, Kirk Lozon, Steve Byrne (author of SKIM) and Rob Kennedy of Local 195 who advised me on union matters.

Editing is a tedious but necessary part of the process. I wouldn't have been able to complete it without the help of my daughter Michelle Zimmer who corrected my grammar and punctuations as well as advising on character development. I hope this final version meets your approval.

To my other daughter, Leesa St. Pierre, owner of LDMedia. The book would not come into existence without your work. From formatting to cover design, WILDCAT is Real!

Finally, to my wife Linda. You allowed me to go to this other world, and other worlds, without interruption and with encouragement. You've stuck by this dreamer for over 44 years, and I am so lucky and grateful. I LOVE YOU!

Micheal Micallef

Author Bio

Micheal Micallef is a retired auto worker after over 32 years of service. He experienced a plant closure in 2010, with 25 years seniority. Through the efforts of the union, he was able to find work in the auto sector for 7.5 more years.

He lives in Southwestern Ontario with his wife Linda. They travel often, mostly cruising. Otherwise, they spend time with their three grown children and seven grandchildren as well as visiting friends and other family.

Mike, as he is normally called, enjoys taking long walks with Linda, playing golf in the warm weather and watching hockey throughout the winter and spring. Go Leafs Go!

Contact at: wildcatmm59@gmail.com

Manufactured by Amazon.ca
Bolton, ON

45409409R00195